BABYMOUSE AND FRIENDS*

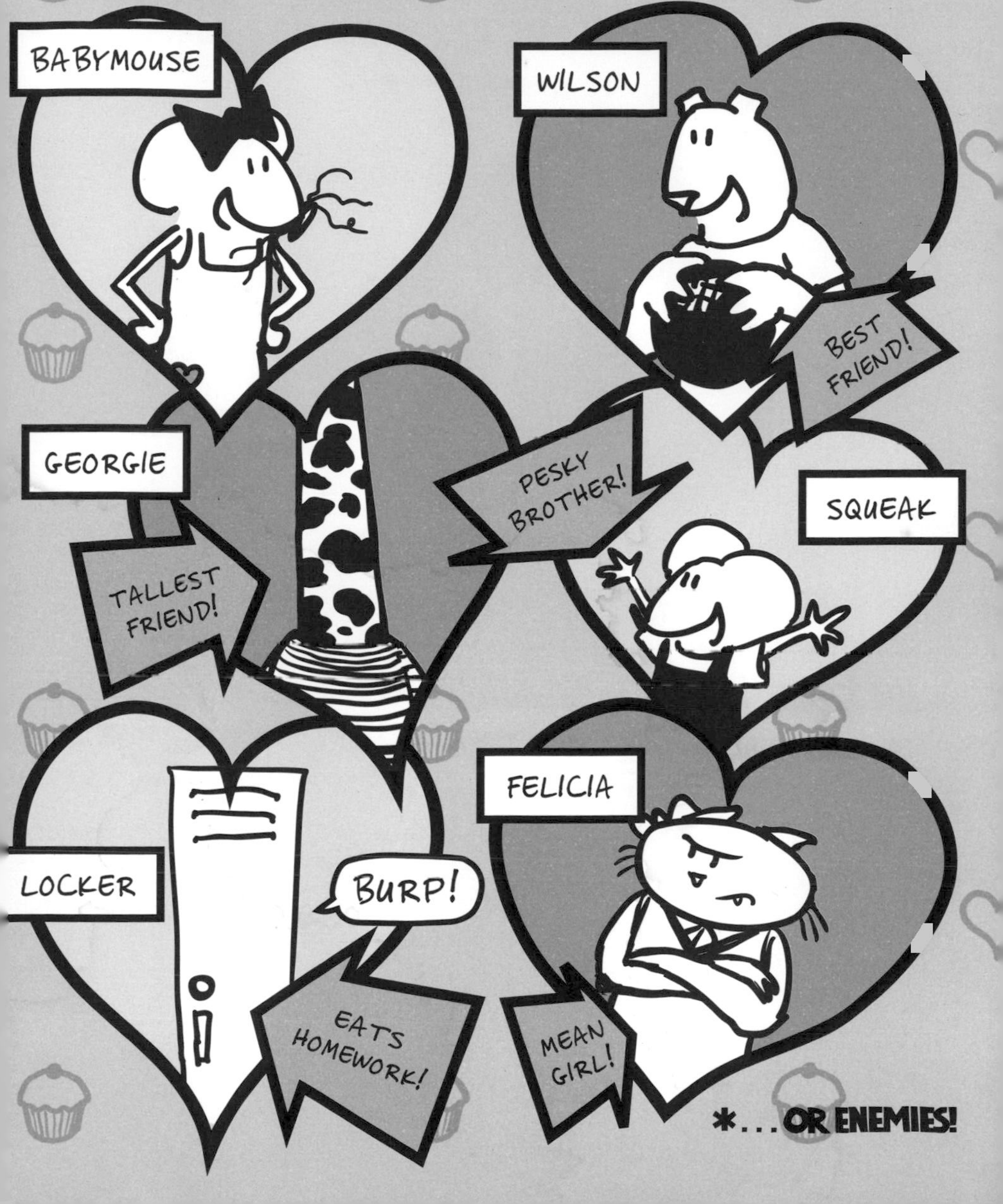
BABYMOUSE
WILSON
BEST FRIEND!
GEORGIE
TALLEST FRIEND!
PESKY BROTHER!
SQUEAK
LOCKER
BURP!
EATS HOMEWORK!
FELICIA
MEAN GIRL!

*. . . OR ENEMIES!

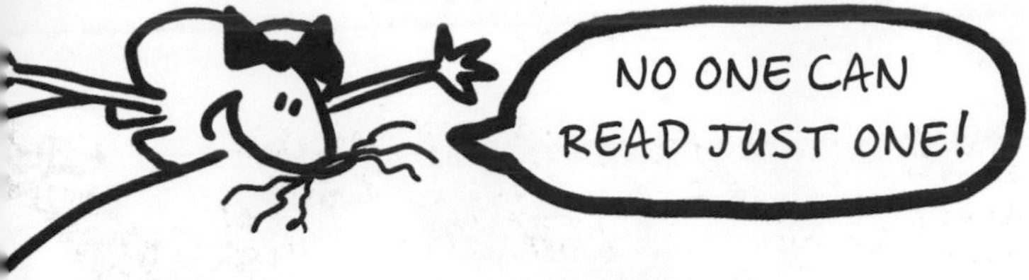
NO ONE CAN
READ JUST ONE!

Be sure to read **ALL** the **BABYMOUSE** books:

#1 BABYMOUSE: Queen of the World!
#2 BABYMOUSE: Our Hero
#3 BABYMOUSE: Beach Babe
#4 BABYMOUSE: Rock Star
#5 BABYMOUSE: Heartbreaker
#6 CAMP BABYMOUSE
#7 BABYMOUSE: Skater Girl
#8 BABYMOUSE: Puppy Love
#9 BABYMOUSE: Monster Mash
#10 BABYMOUSE: The Musical
#11 BABYMOUSE: Dragonslayer
#12 BABYMOUSE: Burns Rubber
#13 BABYMOUSE: Cupcake Tycoon
#14 BABYMOUSE: Mad Scientist
#15 A Very BABYMOUSE Christmas
#16 BABYMOUSE for President
#17 Extreme BABYMOUSE
#18 Happy Birthday, BABYMOUSE

BABYMOUSE
OUR HERO

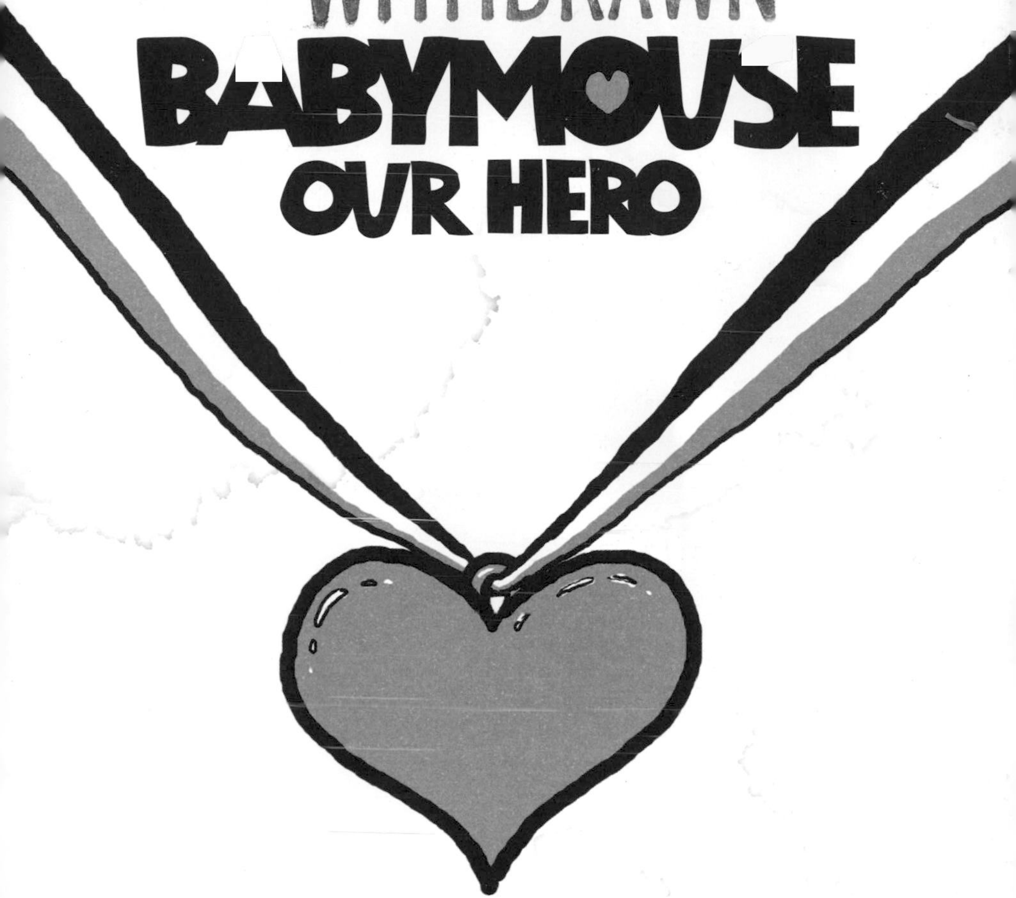

BY JENNIFER L. HOLM & MATTHEW HOLM

RANDOM HOUSE NEW YORK

YAWN
BORING!

Published in the United States by Random House Children's Books, a division of Random House LLC, a Penguin Random House Company, New York. Random House and the colophon are registered trademarks of Random House LLC.

Visit us on the Web!
randomhouse.com/kids
Babymouse.com

Educators and librarians, for a variety of teaching tools, visit us at
RHTeachersLibrarians.com

Library of Congress Cataloging-in-Publication Data
Holm, Jennifer L.
Babymouse : our hero / Jennifer Holm and Matthew Holm
p. cm.
SUMMARY: An imaginative young mouse is terrified to face her enemy in dodgeball, but with the help of her best friend, she not only plays the game, she proves herself a hero.
ISBN 978-0-375-83230-7 (trade) — ISBN 978-0-375-93230-4 (lib. bdg.)
[1. Ball games—Fiction. 2. Fear—Fiction. 3. Schools—Fiction. 4. Heroes—Fiction. 5. Mice—Fiction. 6. Animals—Fiction. 7. Cartoons and comics.]
I. Holm, Matthew. II. Title.
PN6727.H592 B32 2005 741.5'973—dc22 2004051169

MANUFACTURED IN MALAYSIA 16

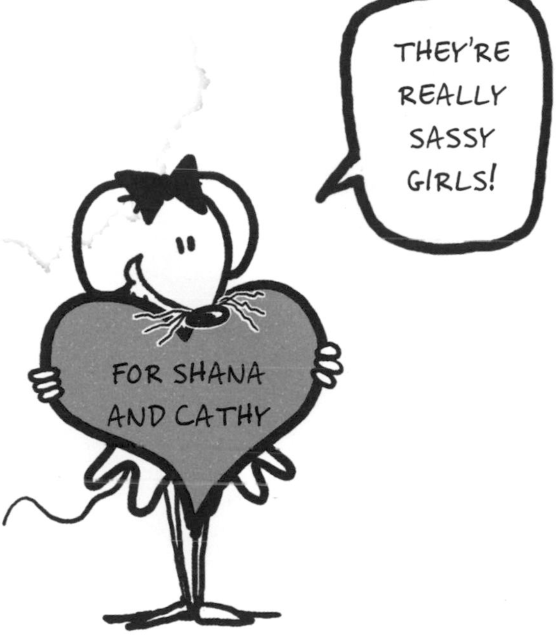
THEY'RE REALLY SASSY GIRLS!
FOR SHANA AND CATHY

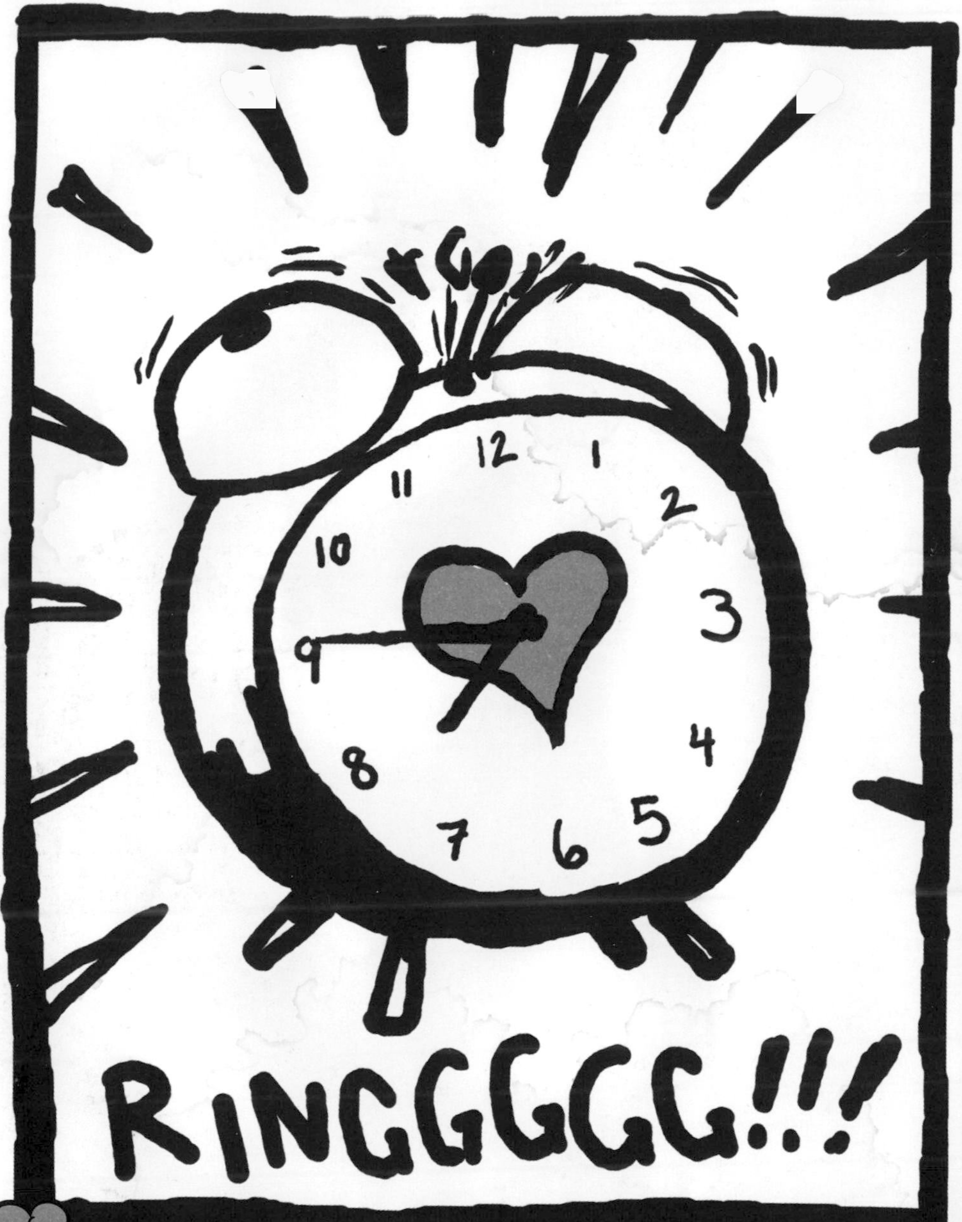
RINGGGGG!!!

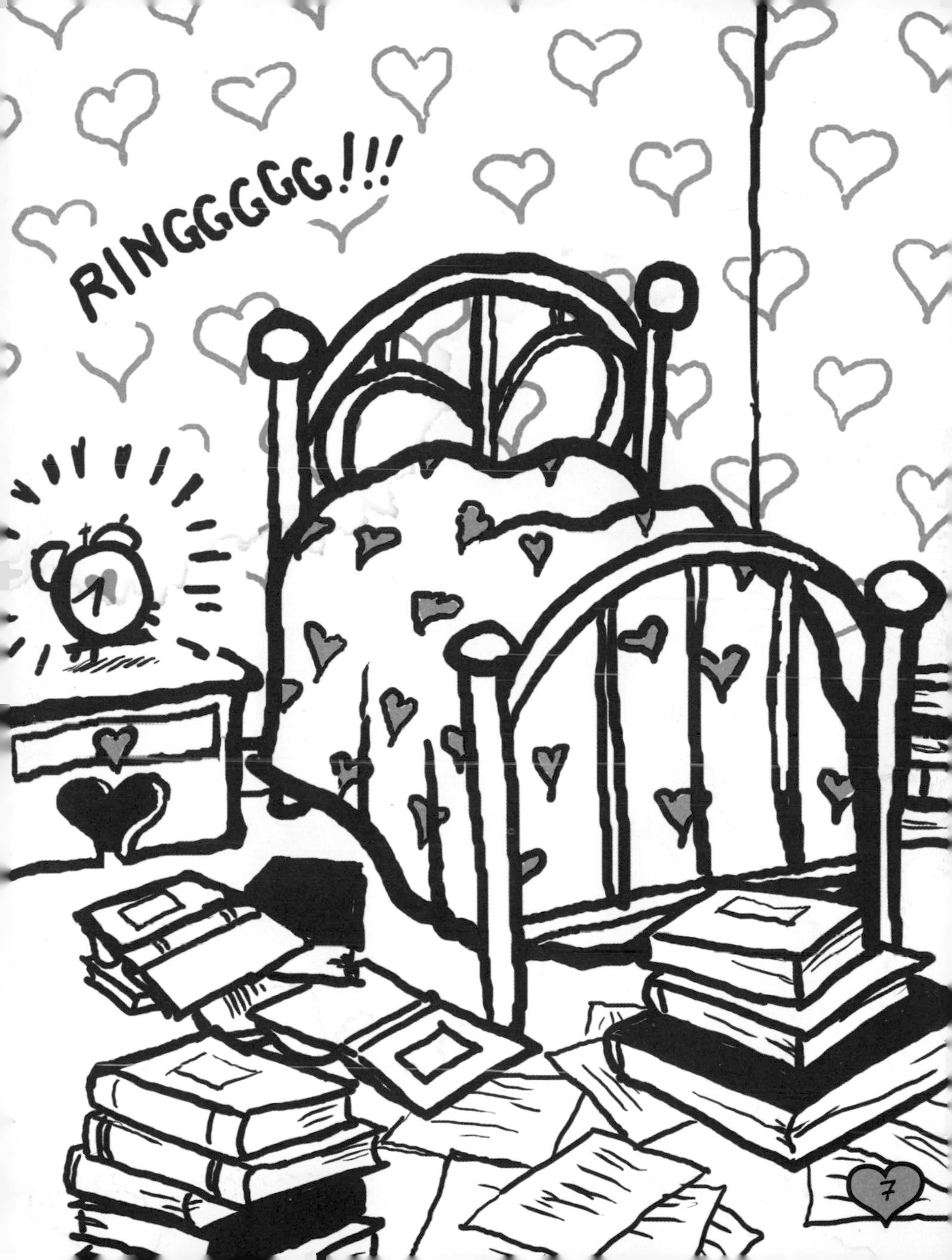
RINGGGGGG!!!

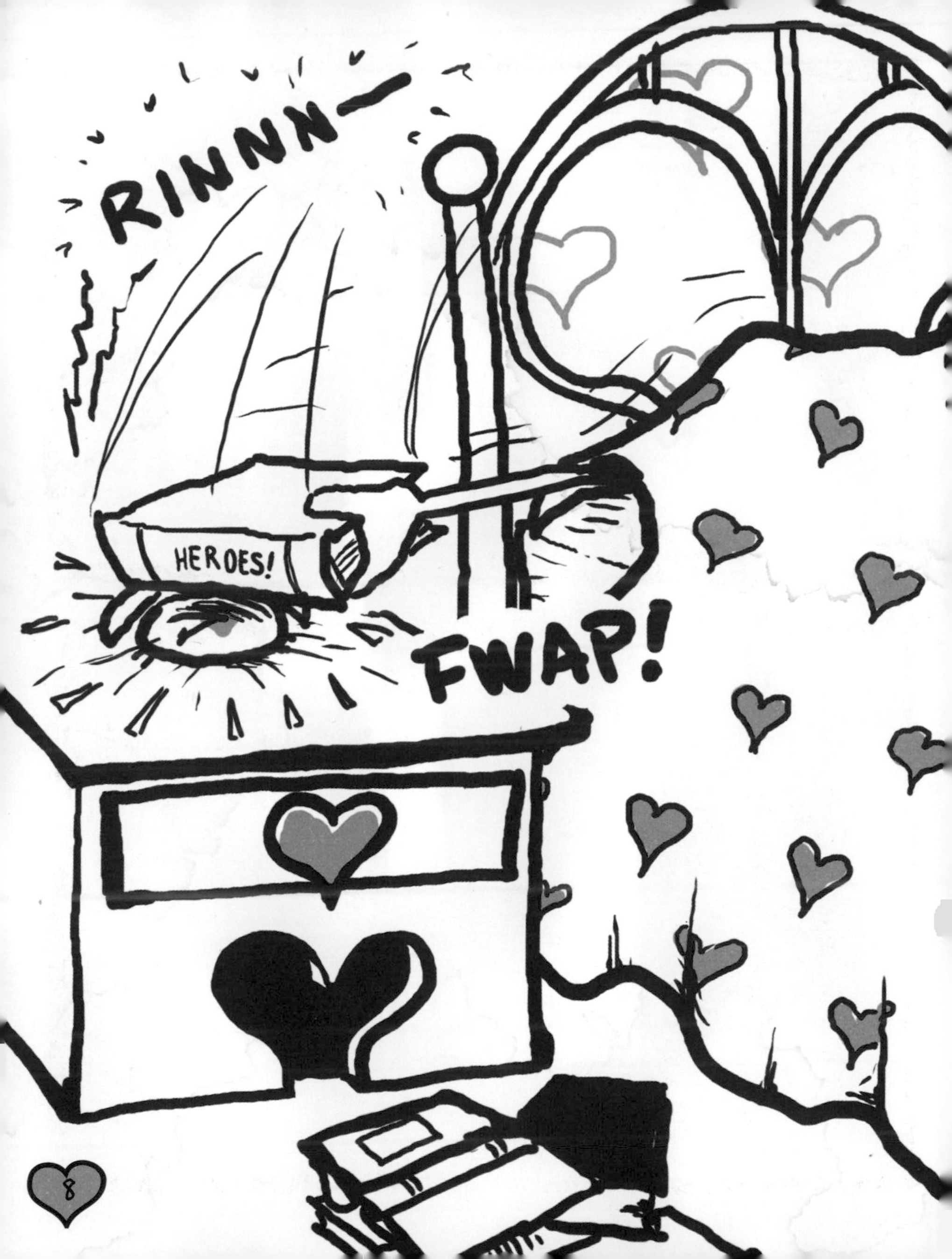
RINNN—
HEROES!
FWAP!

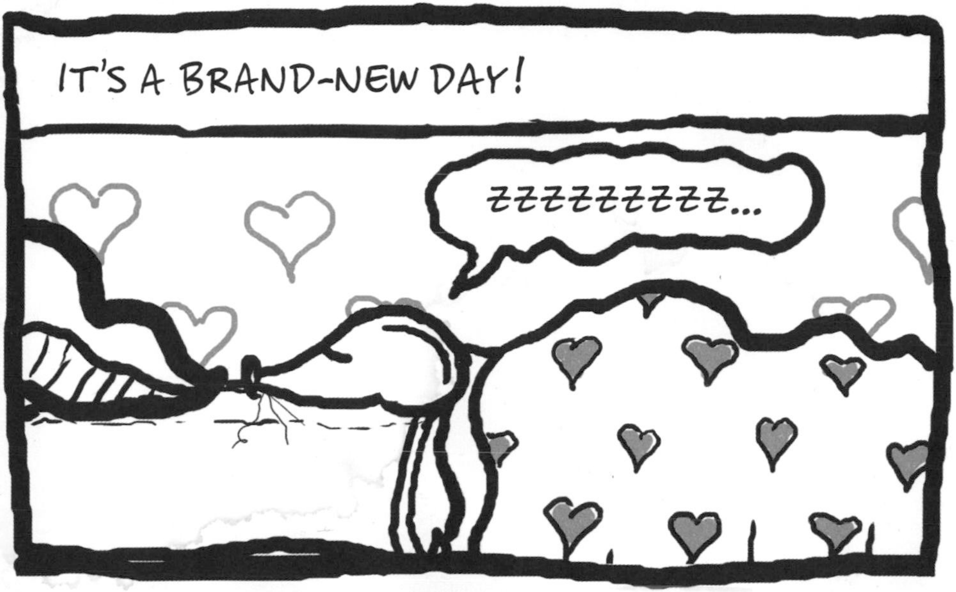
IT'S A BRAND-NEW DAY!
ZZZZZZZZZZ...

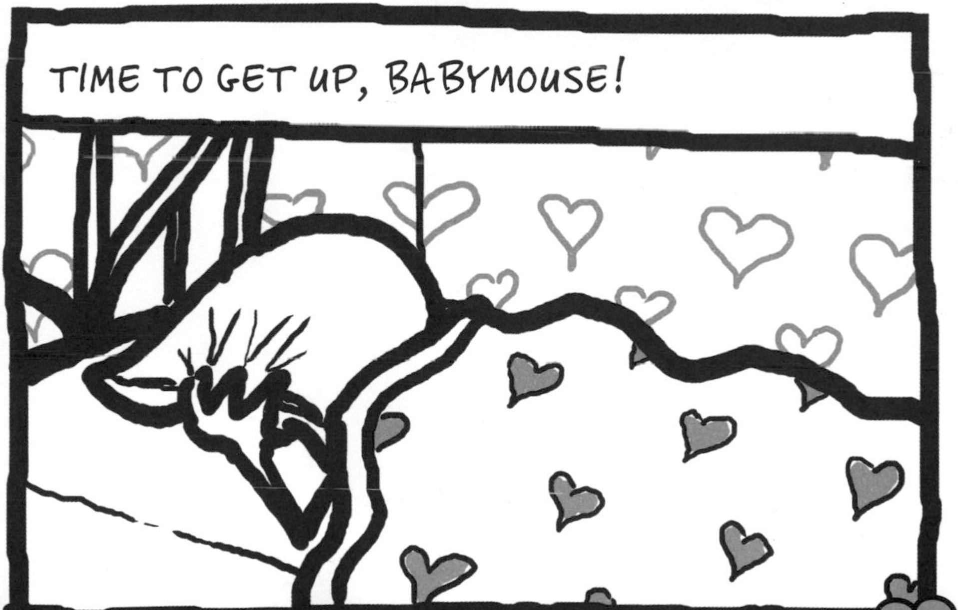
TIME TO GET UP, BABYMOUSE!

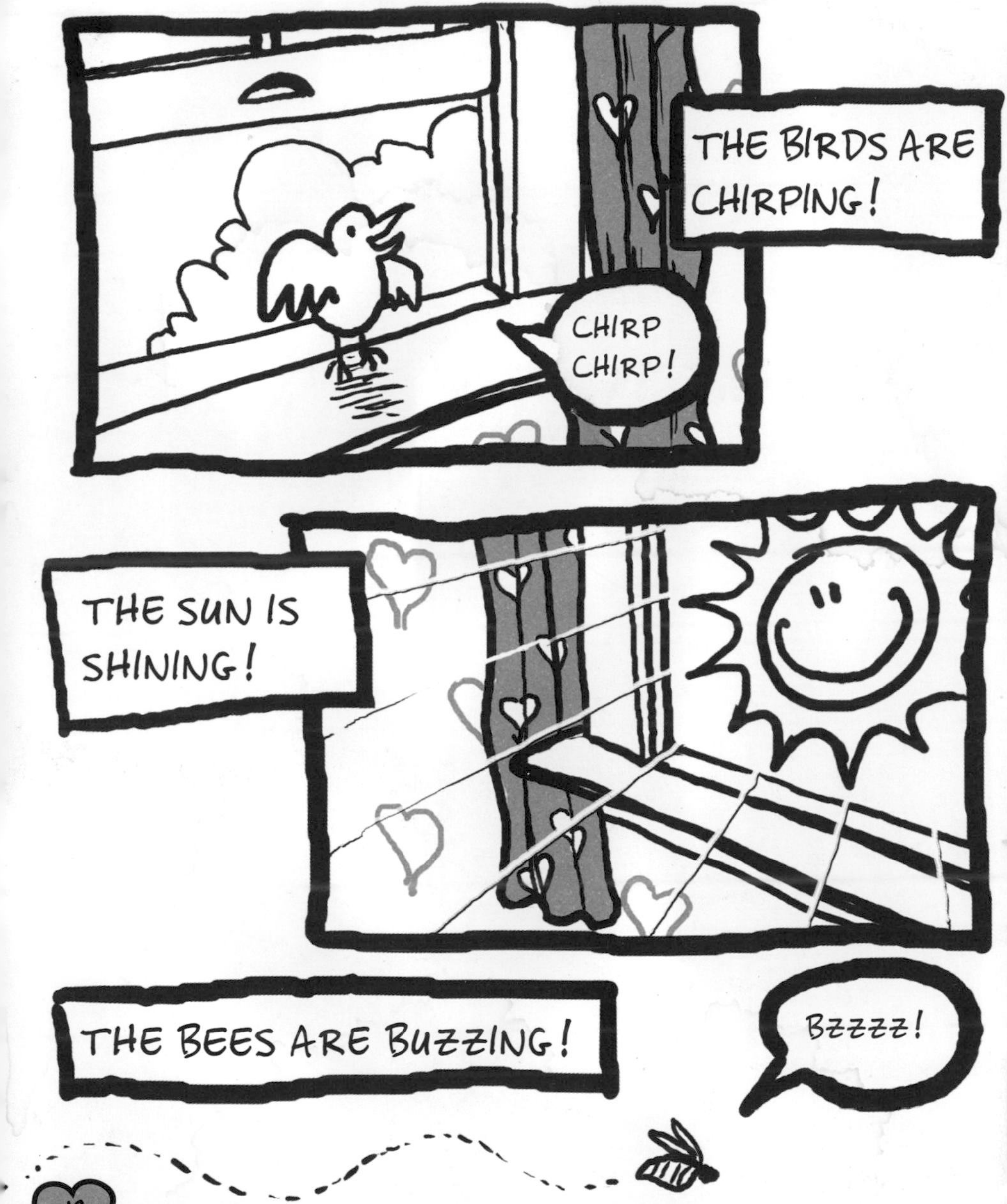
THE BIRDS ARE CHIRPING!
CHIRP CHIRP!
THE SUN IS SHINING!
THE BEES ARE BUZZING!
Bzzzz!

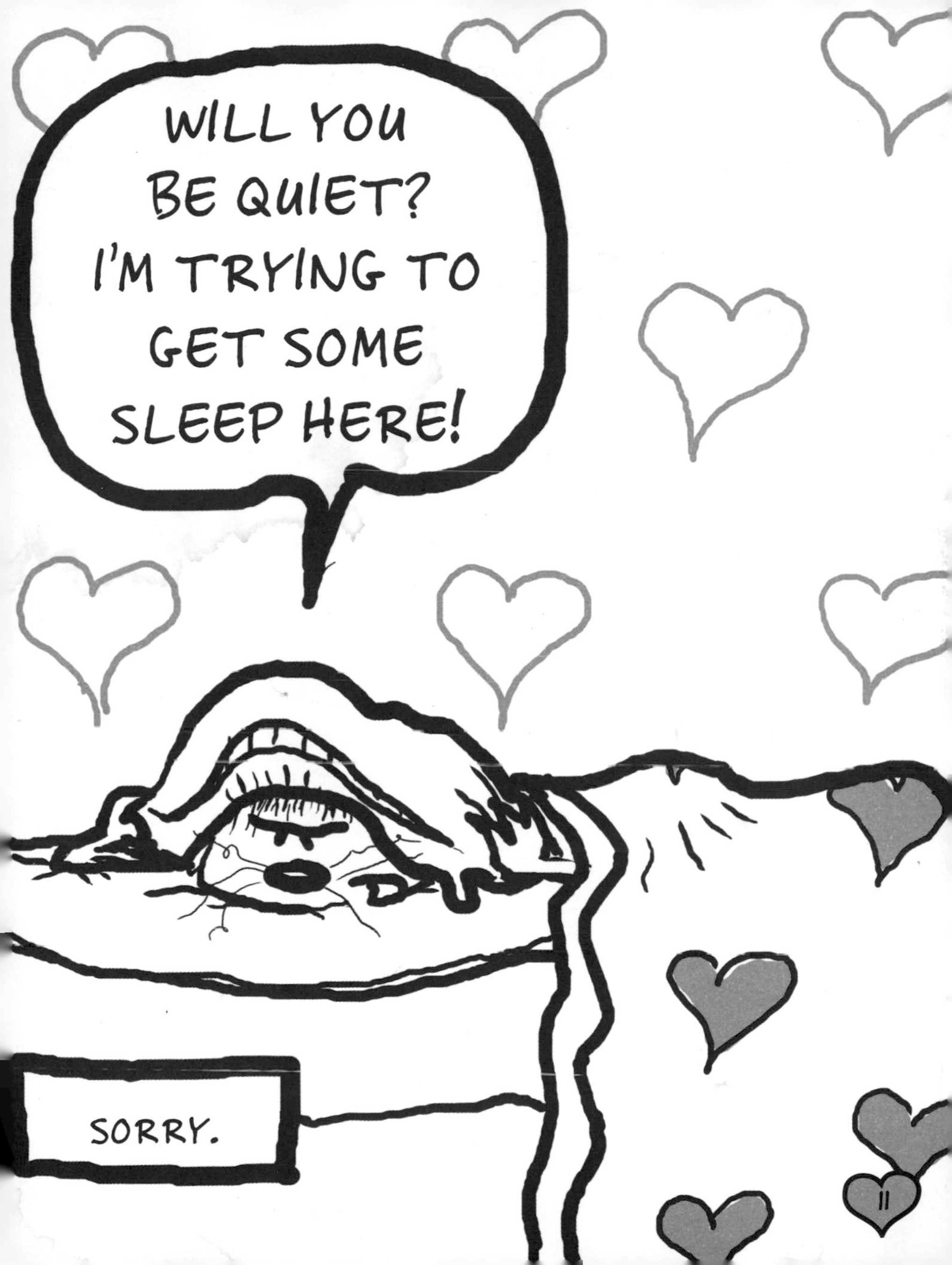
WILL YOU BE QUIET? I'M TRYING TO GET SOME SLEEP HERE!
SORRY.

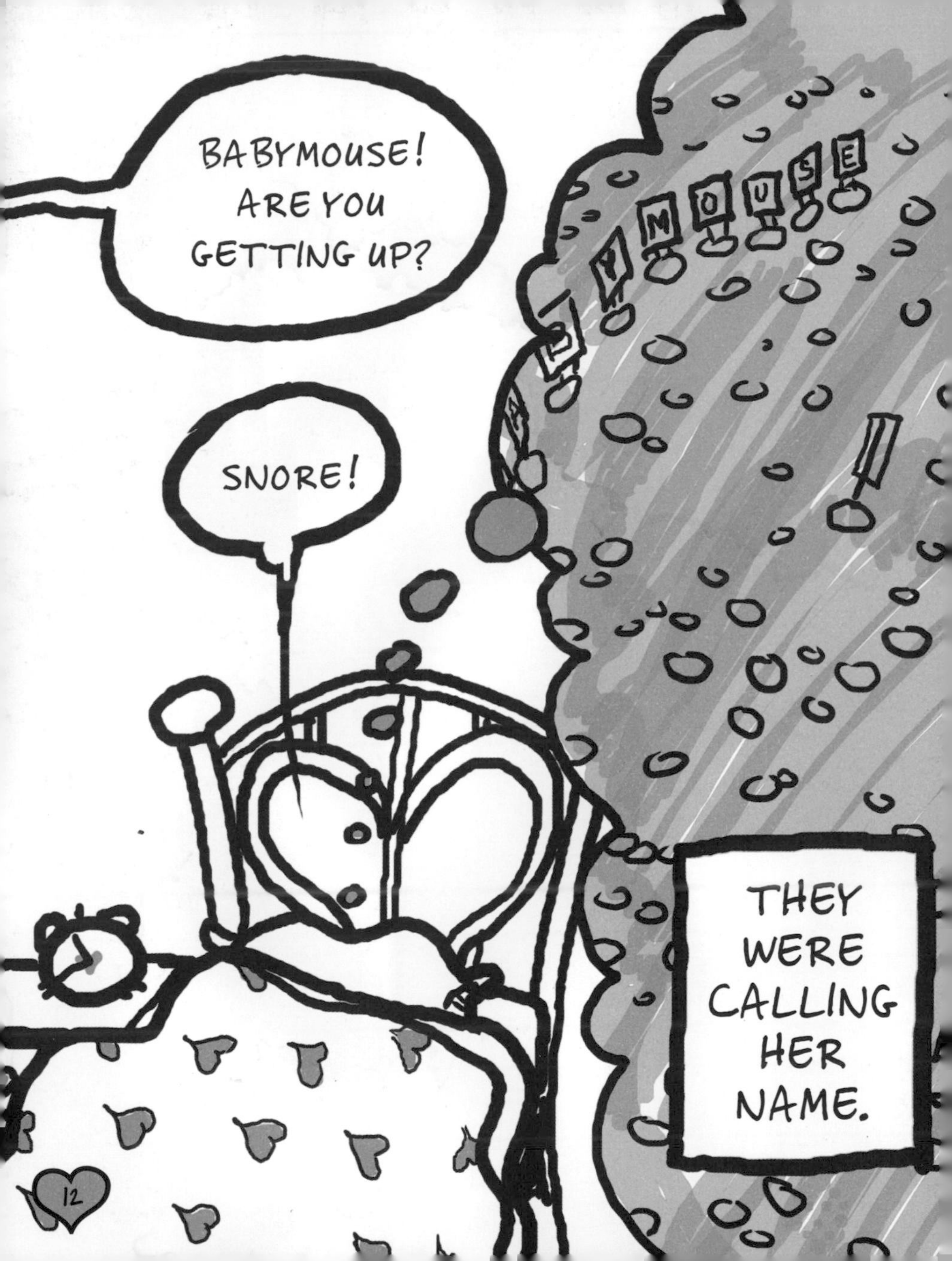
BABYMOUSE! ARE YOU GETTING UP?
SNORE!
THEY WERE CALLING HER NAME.

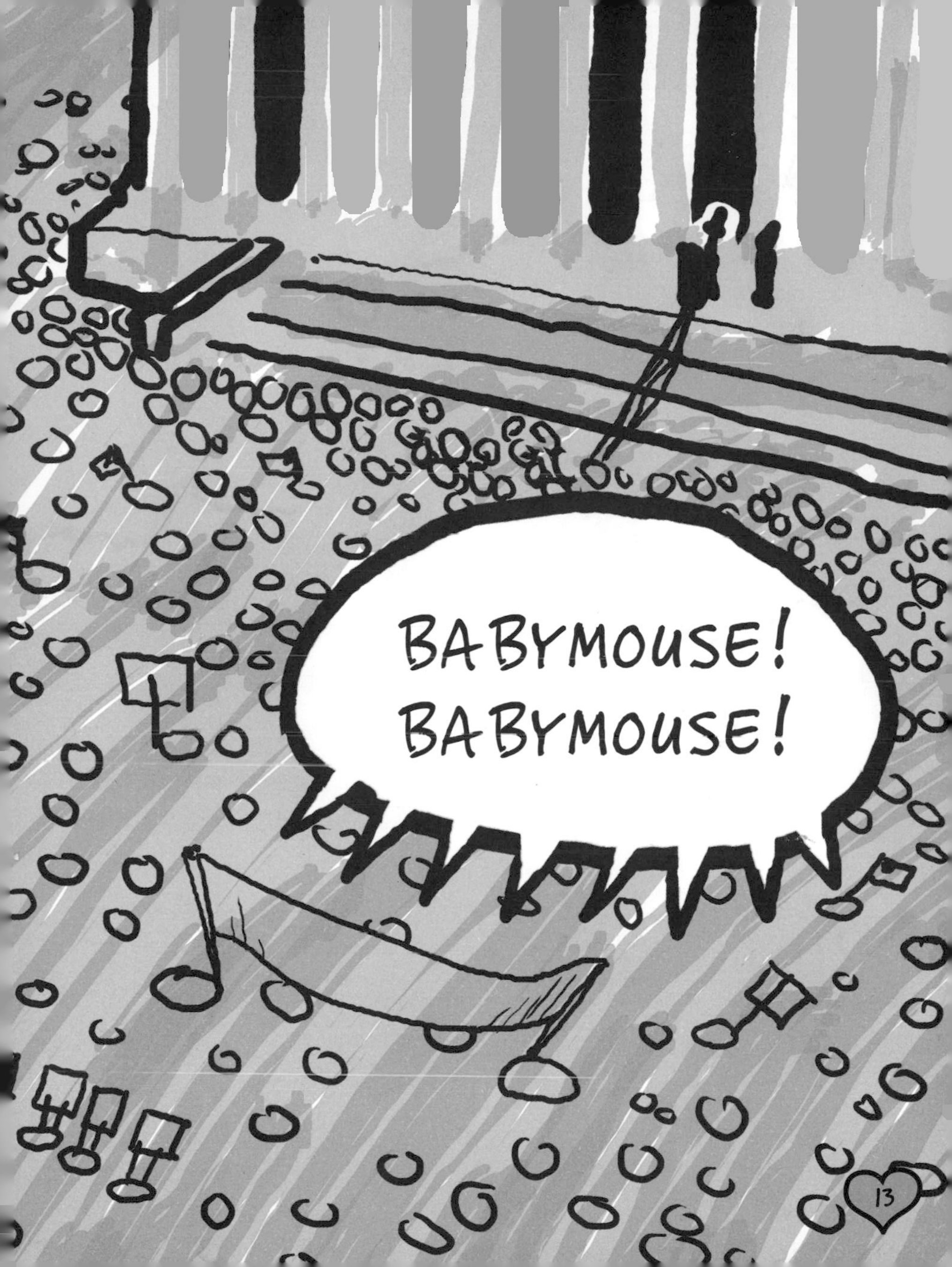
BABYMOUSE!
BABYMOUSE!

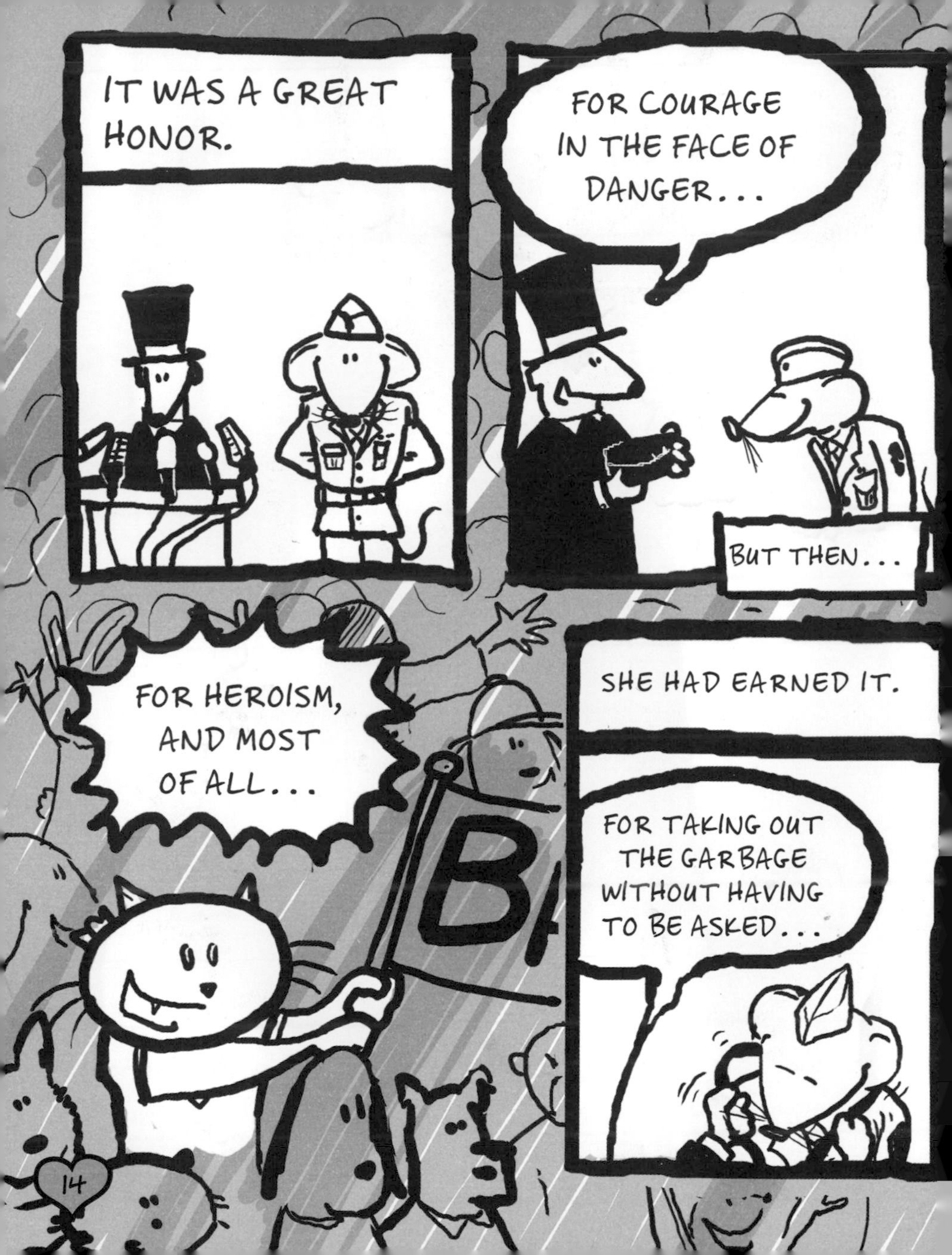
IT WAS A GREAT HONOR.
FOR COURAGE IN THE FACE OF DANGER...
BUT THEN...
FOR HEROISM, AND MOST OF ALL...
SHE HAD EARNED IT.
FOR TAKING OUT THE GARBAGE WITHOUT HAVING TO BE ASKED...

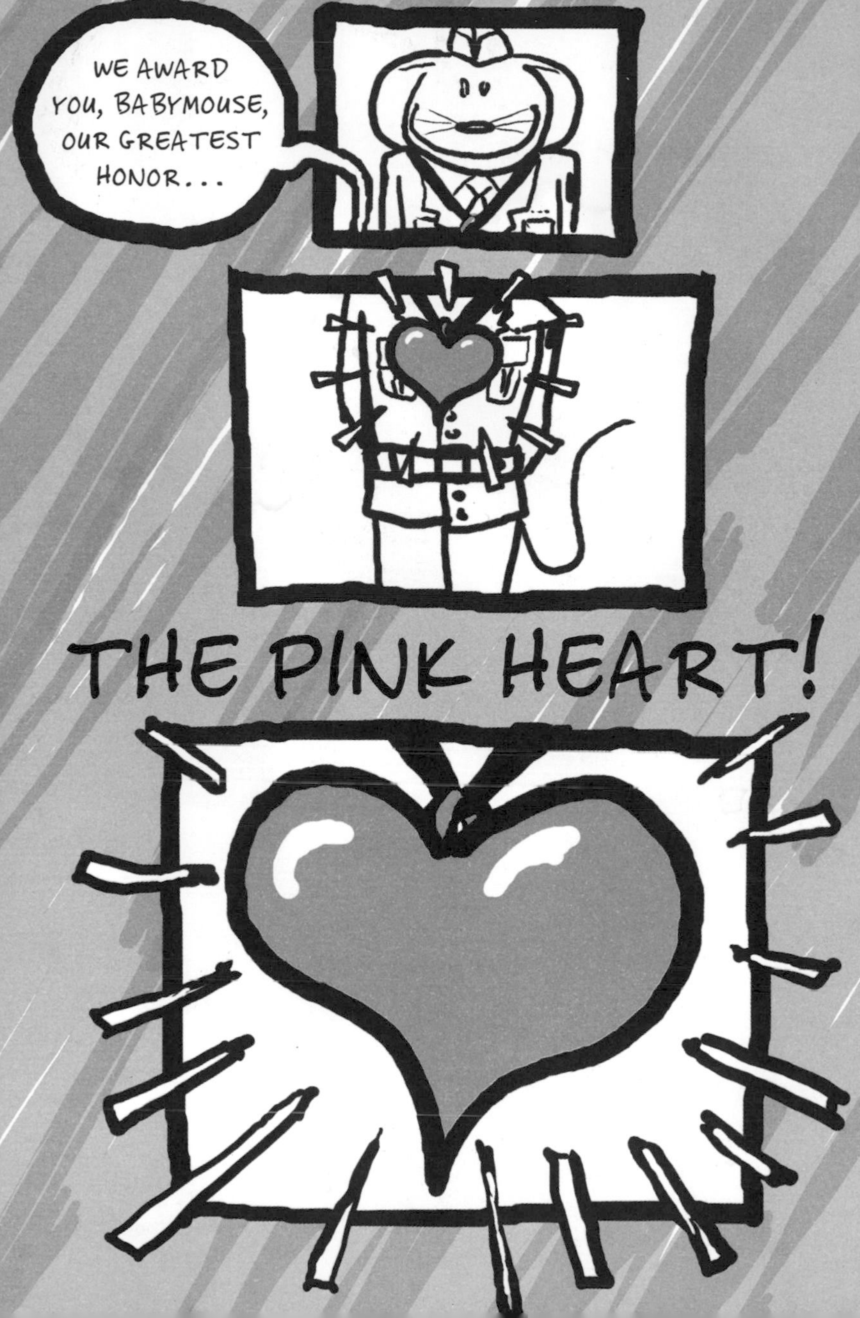
WE AWARD YOU, BABYMOUSE, OUR GREATEST HONOR...
THE PINK HEART!

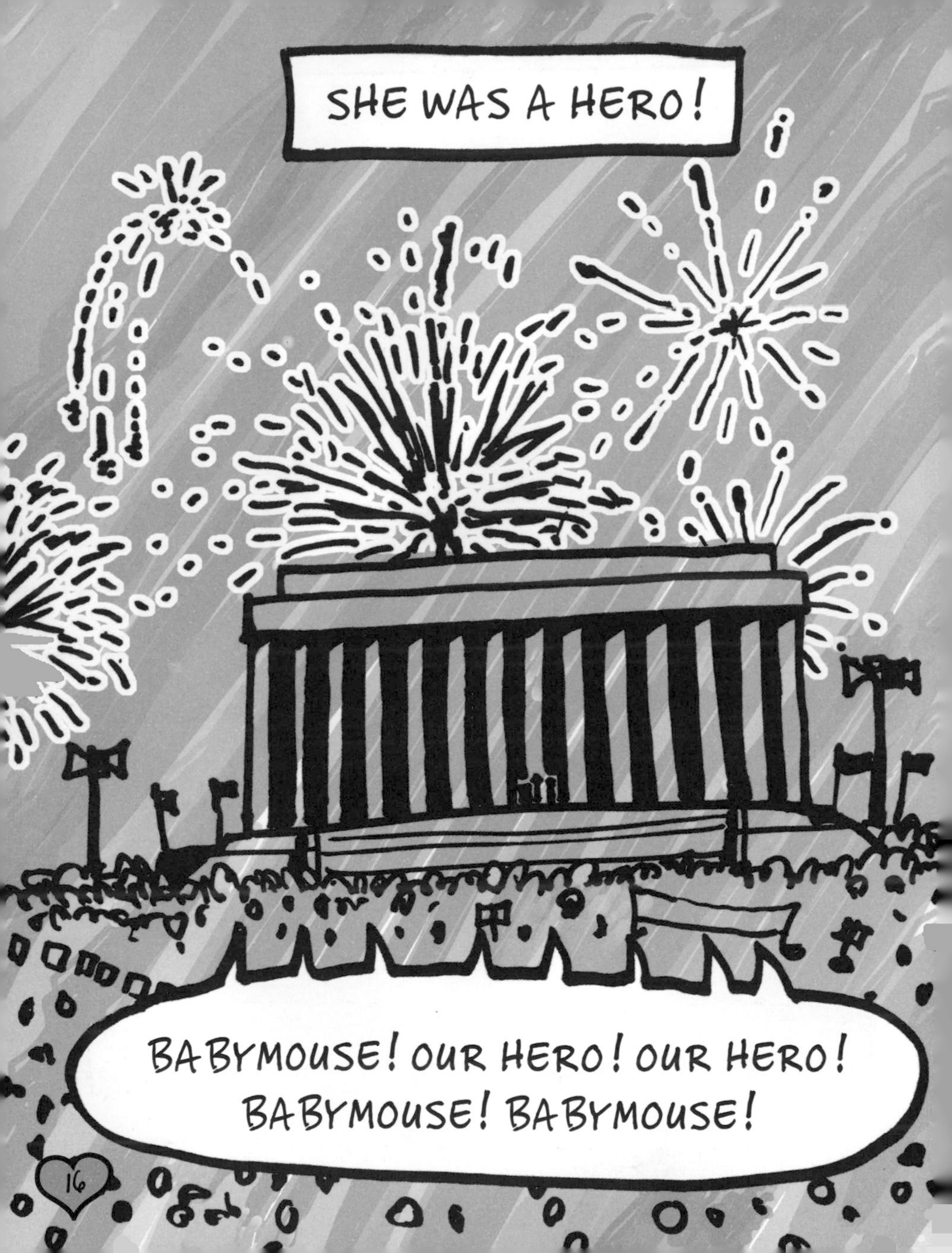
SHE WAS A HERO!
BABYMOUSE! OUR HERO! OUR HERO! BABYMOUSE! BABYMOUSE!

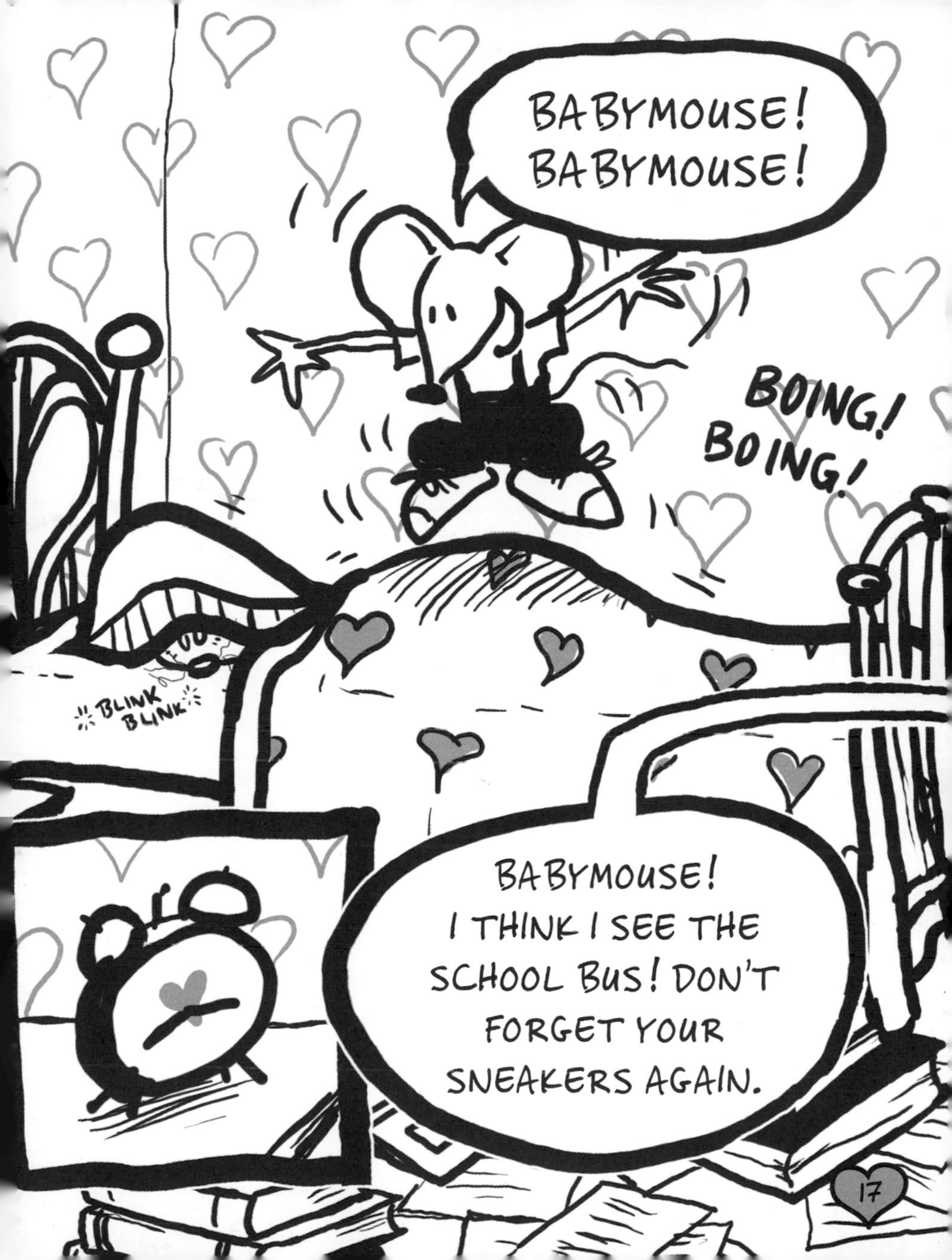
BABYMOUSE! BABYMOUSE!
BOING! BOING!
BLINK BLINK
BABYMOUSE! I THINK I SEE THE SCHOOL BUS! DON'T FORGET YOUR SNEAKERS AGAIN.

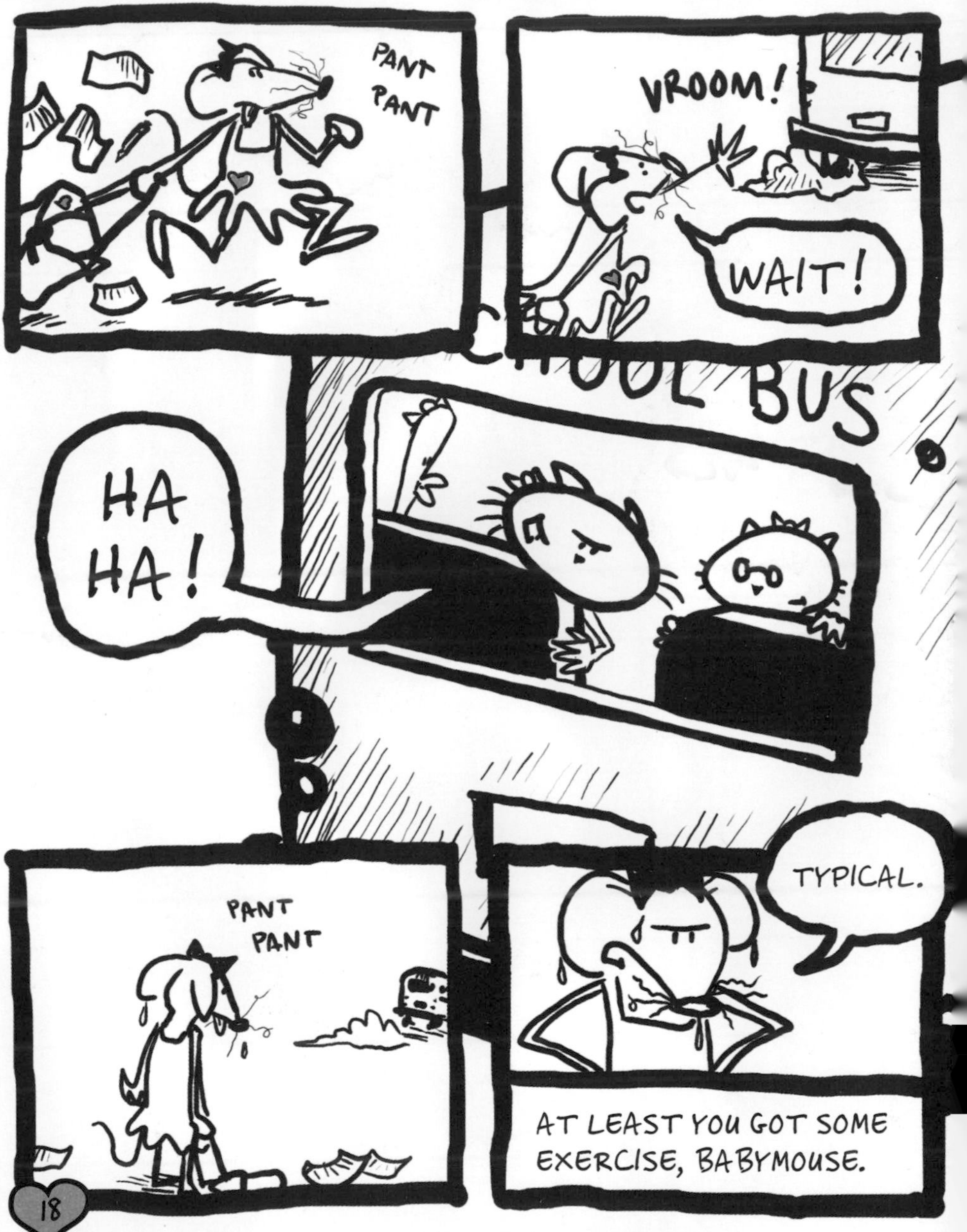
PANT
PANT
VROOM!
WAIT!
CHOOL BUS
HA HA!
PANT
PANT
TYPICAL.
AT LEAST YOU GOT SOME EXERCISE, BABYMOUSE.

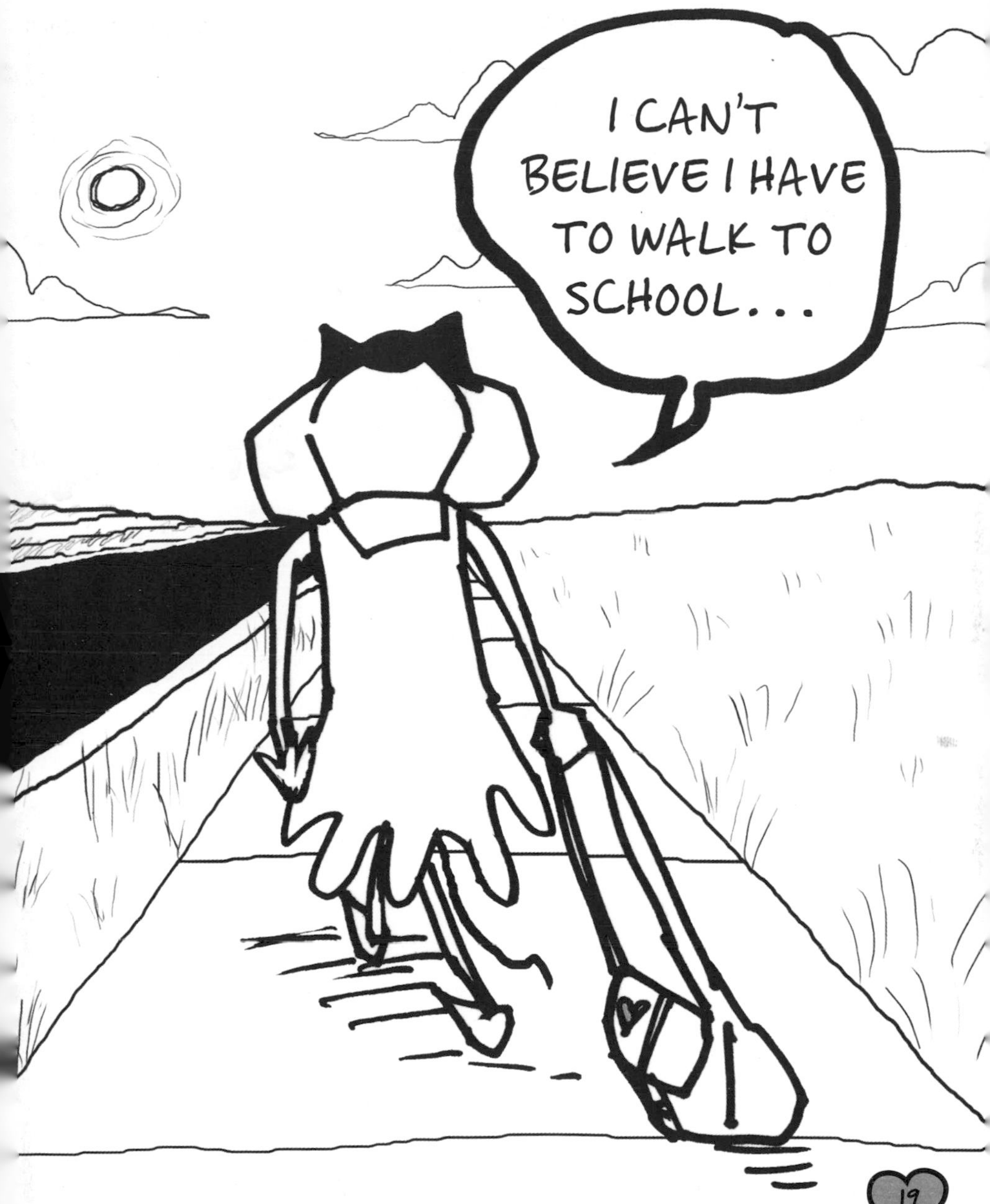
I CAN'T BELIEVE I HAVE TO WALK TO SCHOOL...

BABYMOUSE WONDERED IF SHE'D EVER MAKE IT TO SCHOOL.

I'LL NEVER MAKE IT.

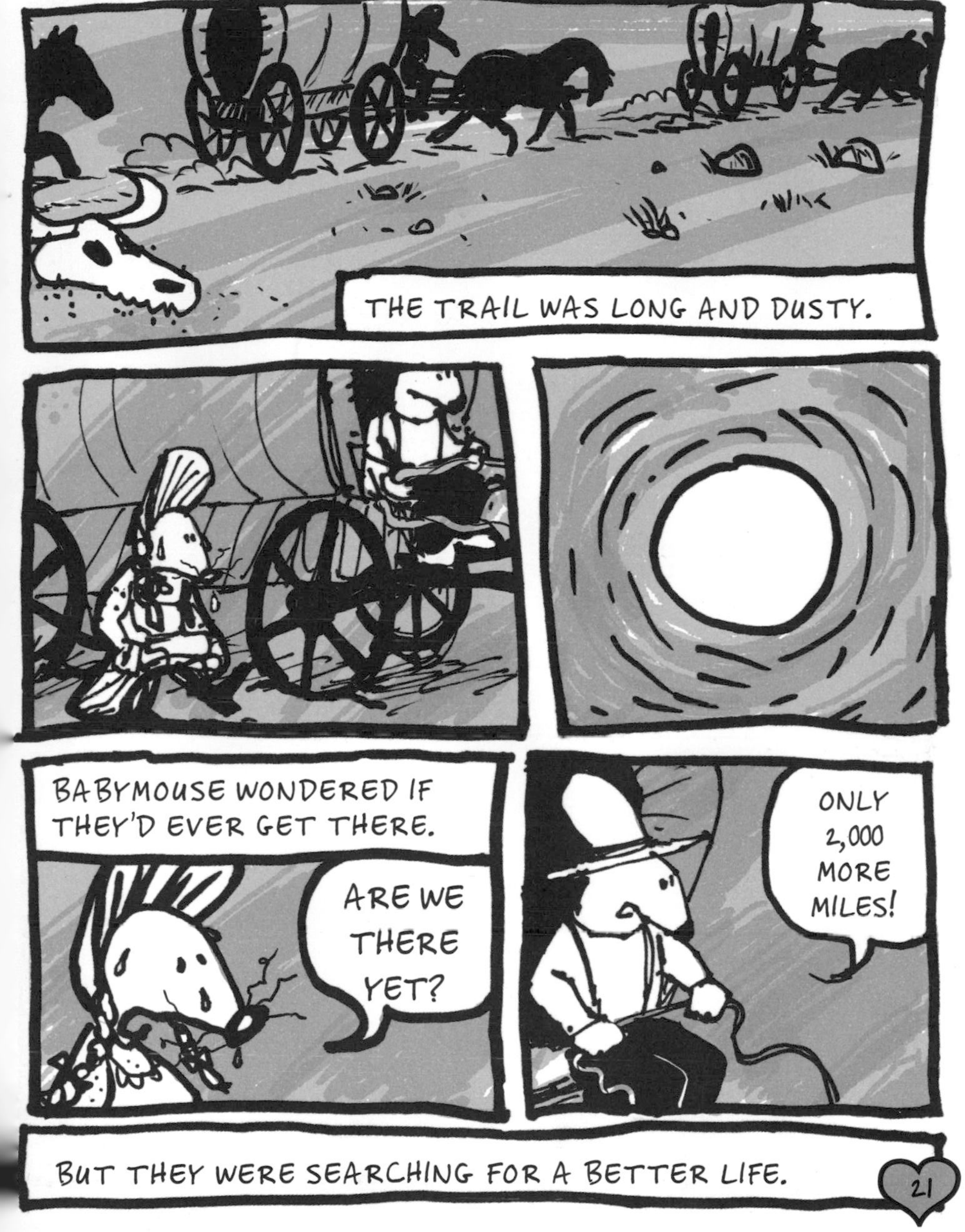
THE TRAIL WAS LONG AND DUSTY.
BABYMOUSE WONDERED IF THEY'D EVER GET THERE.
ARE WE THERE YET?
ONLY 2,000 MORE MILES!
BUT THEY WERE SEARCHING FOR A BETTER LIFE.

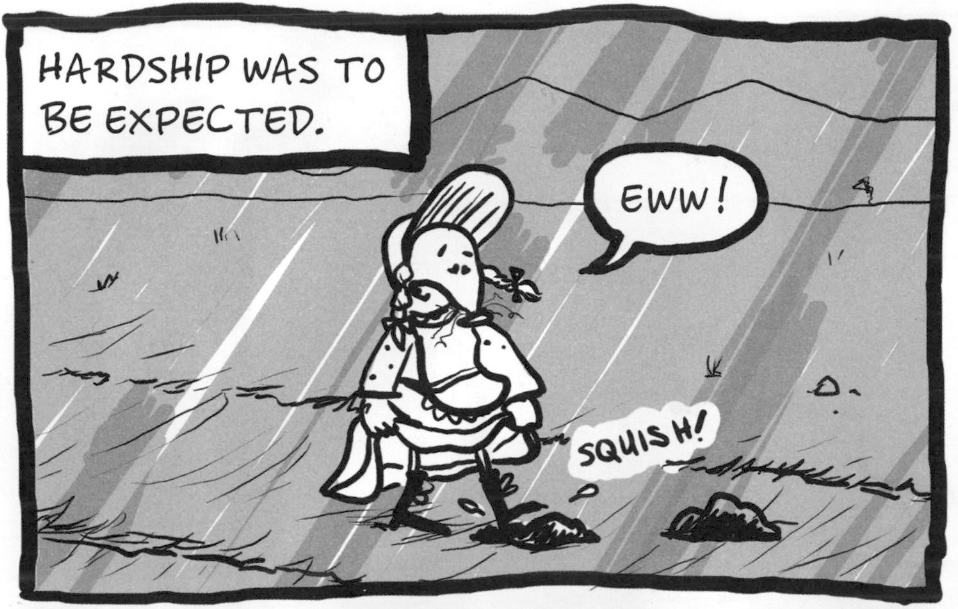
HARDSHIP WAS TO BE EXPECTED.
EWW!
SQUISH!

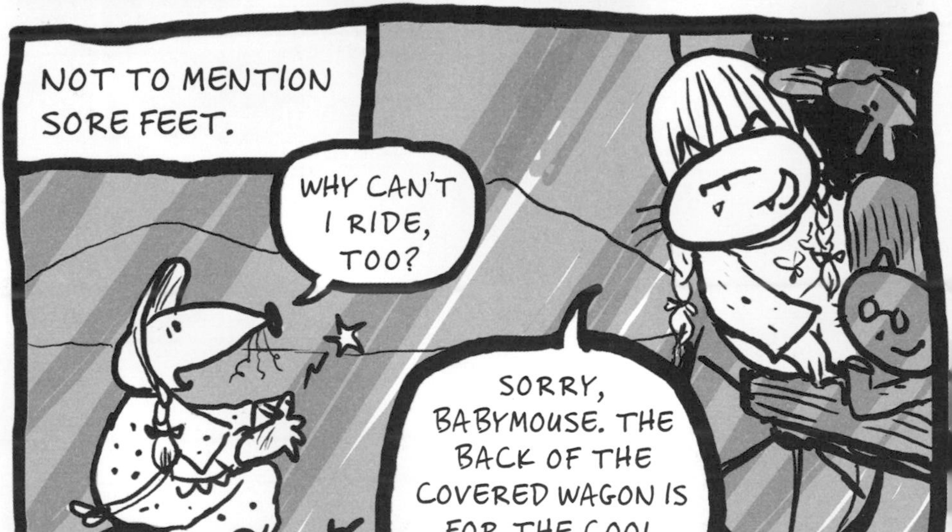
NOT TO MENTION SORE FEET.
WHY CAN'T I RIDE, TOO?
SORRY, BABYMOUSE. THE BACK OF THE COVERED WAGON IS FOR THE COOL PIONEER KIDS.

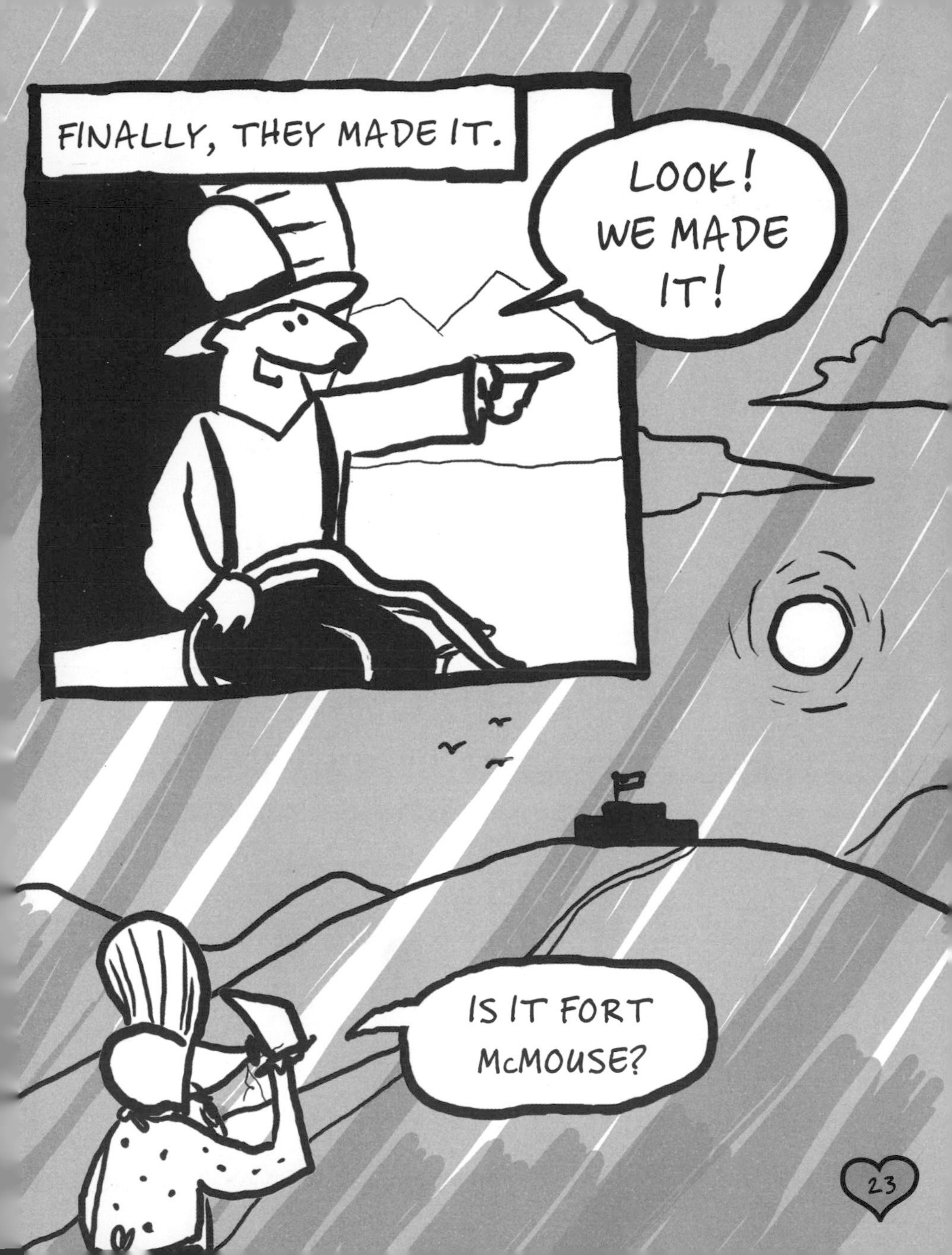
FINALLY, THEY MADE IT.
LOOK! WE MADE IT!
IS IT FORT McMOUSE?

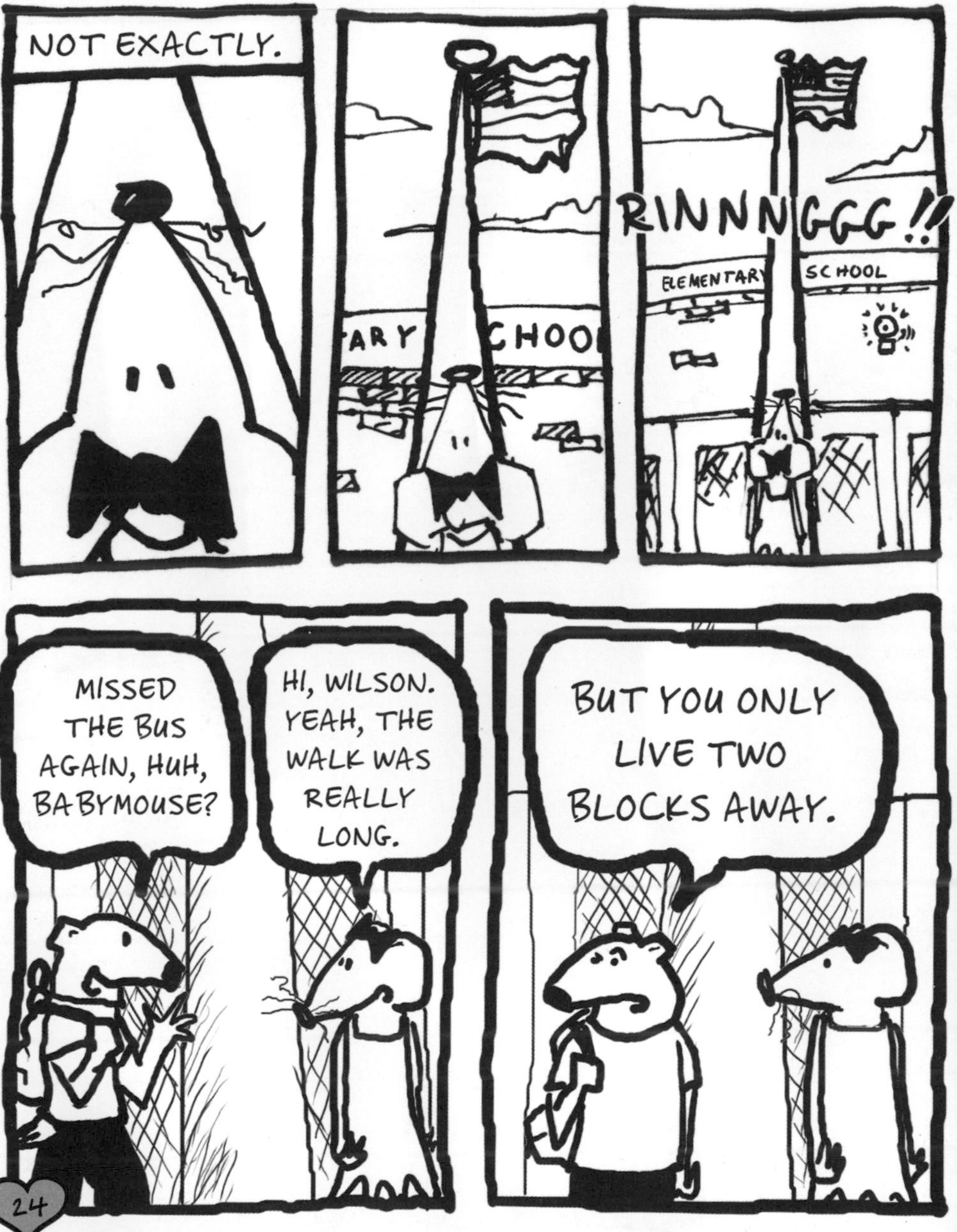
NOT EXACTLY.
ARY
CHOO
RINNNGGG!!
ELEMENTARY
SCHOOL
MISSED THE BUS AGAIN, HUH, BABYMOUSE?
HI, WILSON. YEAH, THE WALK WAS REALLY LONG.
BUT YOU ONLY LIVE TWO BLOCKS AWAY.

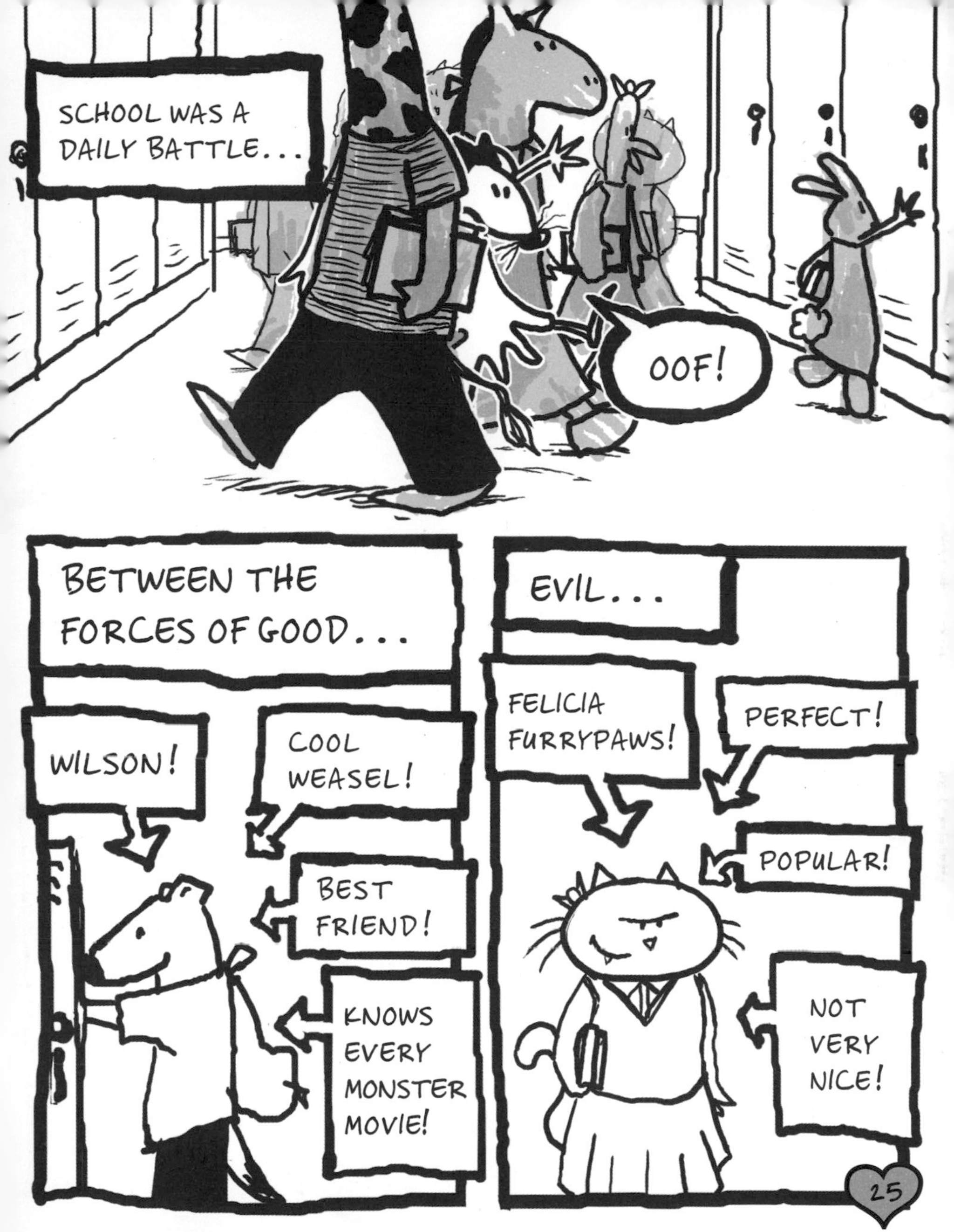
SCHOOL WAS A DAILY BATTLE...
OOF!
BETWEEN THE FORCES OF GOOD...
WILSON!
COOL WEASEL!
BEST FRIEND!
KNOWS EVERY MONSTER MOVIE!
EVIL...
FELICIA FURRYPAWS!
PERFECT!
POPULAR!
NOT VERY NICE!

...AND LOCKER!

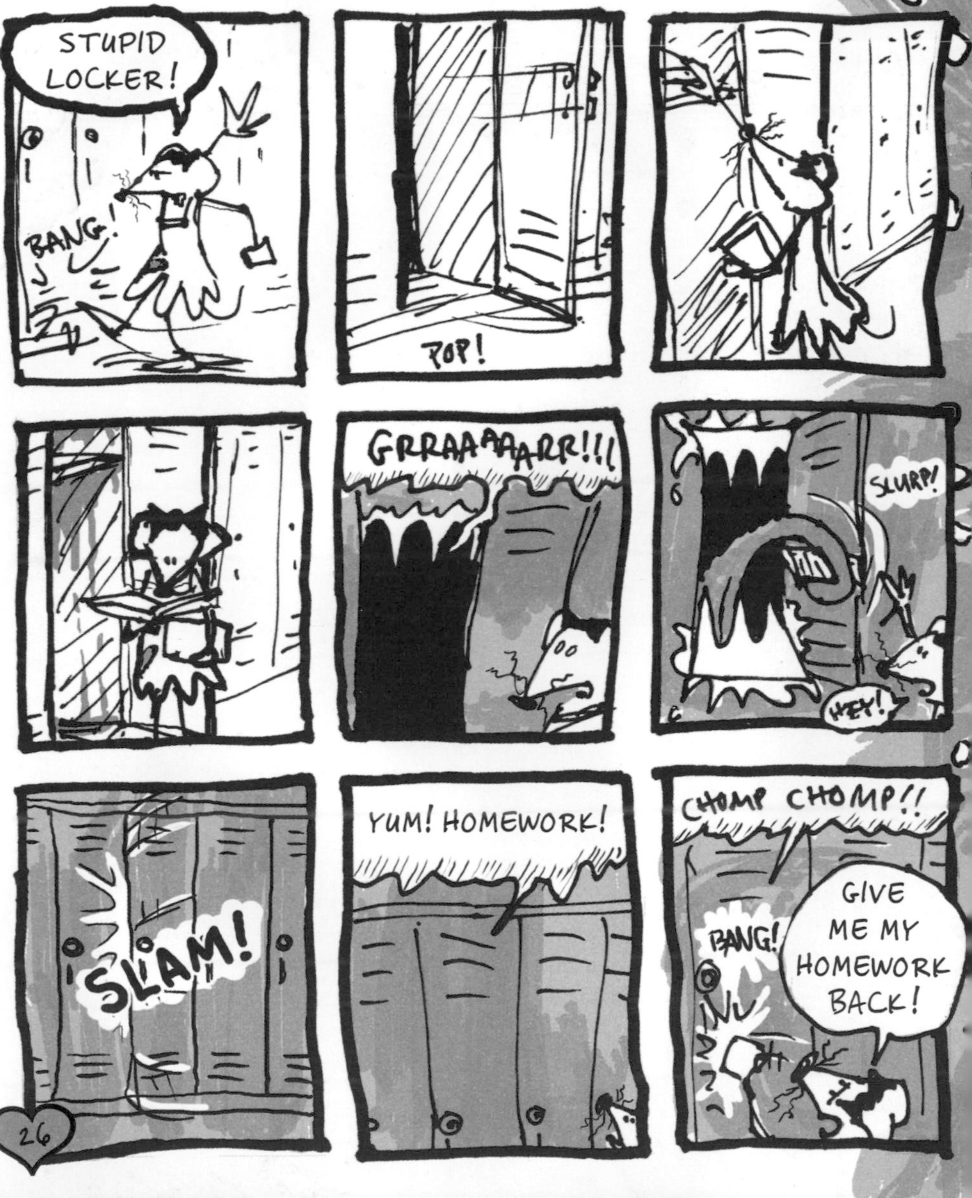
STUPID LOCKER!
BANG!
POP!
GRRAAAAARR!!!
SLURP!
HEY!
SLAM!
YUM! HOMEWORK!
CHOMP CHOMP!!
BANG!
GIVE ME MY HOMEWORK BACK!

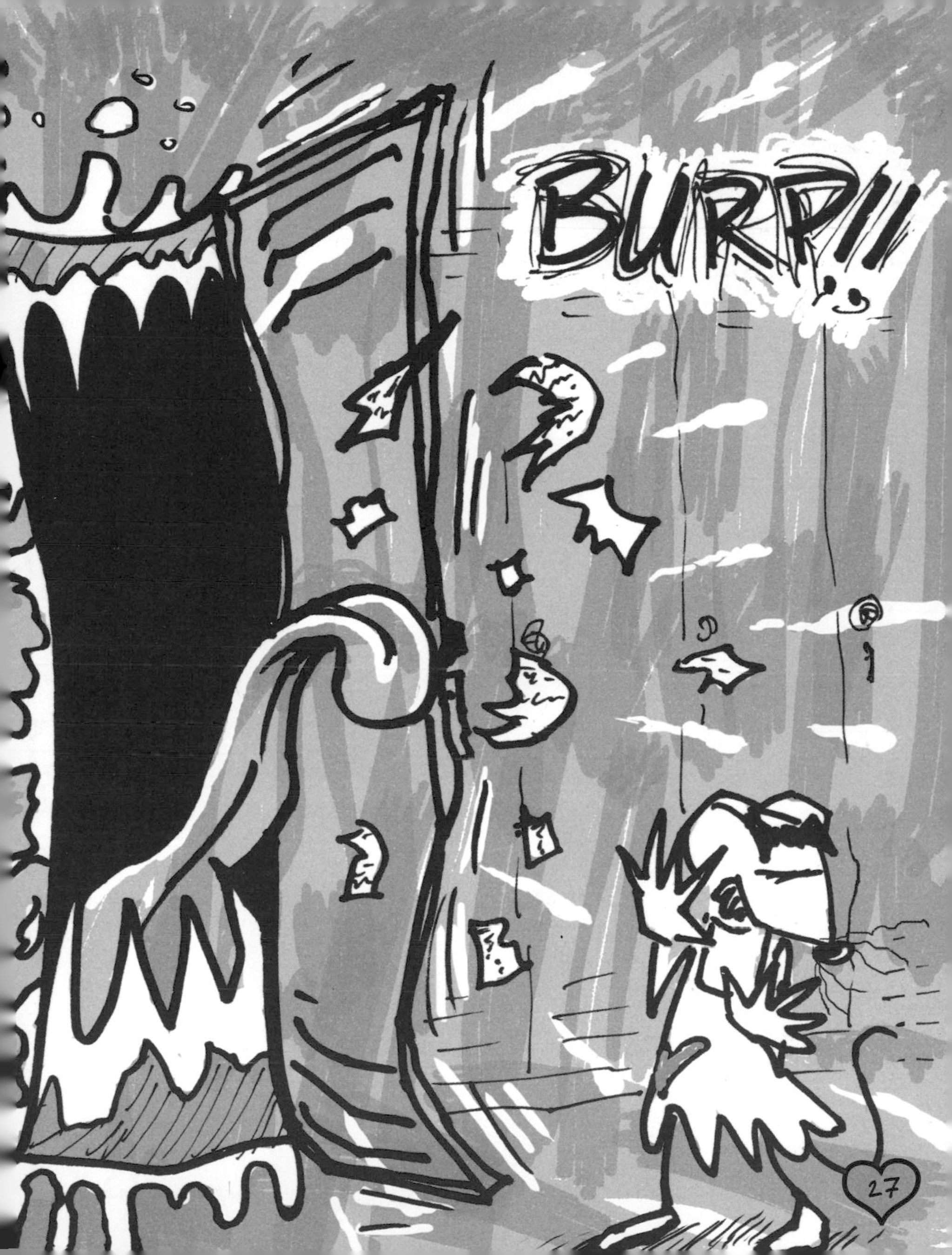
BURP!!

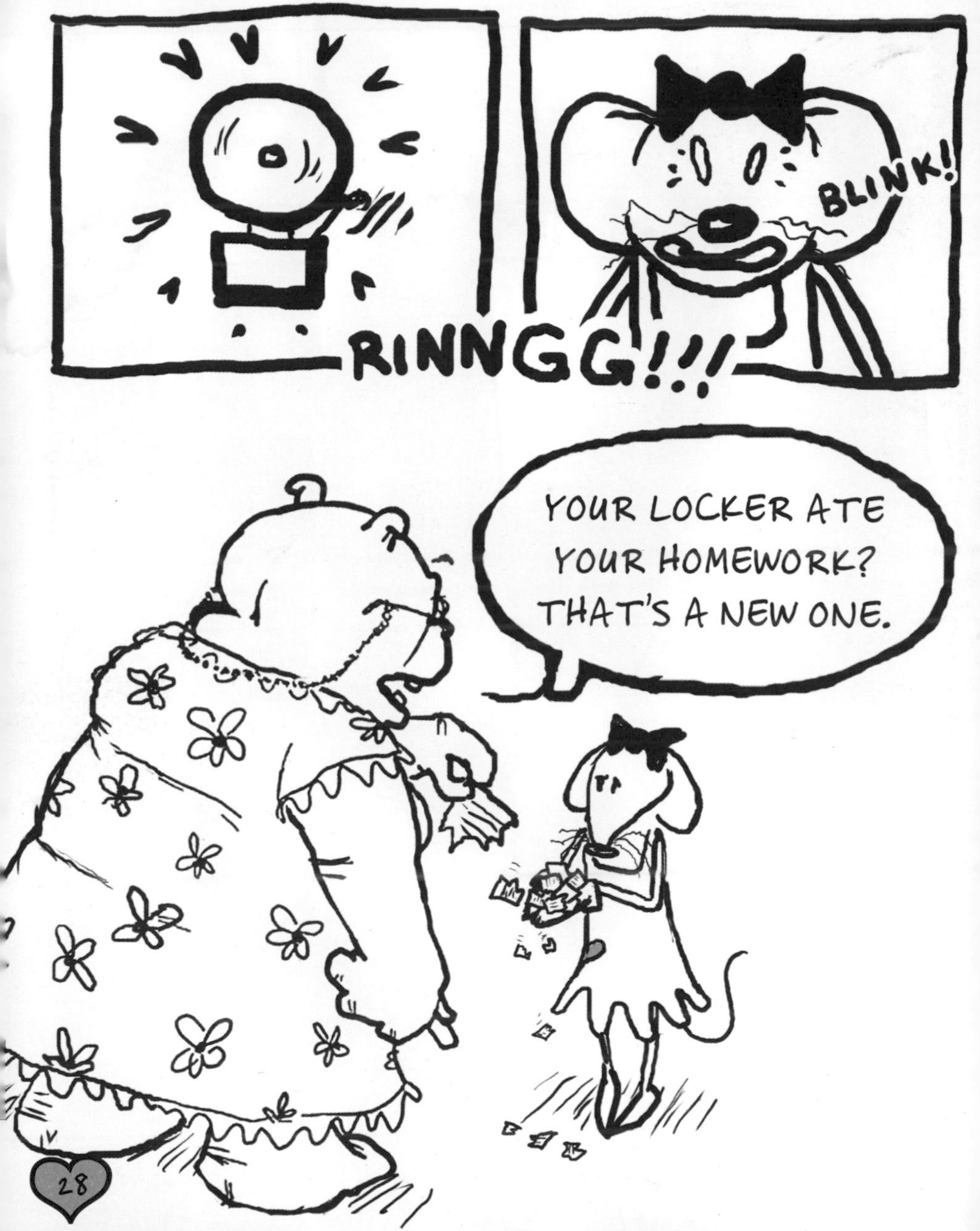
RINNGG!!!
BLINK!
YOUR LOCKER ATE YOUR HOMEWORK? THAT'S A NEW ONE.

MATH.

. . . CARRY THE ONE . . .

SIGH.

FRACTIONS IN ACTION!

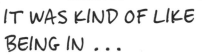

IT WAS KIND OF LIKE BEING IN . . .

PRISON!!!

CLICK!

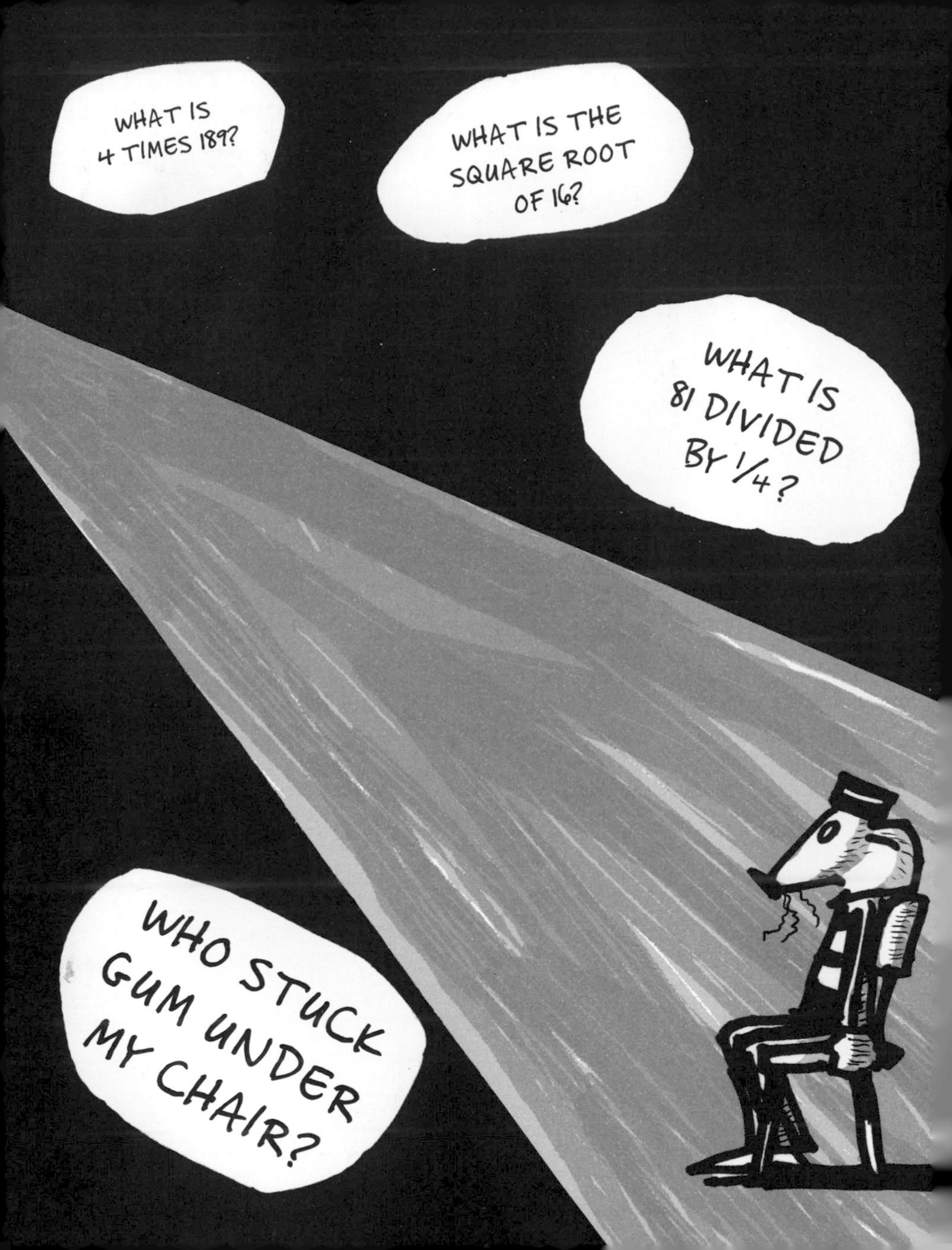
WHAT IS 4 TIMES 189?
WHAT IS THE SQUARE ROOT OF 16?
WHAT IS 81 DIVIDED BY 1/4?
WHO STUCK GUM UNDER MY CHAIR?

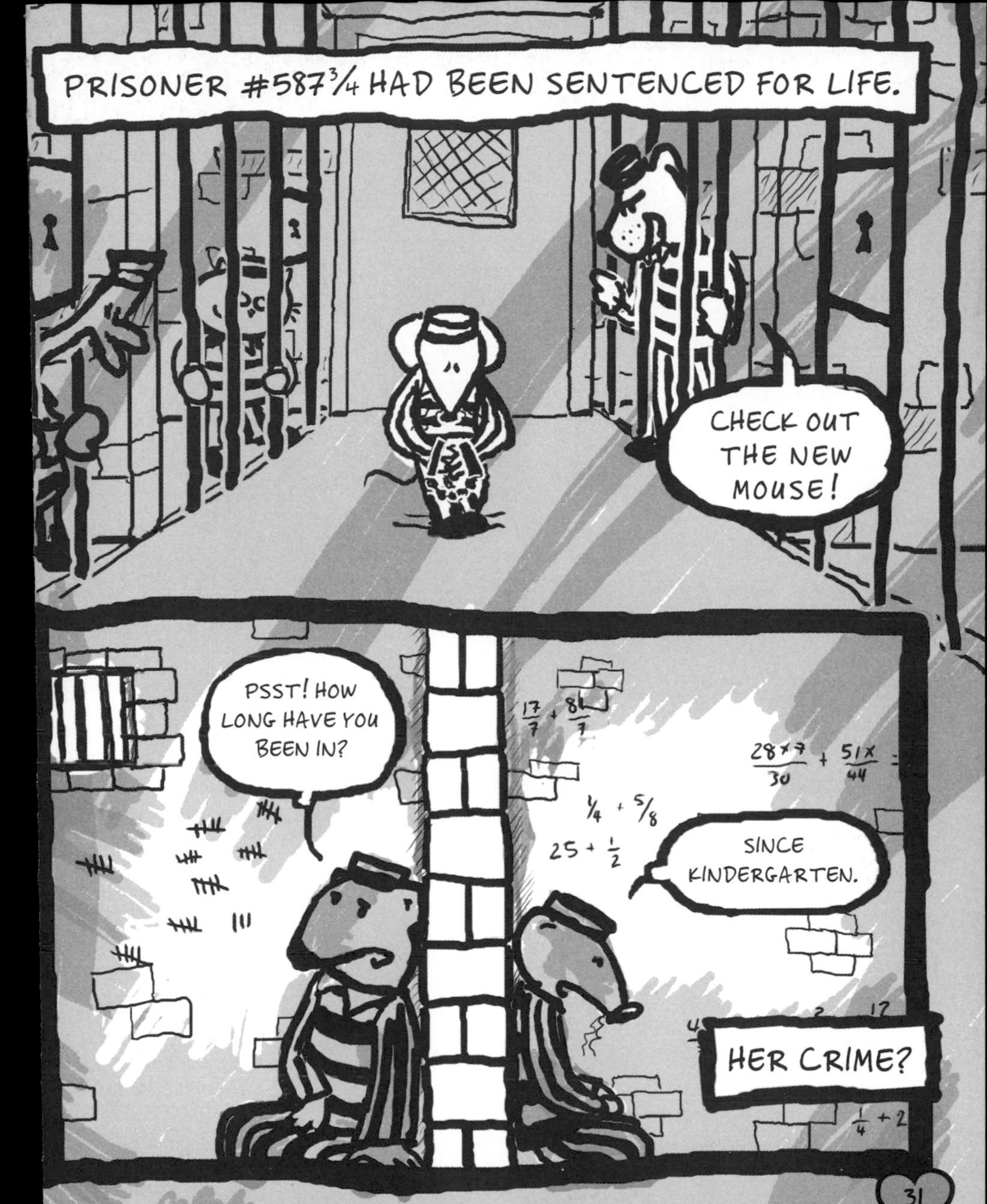
PRISONER #587¾ HAD BEEN SENTENCED FOR LIFE.
CHECK OUT THE NEW MOUSE!
PSST! HOW LONG HAVE YOU BEEN IN?
SINCE KINDERGARTEN.
HER CRIME?

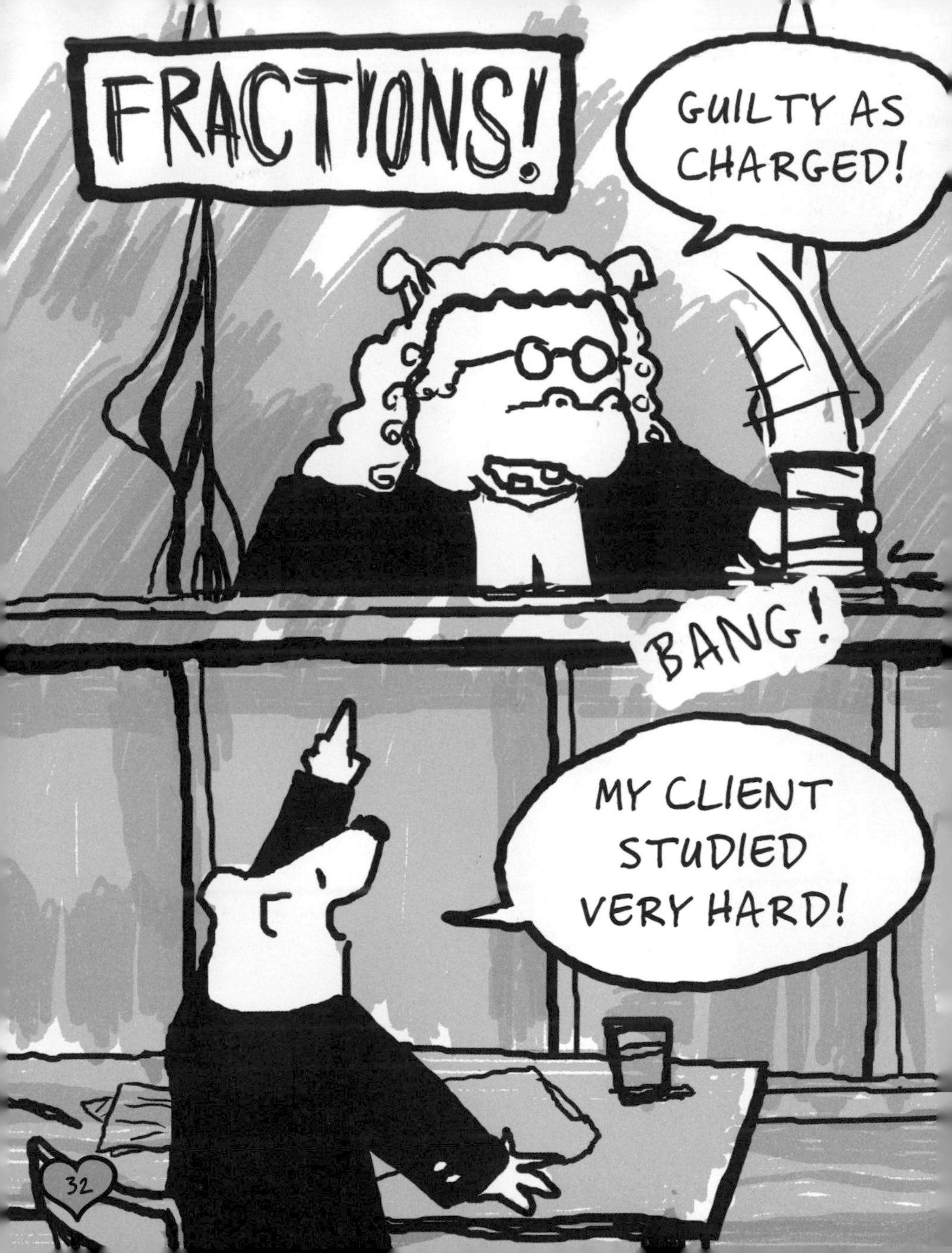
FRACTIONS!
GUILTY AS CHARGED!
BANG!
MY CLIENT STUDIED VERY HARD!

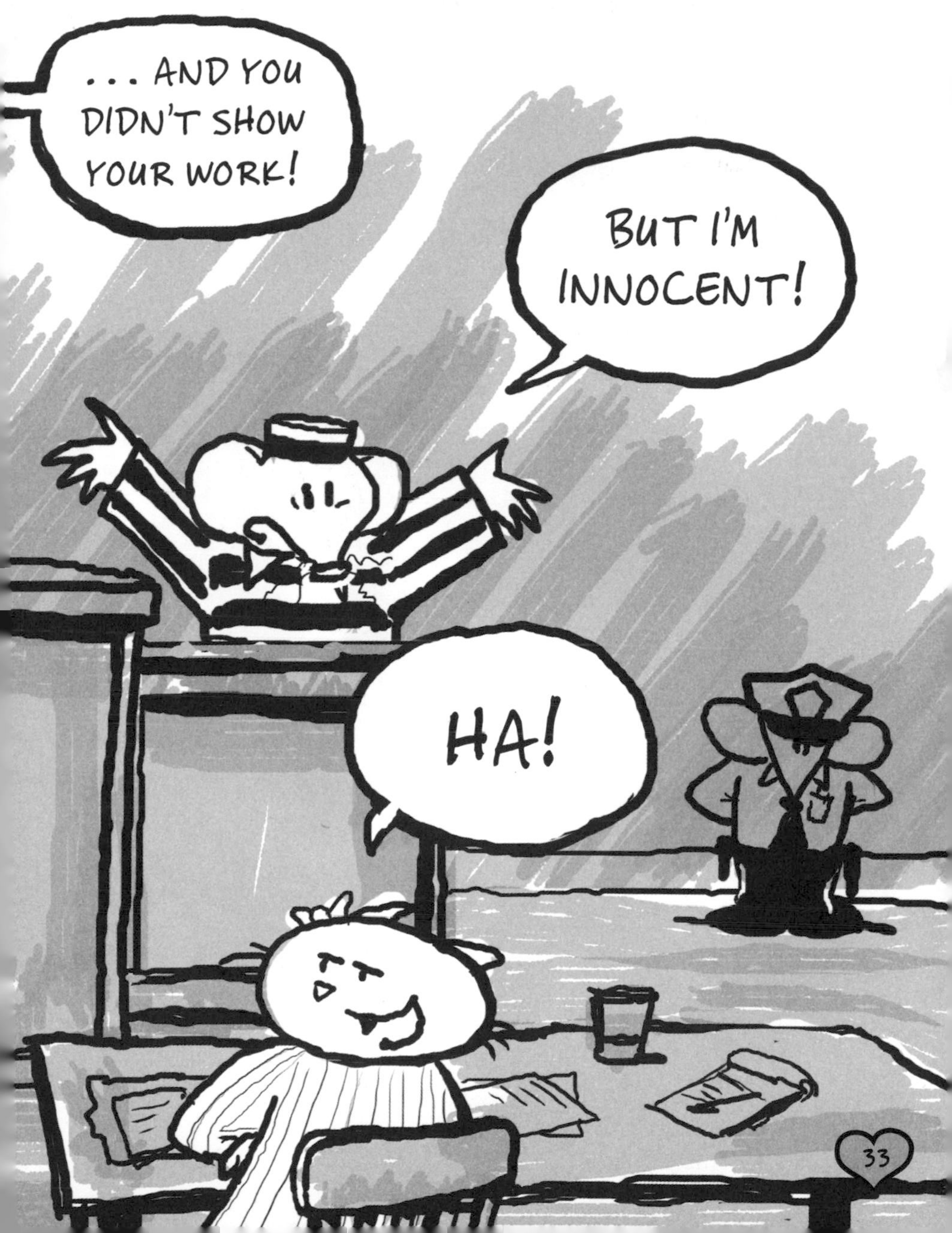
. . . AND YOU DIDN'T SHOW YOUR WORK!
BUT I'M INNOCENT!
HA!

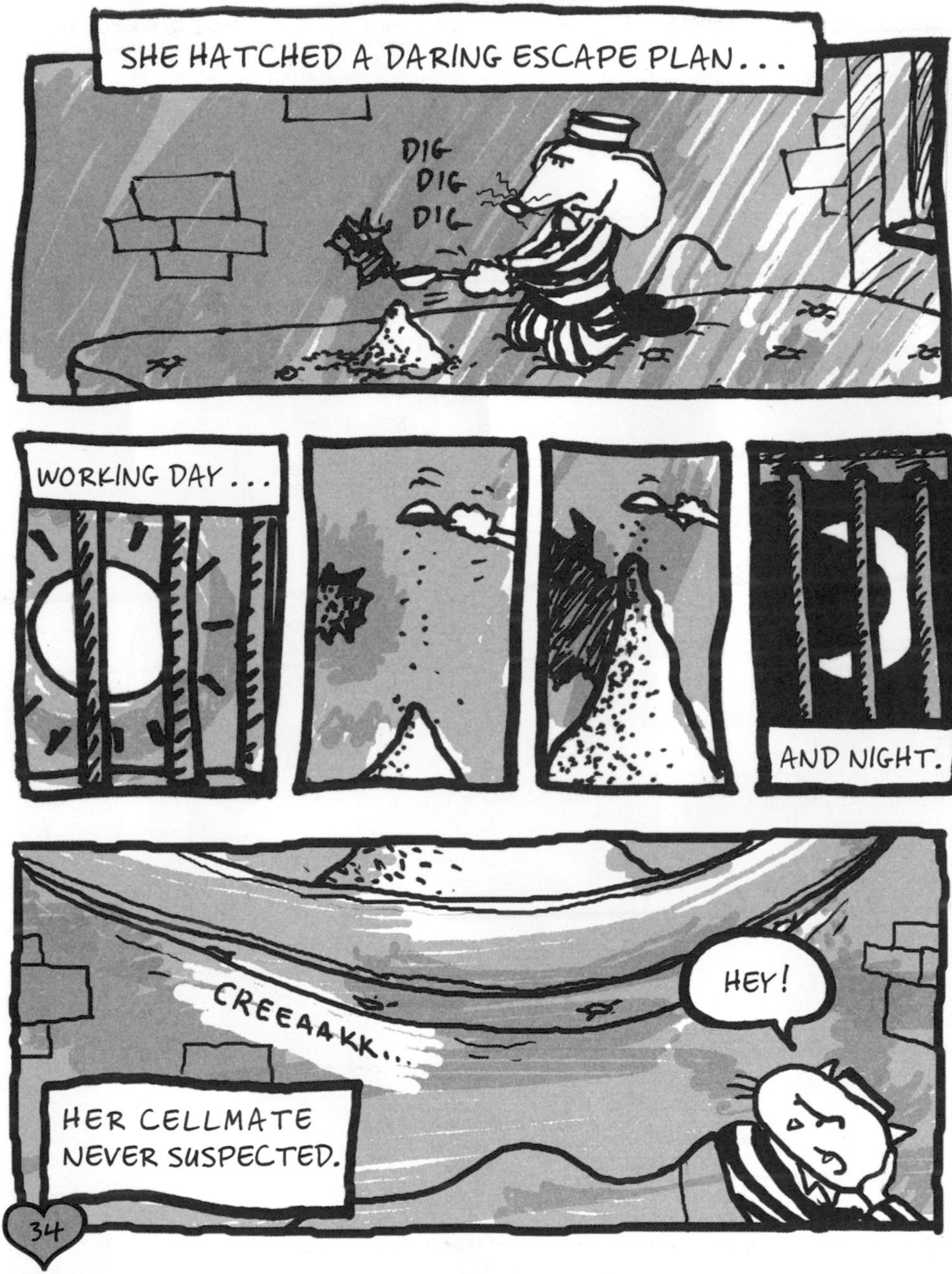
SHE HATCHED A DARING ESCAPE PLAN...
DIG
DIG
DIG
WORKING DAY...
AND NIGHT.
CREEAAKK...
HEY!
HER CELLMATE NEVER SUSPECTED.

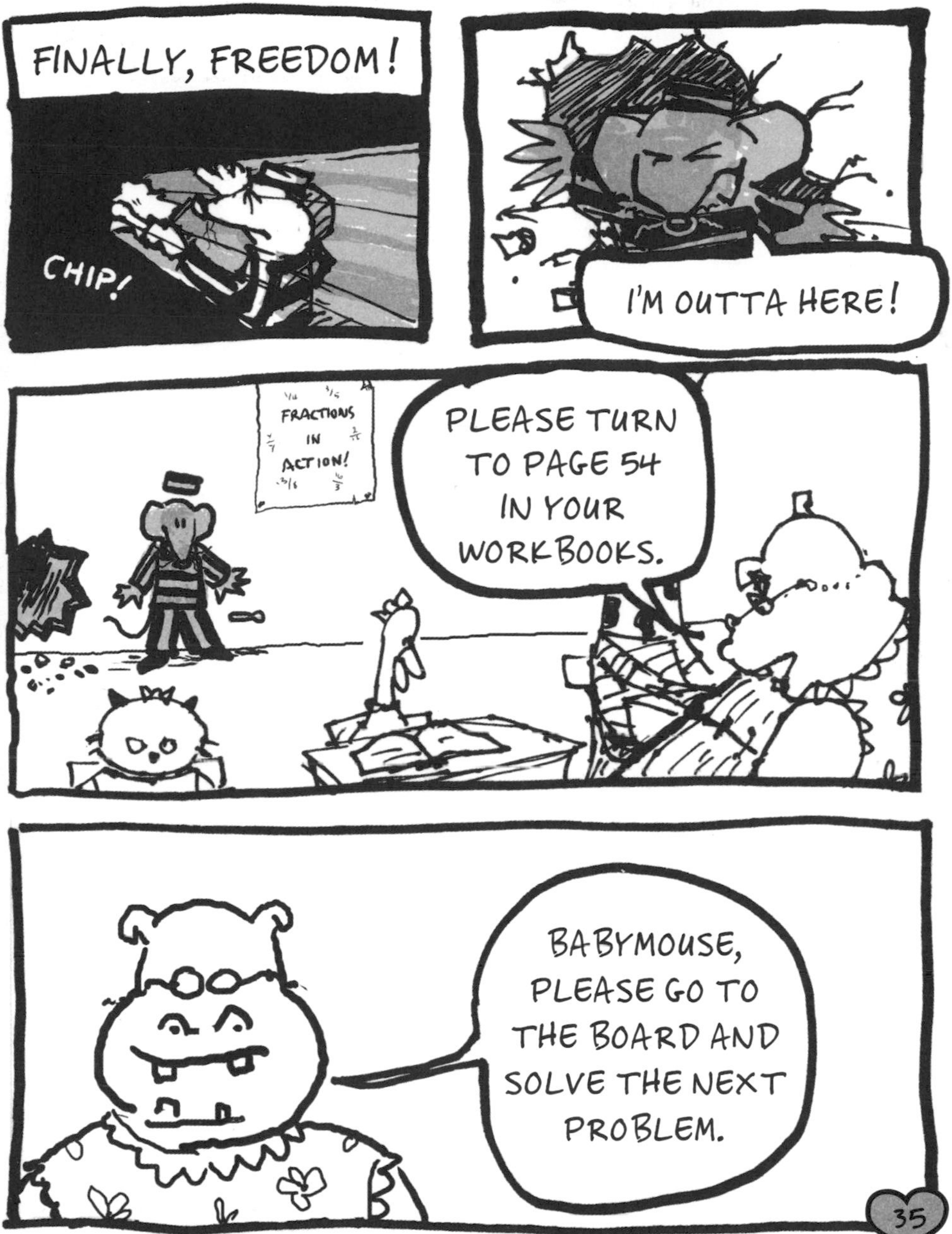
FINALLY, FREEDOM!
CHIP!
I'M OUTTA HERE!
FRACTIONS IN ACTION!
PLEASE TURN TO PAGE 54 IN YOUR WORKBOOKS.
BABYMOUSE, PLEASE GO TO THE BOARD AND SOLVE THE NEXT PROBLEM.

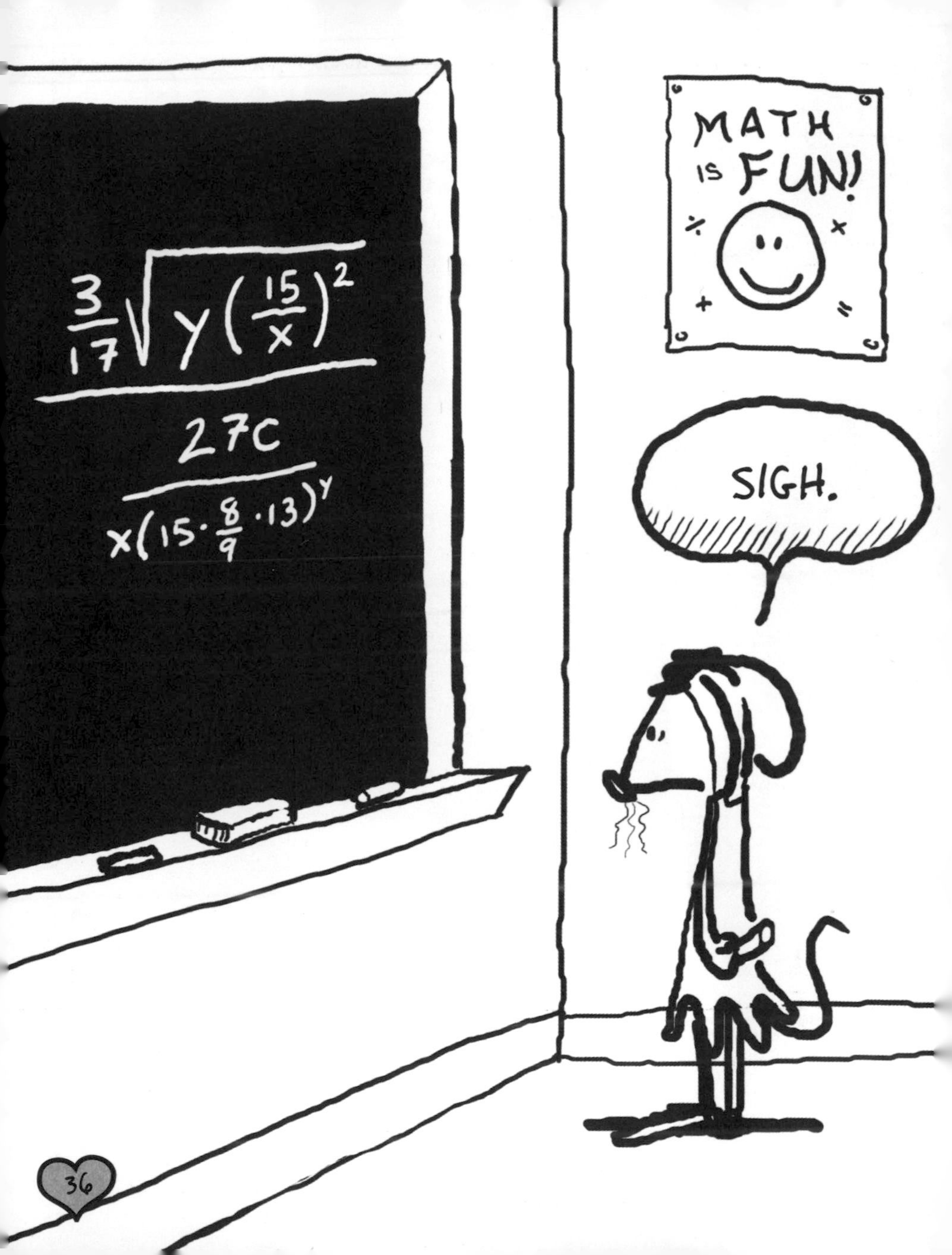
MATH IS FUN!
SIGH.

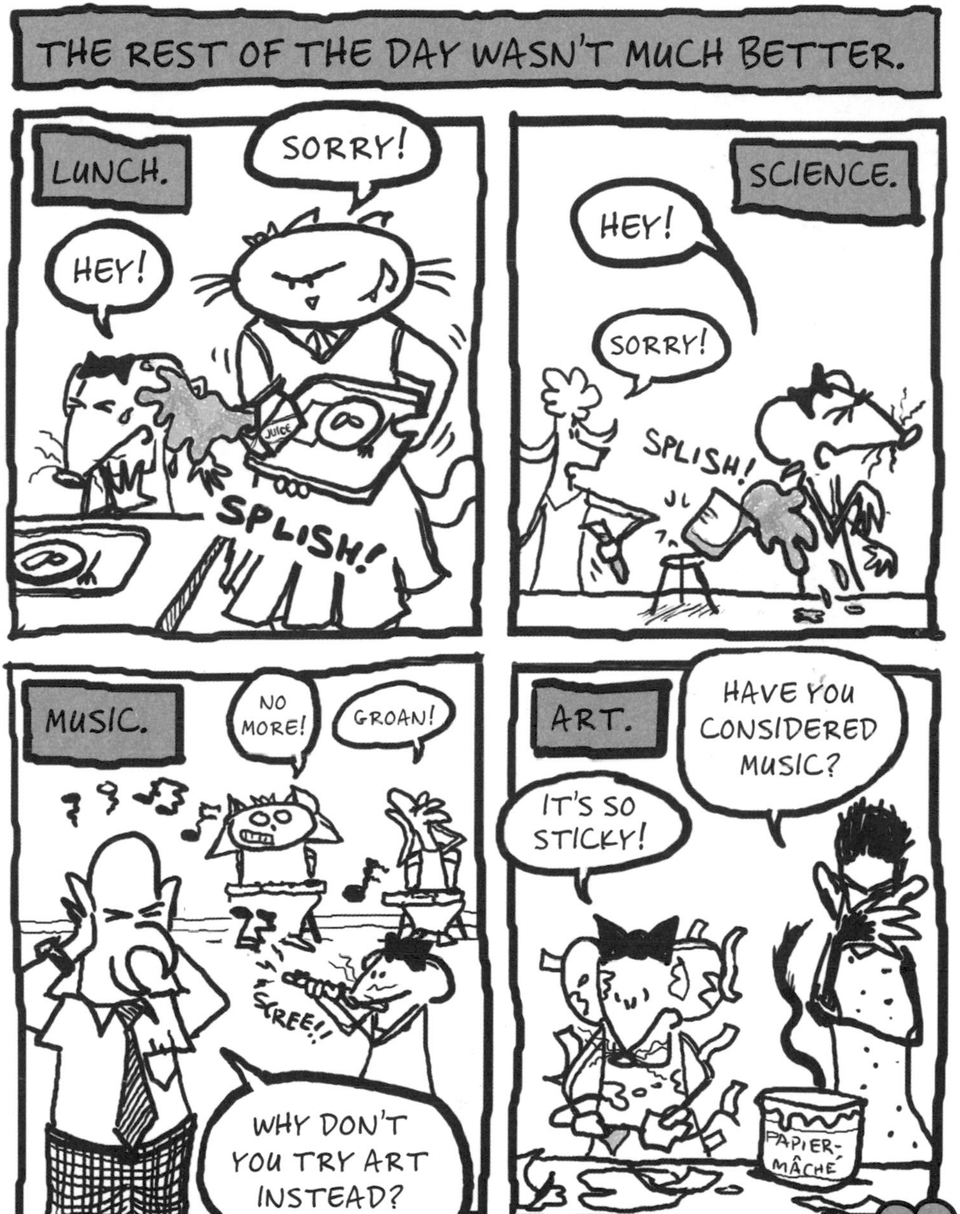
THE REST OF THE DAY WASN'T MUCH BETTER.
LUNCH.
SORRY!
HEY!
JUICE
SPLISH!
SCIENCE.
HEY!
SORRY!
SPLISH!
MUSIC.
NO MORE!
GROAN!
SCREE!!
WHY DON'T YOU TRY ART INSTEAD?
ART.
HAVE YOU CONSIDERED MUSIC?
IT'S SO STICKY!
PAPIER-MÂCHE

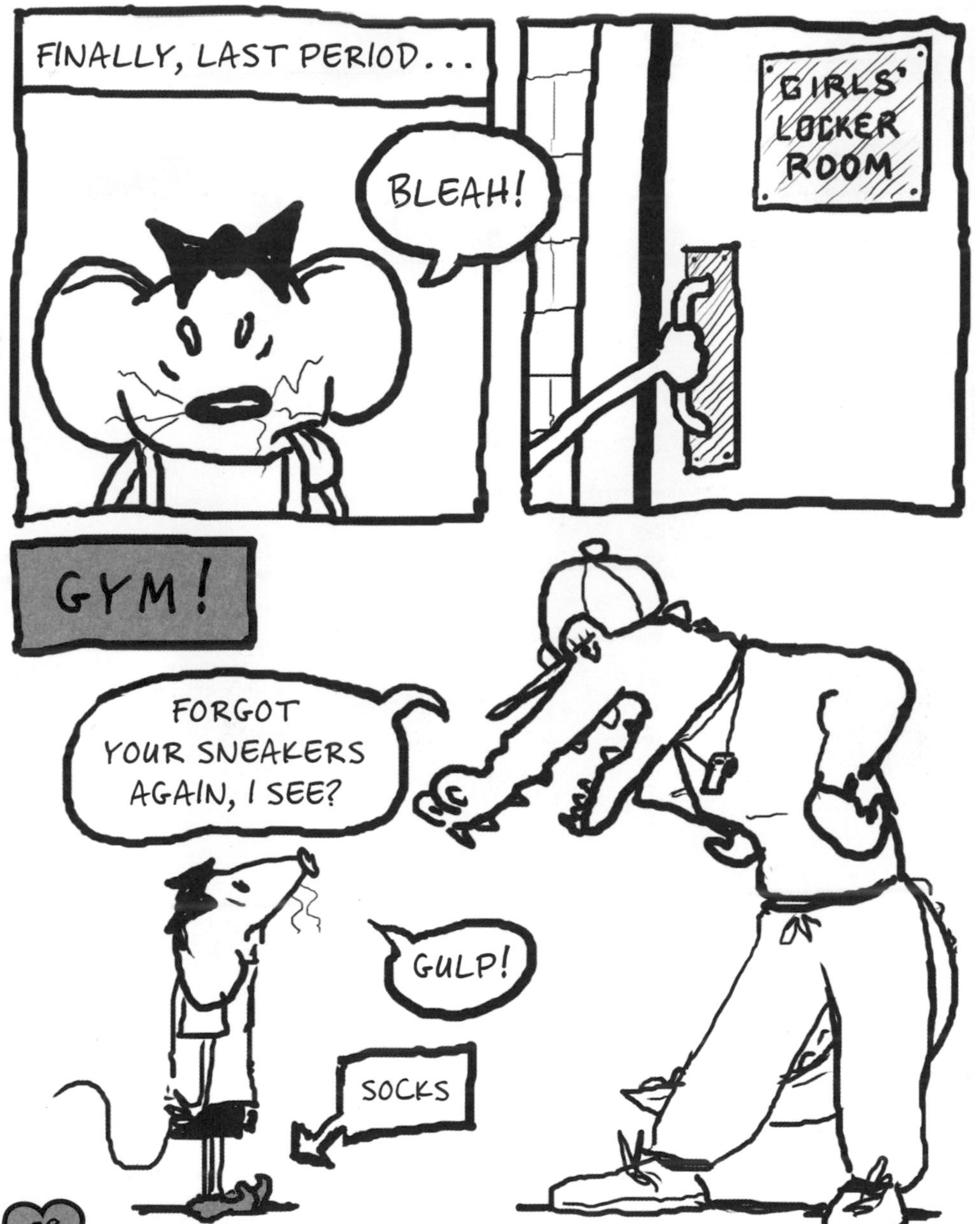
FINALLY, LAST PERIOD...
BLEAH!
GIRLS' LOCKER ROOM
GYM!
FORGOT YOUR SNEAKERS AGAIN, I SEE?
GULP!
SOCKS

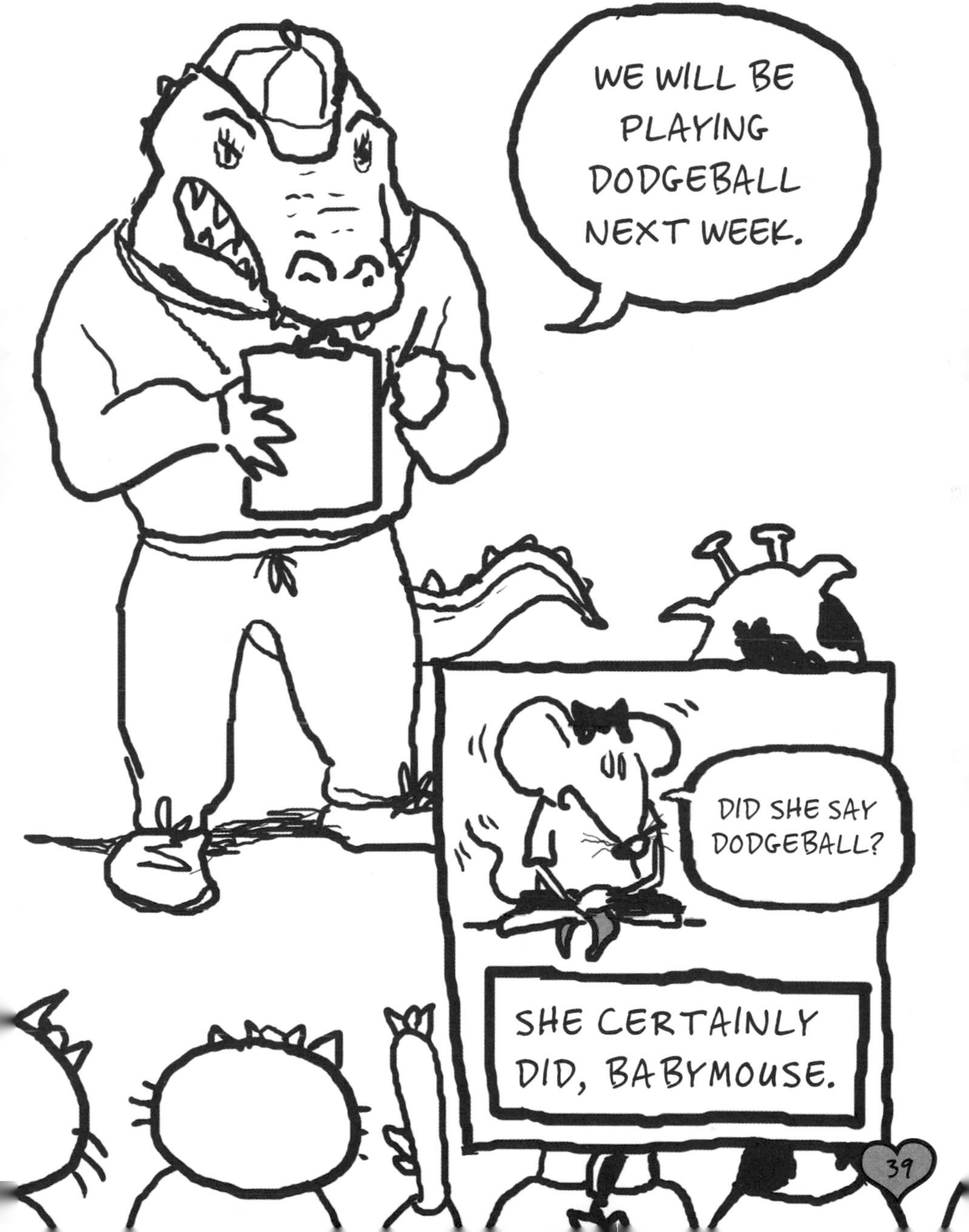
WE WILL BE PLAYING DODGEBALL NEXT WEEK.
DID SHE SAY DODGEBALL?
SHE CERTAINLY DID, BABYMOUSE.

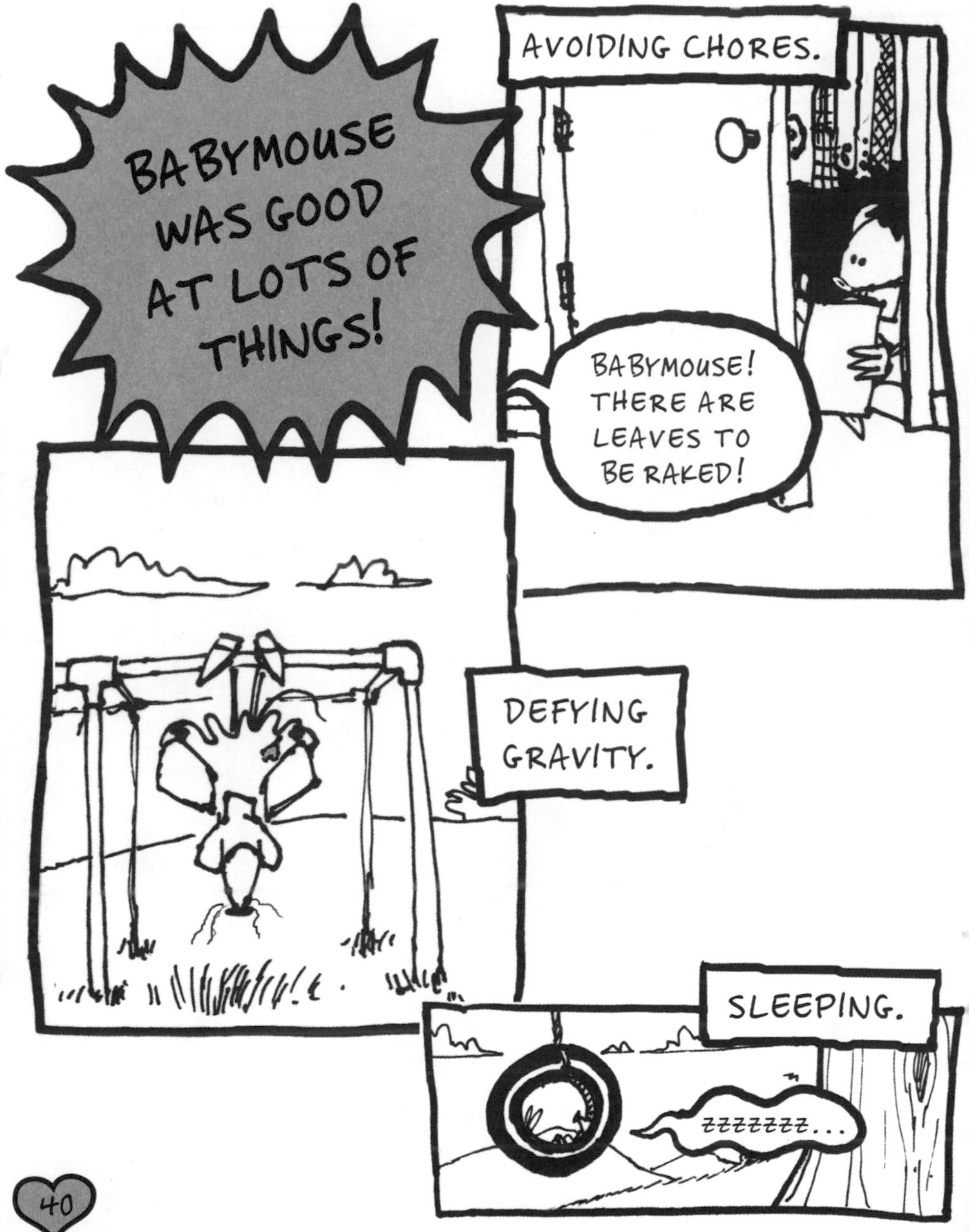
BABYMOUSE WAS GOOD AT LOTS OF THINGS!
AVOIDING CHORES.
BABYMOUSE! THERE ARE LEAVES TO BE RAKED!
DEFYING GRAVITY.
SLEEPING.
ZZZZZZZ...

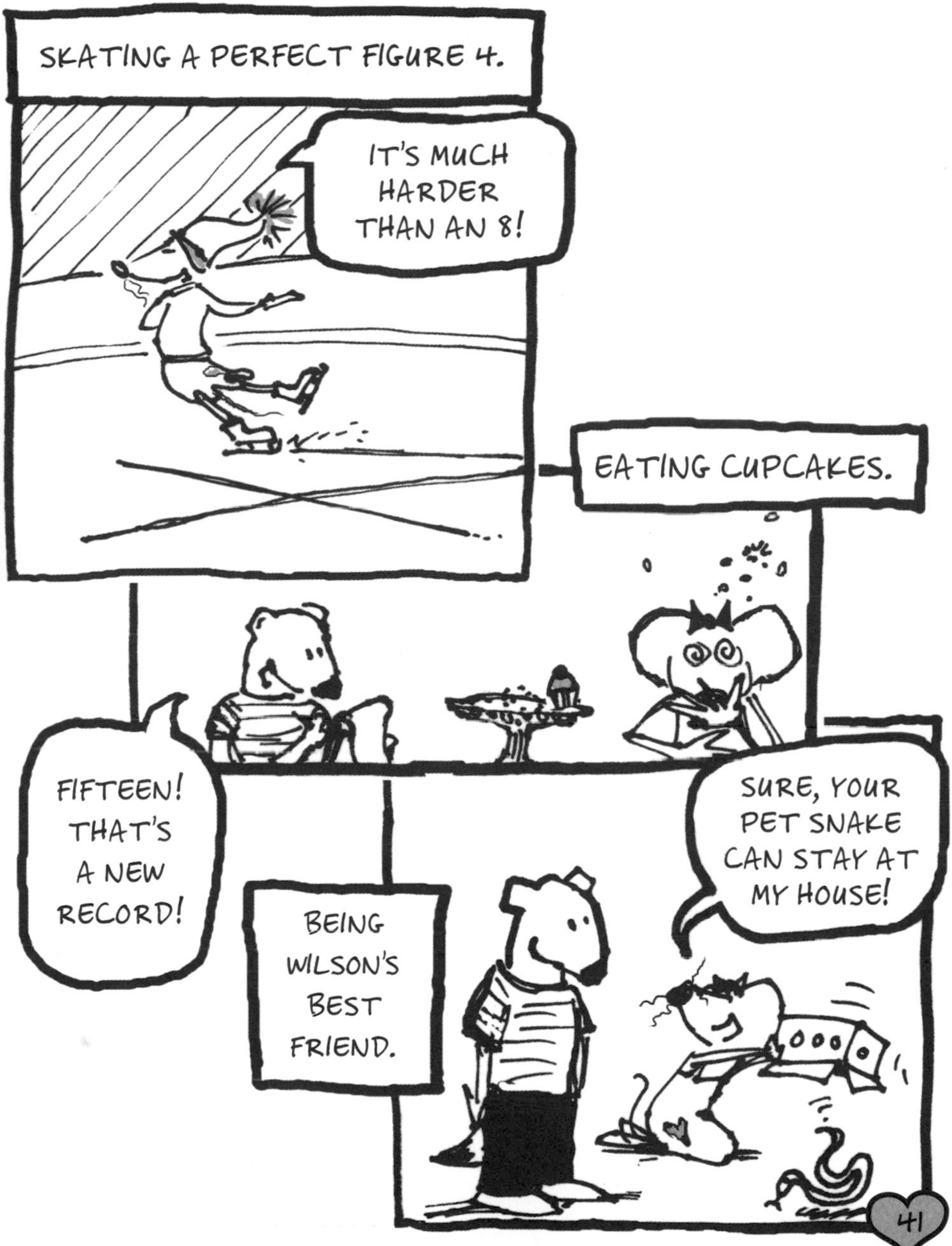
SKATING A PERFECT FIGURE 4.
IT'S MUCH HARDER THAN AN 8!
EATING CUPCAKES.
FIFTEEN! THAT'S A NEW RECORD!
BEING WILSON'S BEST FRIEND.
SURE, YOUR PET SNAKE CAN STAY AT MY HOUSE!

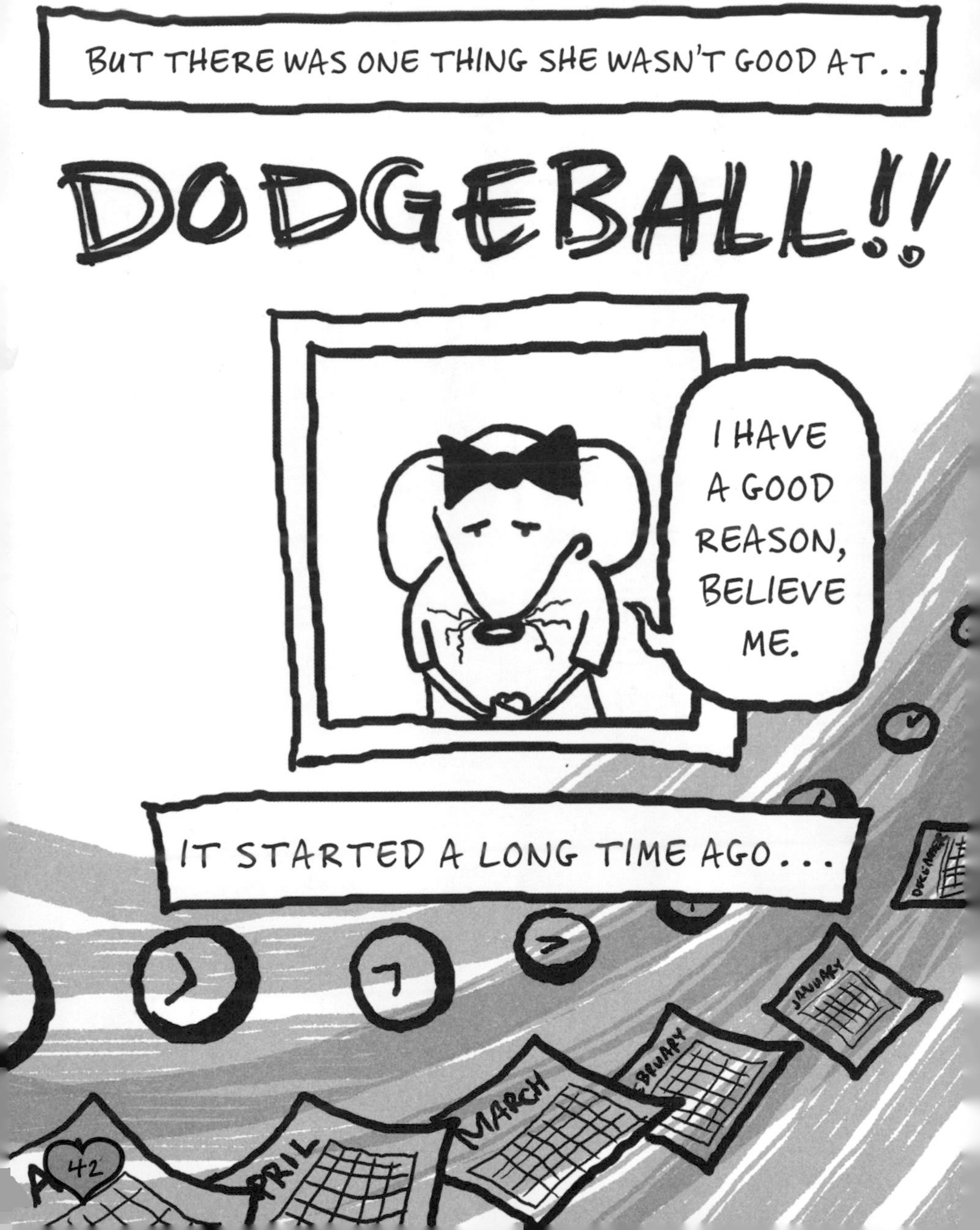
BUT THERE WAS ONE THING SHE WASN'T GOOD AT...
DODGEBALL!!
I HAVE A GOOD REASON, BELIEVE ME.
IT STARTED A LONG TIME AGO...
JANUARY
FEBRUARY
MARCH
APRIL

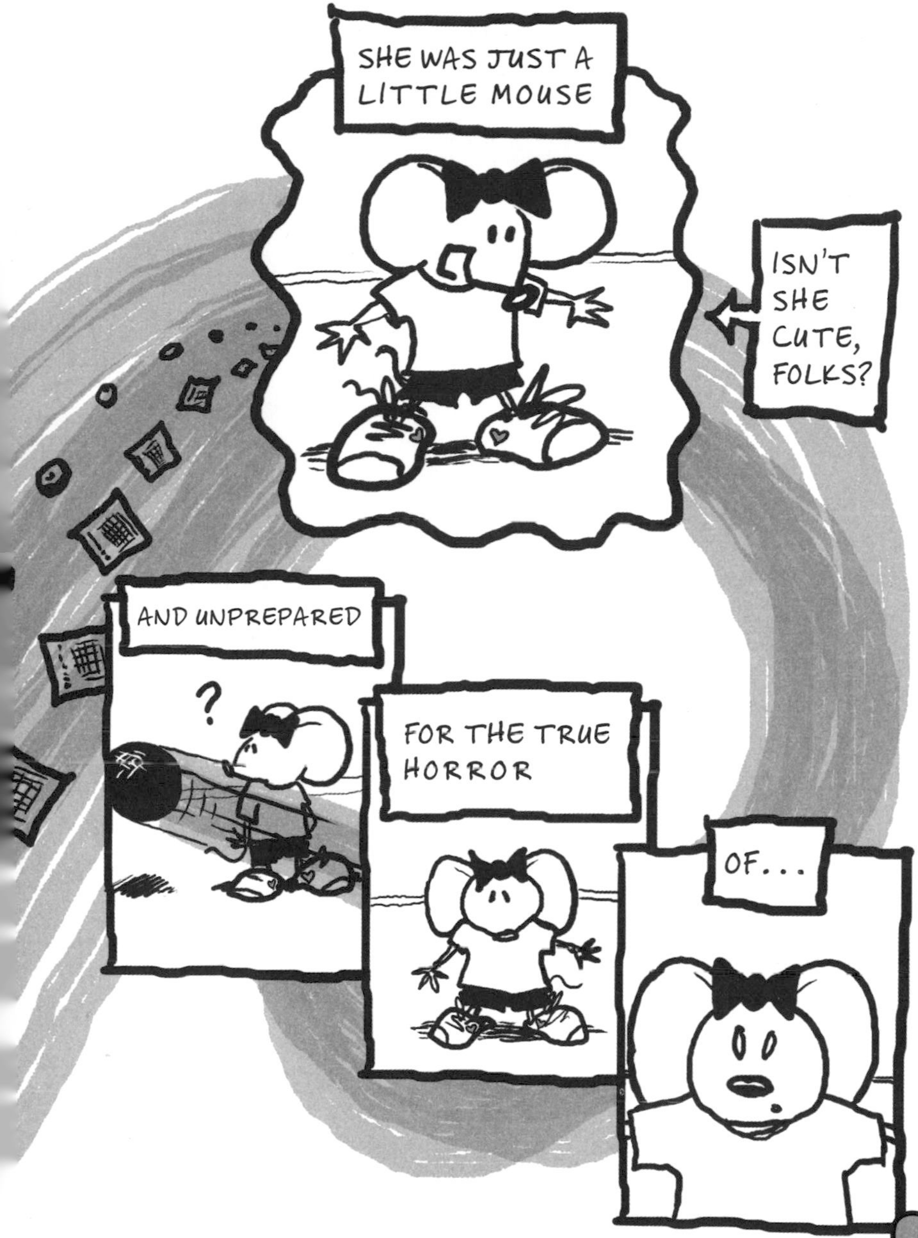
SHE WAS JUST A LITTLE MOUSE
ISN'T SHE CUTE, FOLKS?
AND UNPREPARED
?
FOR THE TRUE HORROR
OF...

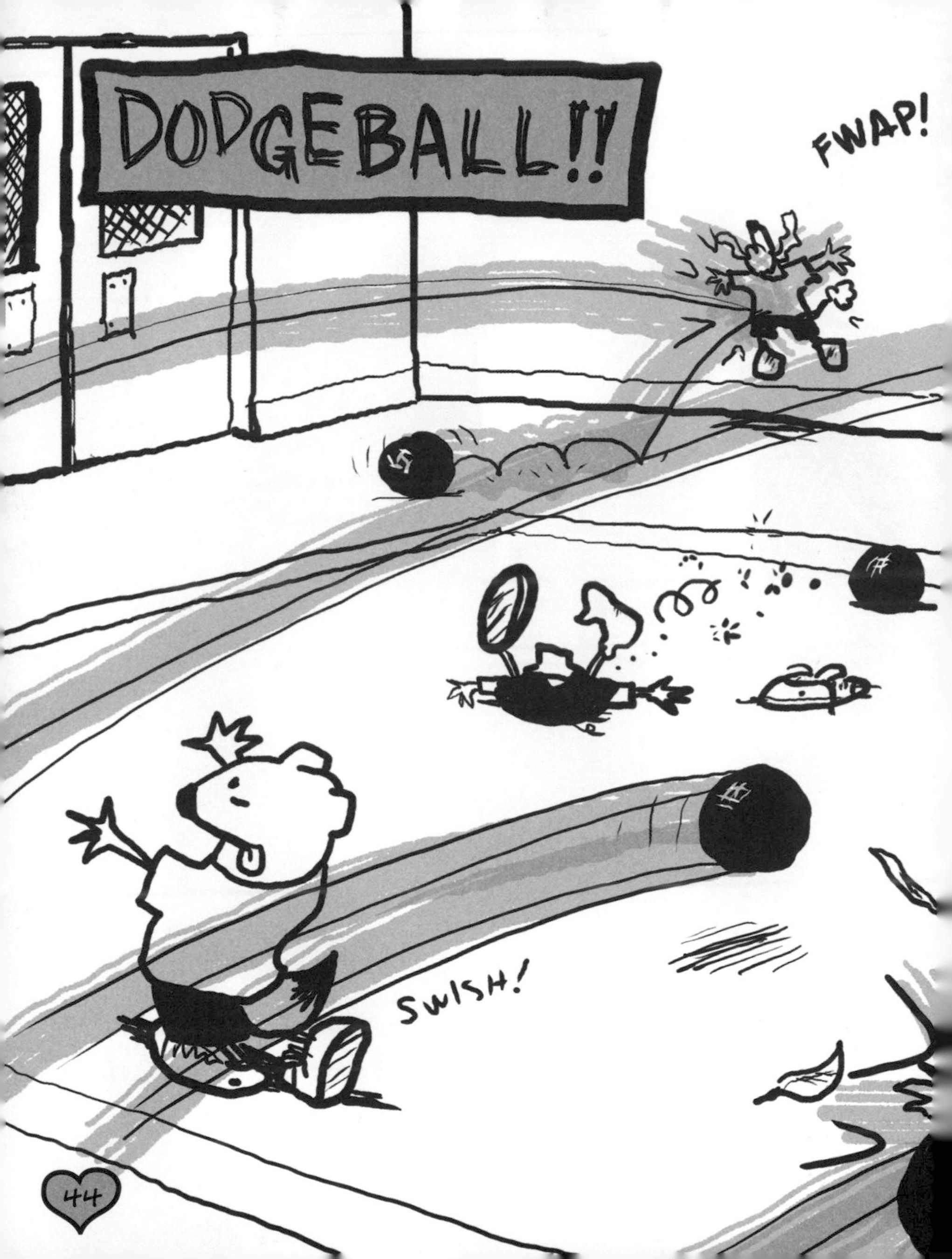
DODGEBALL!!
FWAP!
SWISH!

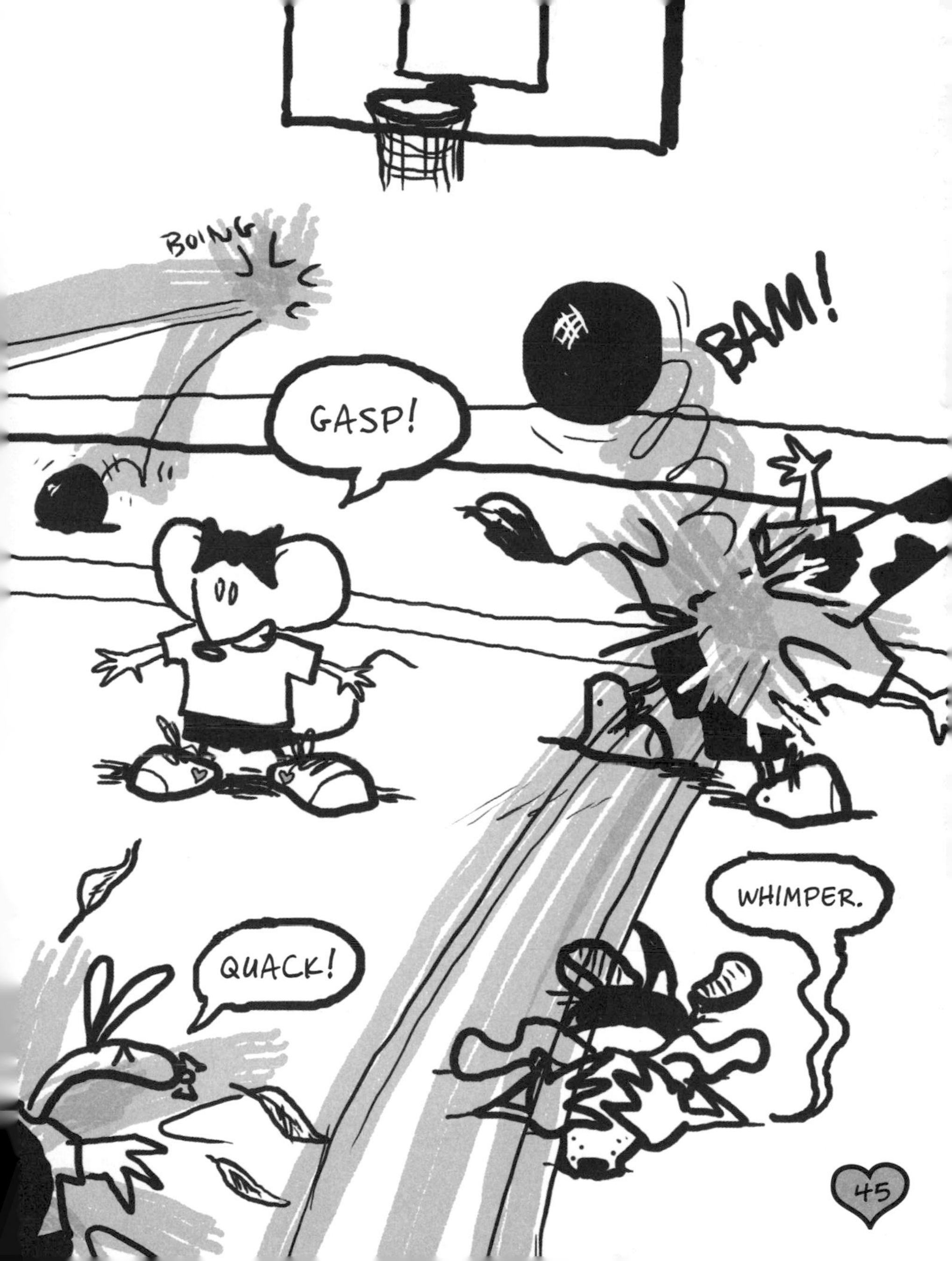
BOING
BAM!
GASP!
WHIMPER.
QUACK!

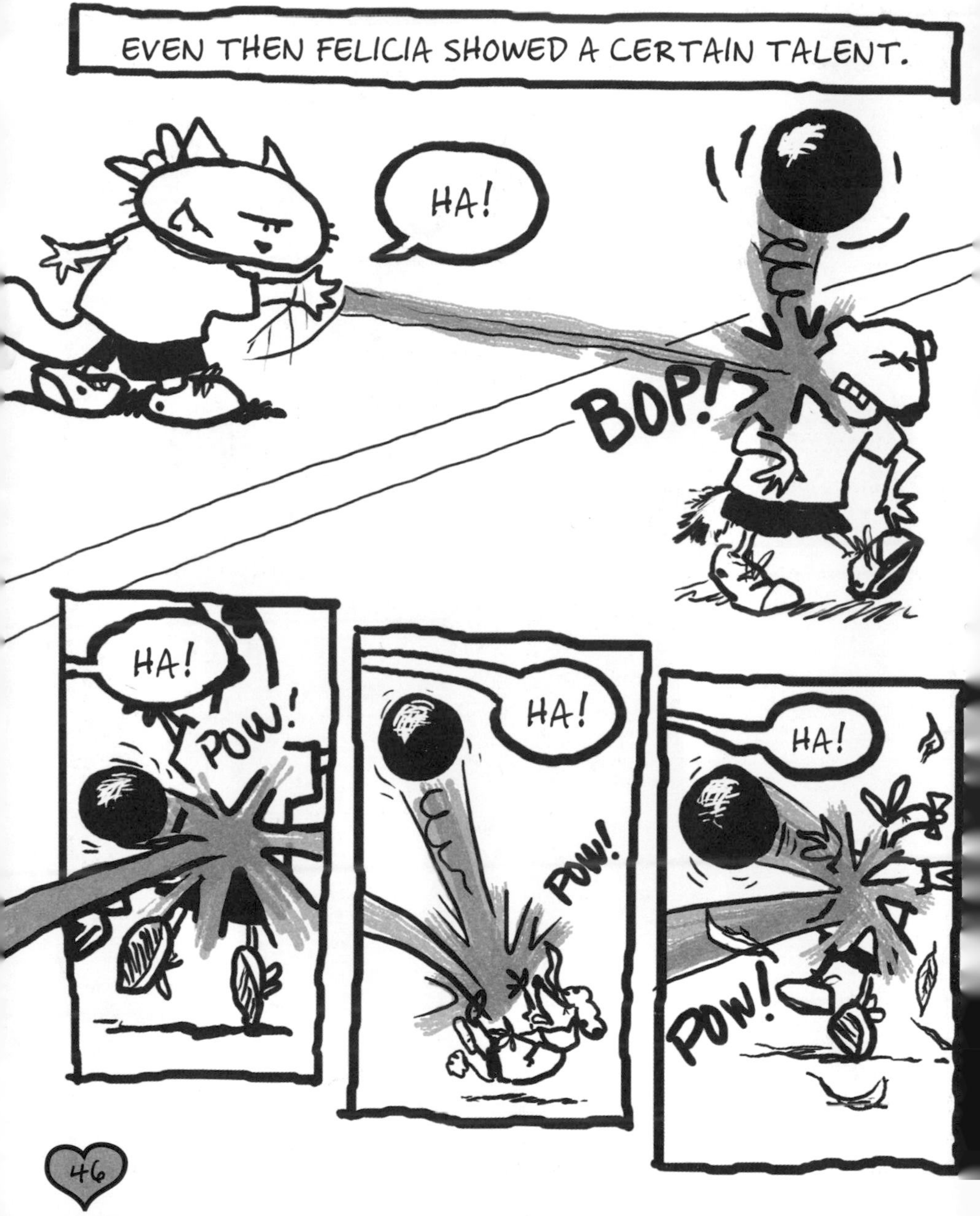
EVEN THEN FELICIA SHOWED A CERTAIN TALENT.
HA!
BOP!
HA!
POW!
HA!
POW!
HA!
POW!

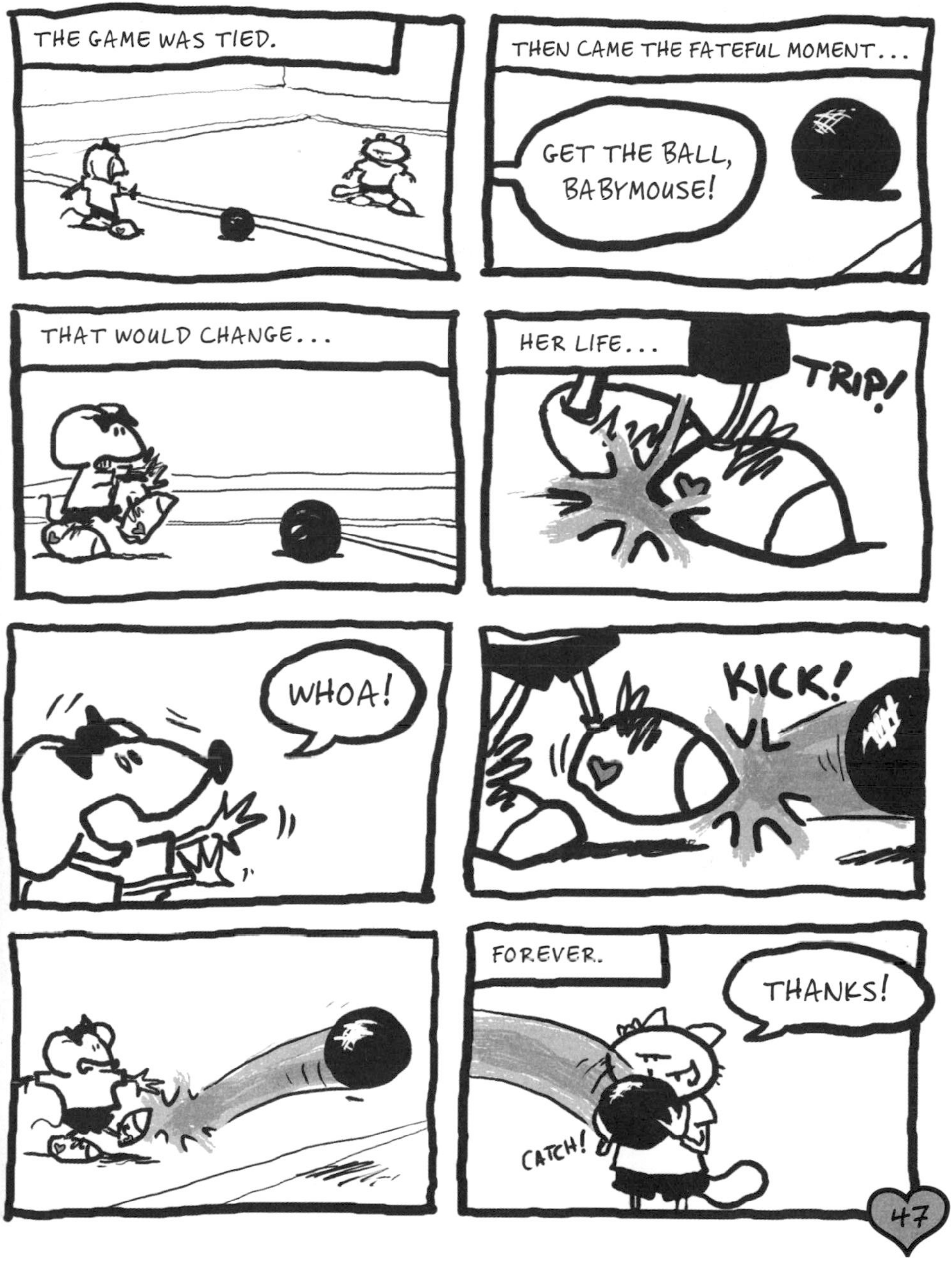
THE GAME WAS TIED.
THEN CAME THE FATEFUL MOMENT...
GET THE BALL, BABYMOUSE!
THAT WOULD CHANGE...
HER LIFE...
TRIP!
WHOA!
KICK!
FOREVER.
THANKS!
CATCH!

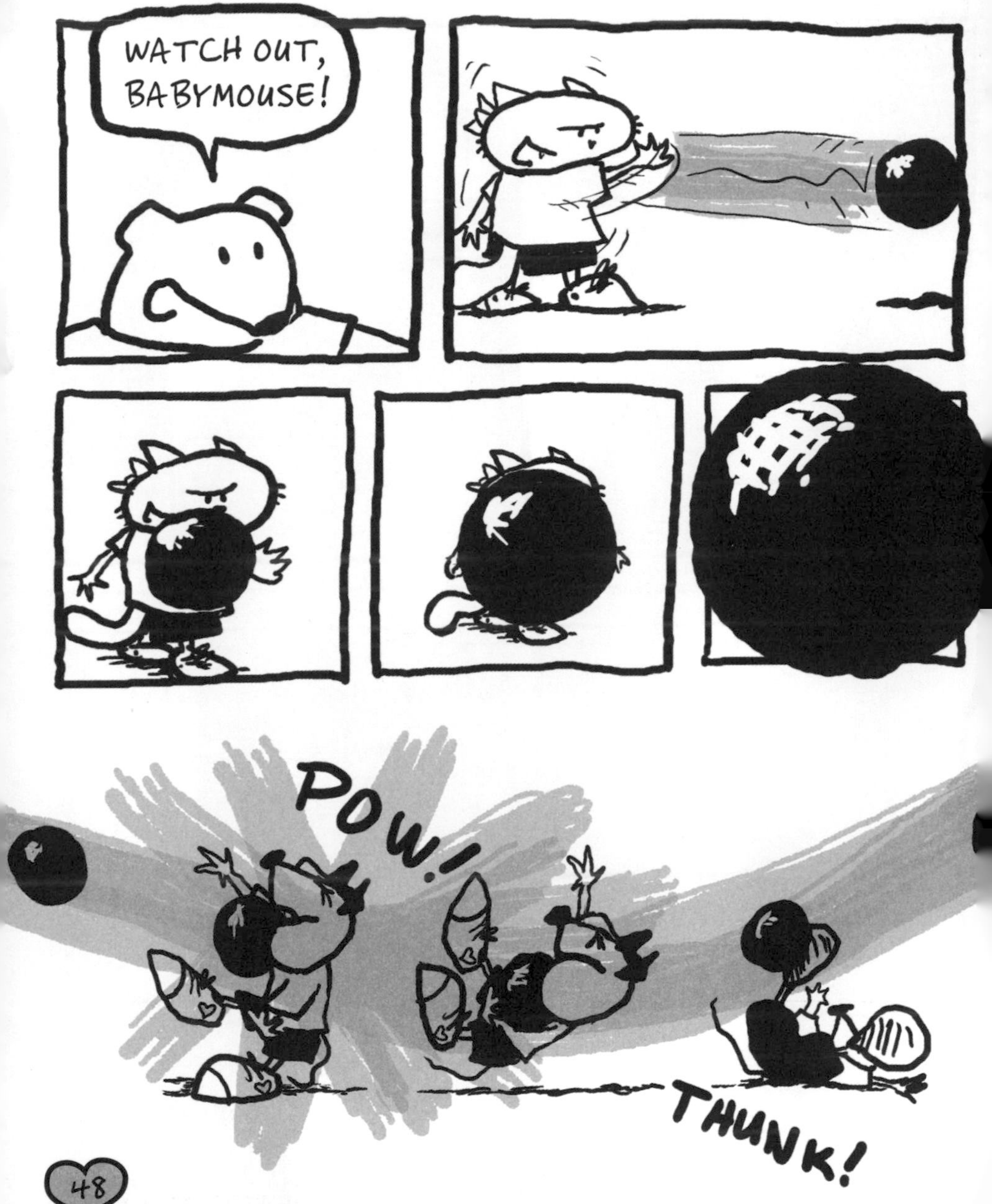
WATCH OUT, BABYMOUSE!
POW!
THUNK!

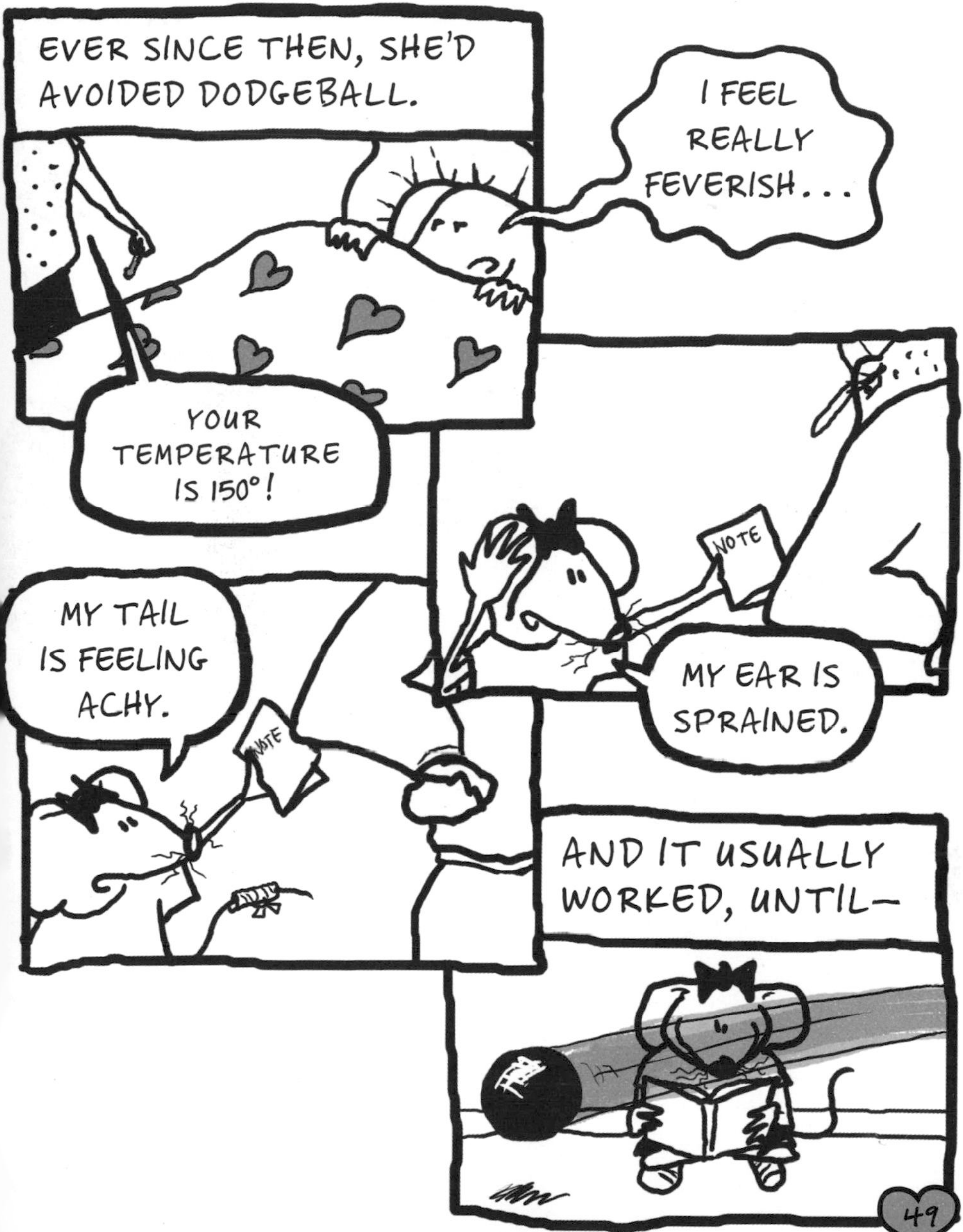
EVER SINCE THEN, SHE'D AVOIDED DODGEBALL.
I FEEL REALLY FEVERISH...
YOUR TEMPERATURE IS 150°!
NOTE
MY EAR IS SPRAINED.
MY TAIL IS FEELING ACHY.
NOTE
AND IT USUALLY WORKED, UNTIL—

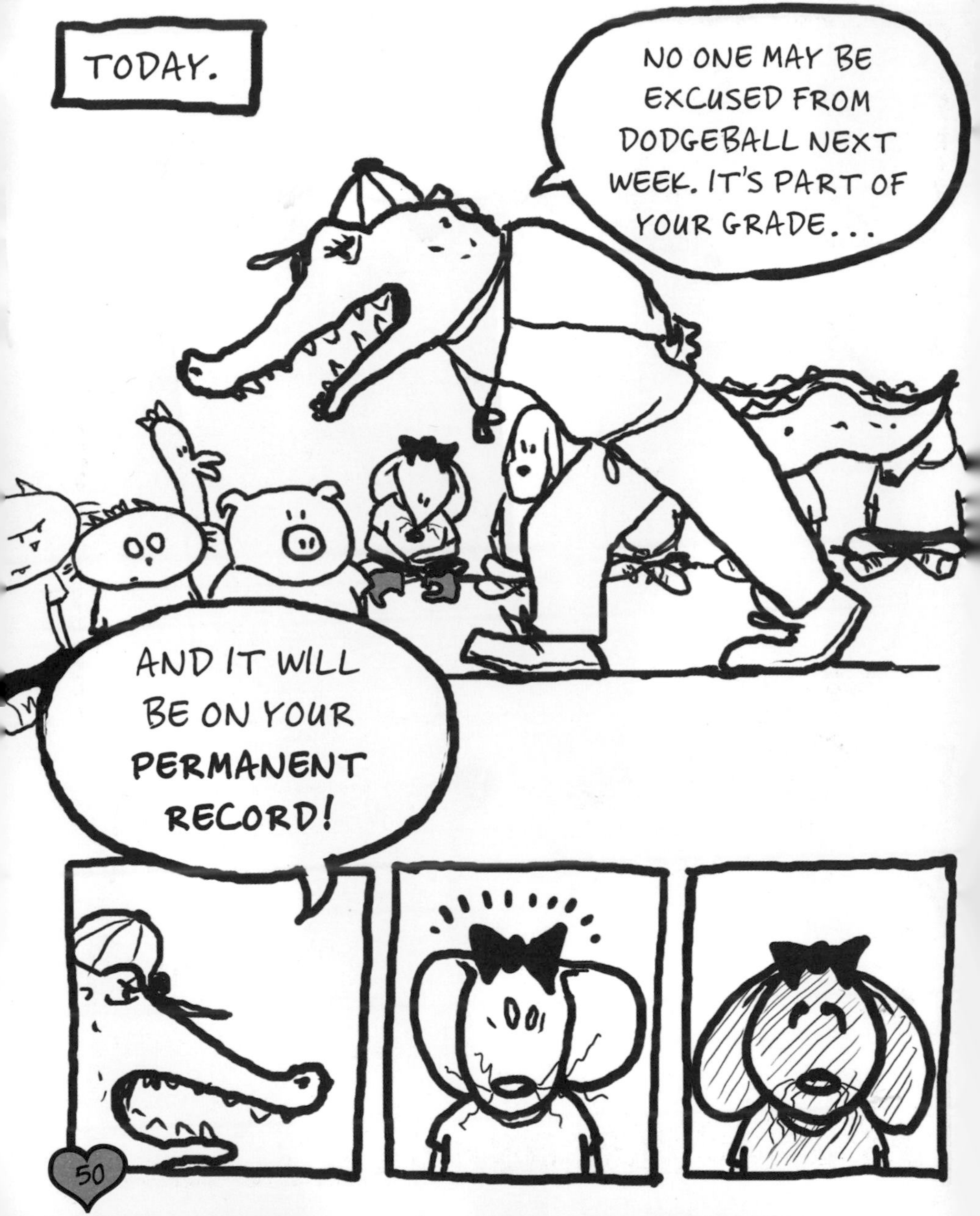
TODAY.
NO ONE MAY BE EXCUSED FROM DODGEBALL NEXT WEEK. IT'S PART OF YOUR GRADE...
AND IT WILL BE ON YOUR PERMANENT RECORD!

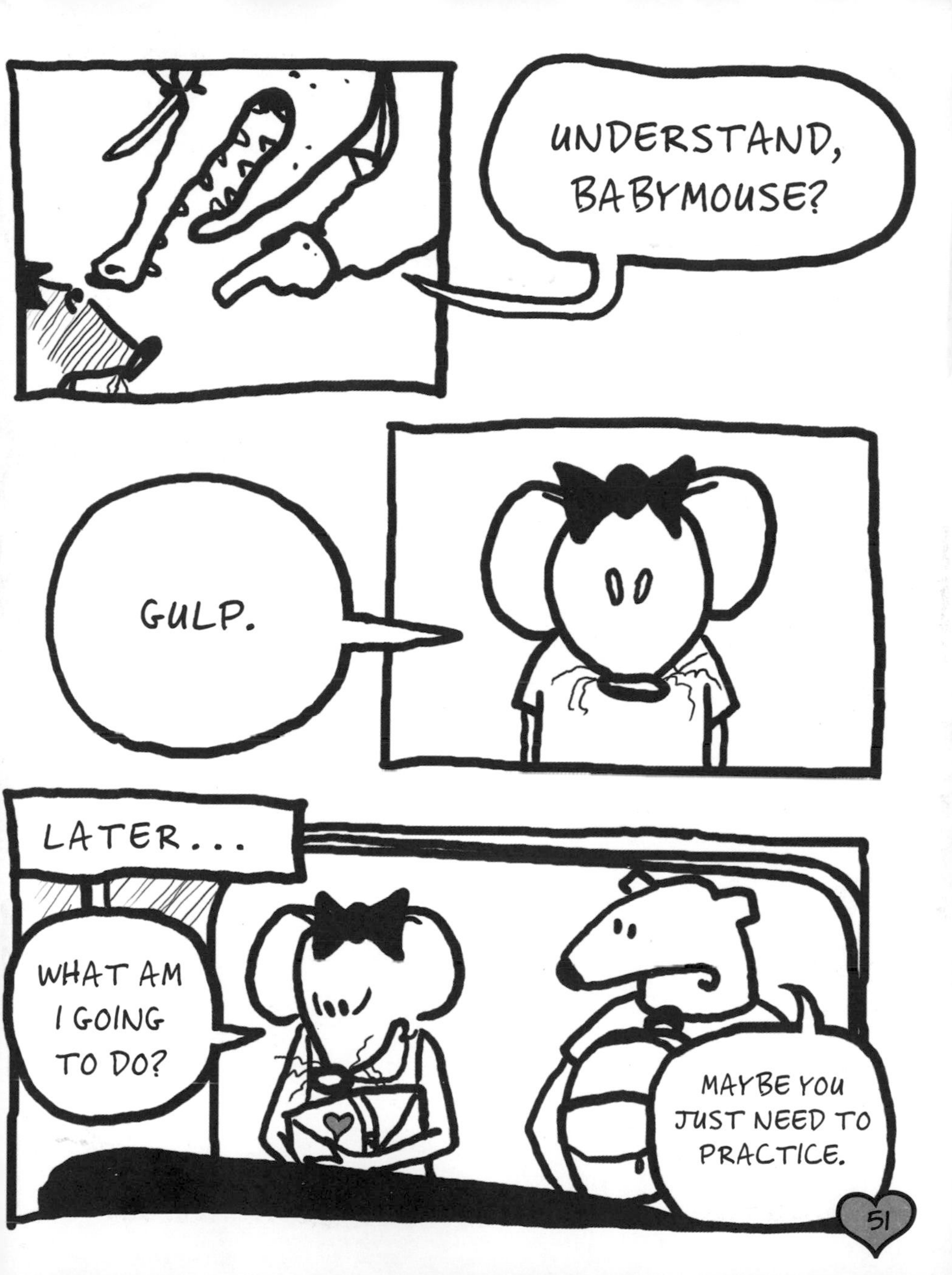
UNDERSTAND, BABYMOUSE?
GULP.
LATER...
WHAT AM I GOING TO DO?
MAYBE YOU JUST NEED TO PRACTICE.

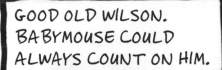
GOOD OLD WILSON. BABYMOUSE COULD ALWAYS COUNT ON HIM.

OKAY.

WOW! IT LOOKS LIKE NEW! MOM WILL NEVER KNOW.

WHO COULD FORGET THE TIME HE FIXED THE VASE SHE DROPPED?

GLUE

AND PULLED THE CACTUS NEEDLES OUT OF HER TAIL?

OW!

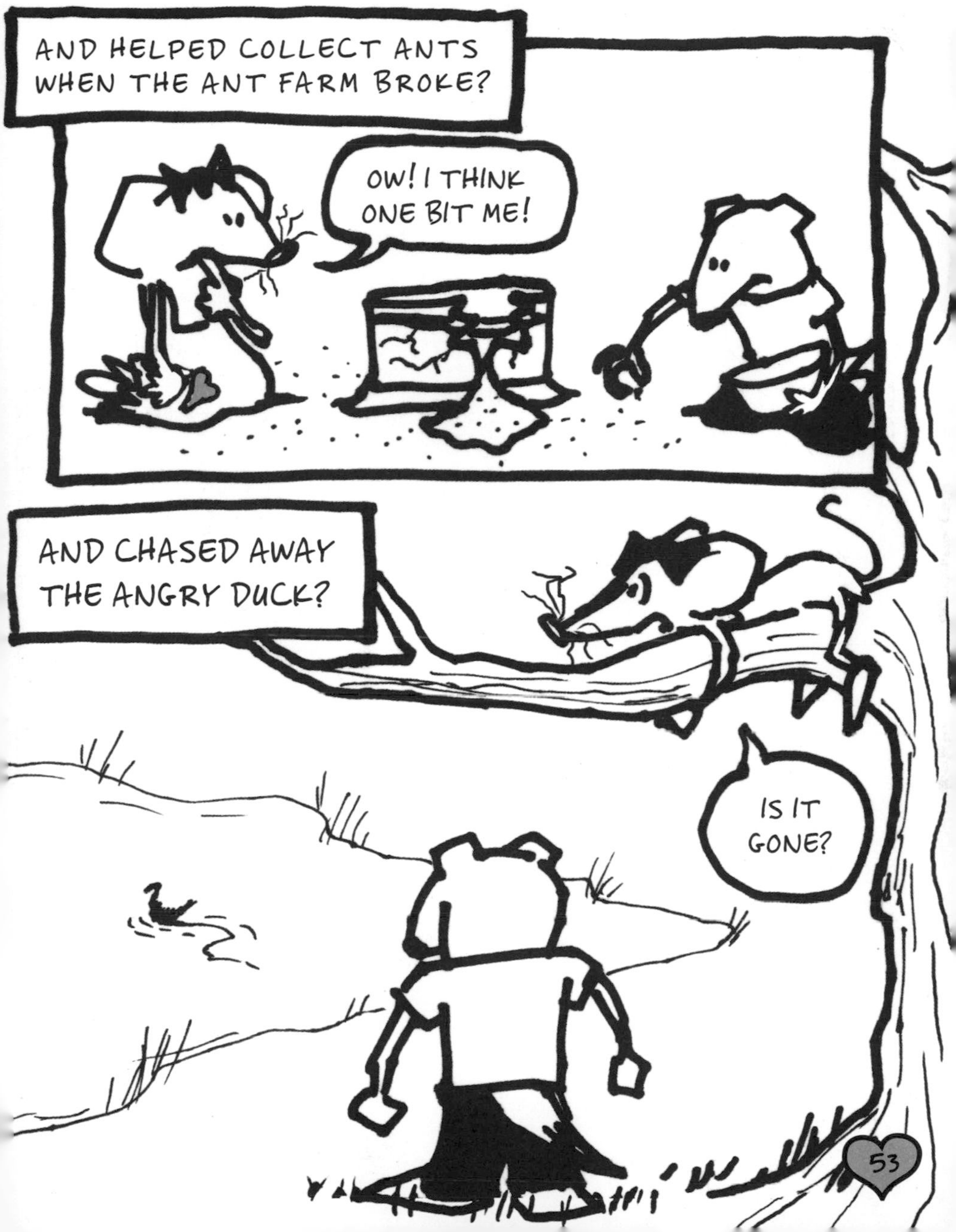
AND HELPED COLLECT ANTS WHEN THE ANT FARM BROKE?
OW! I THINK ONE BIT ME!
AND CHASED AWAY THE ANGRY DUCK?
IS IT GONE?

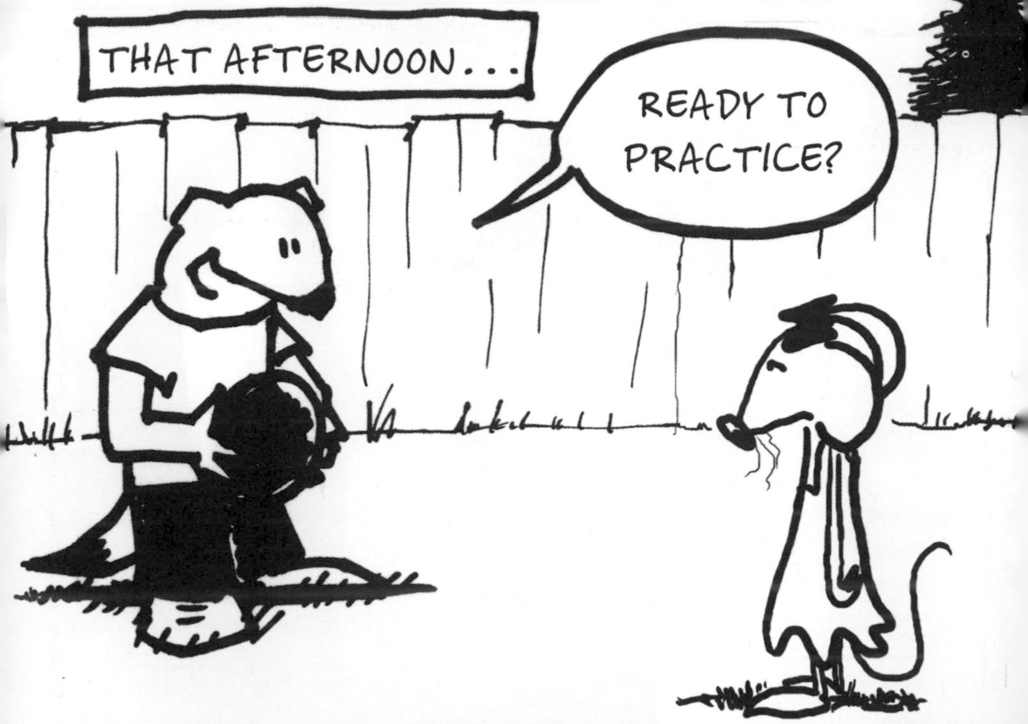
THAT AFTERNOON...
READY TO PRACTICE?

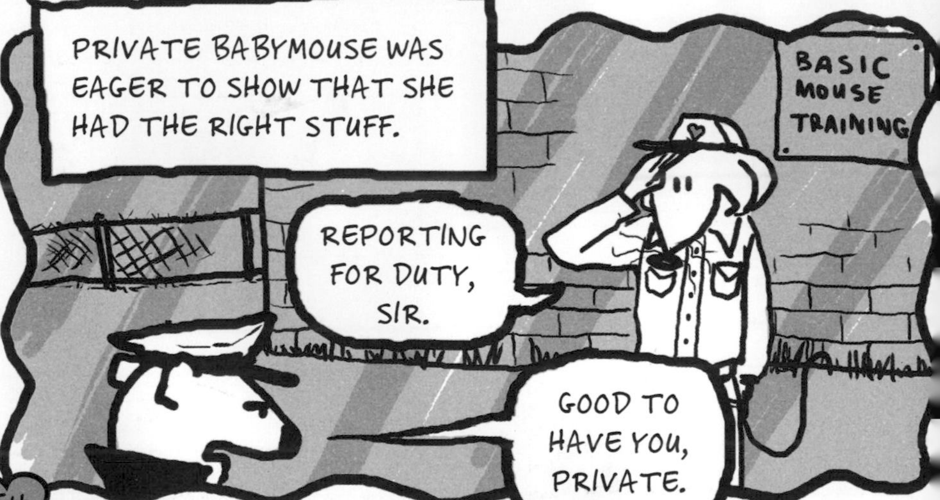
PRIVATE BABYMOUSE WAS EAGER TO SHOW THAT SHE HAD THE RIGHT STUFF.
BASIC MOUSE TRAINING
REPORTING FOR DUTY, SIR.
GOOD TO HAVE YOU, PRIVATE.

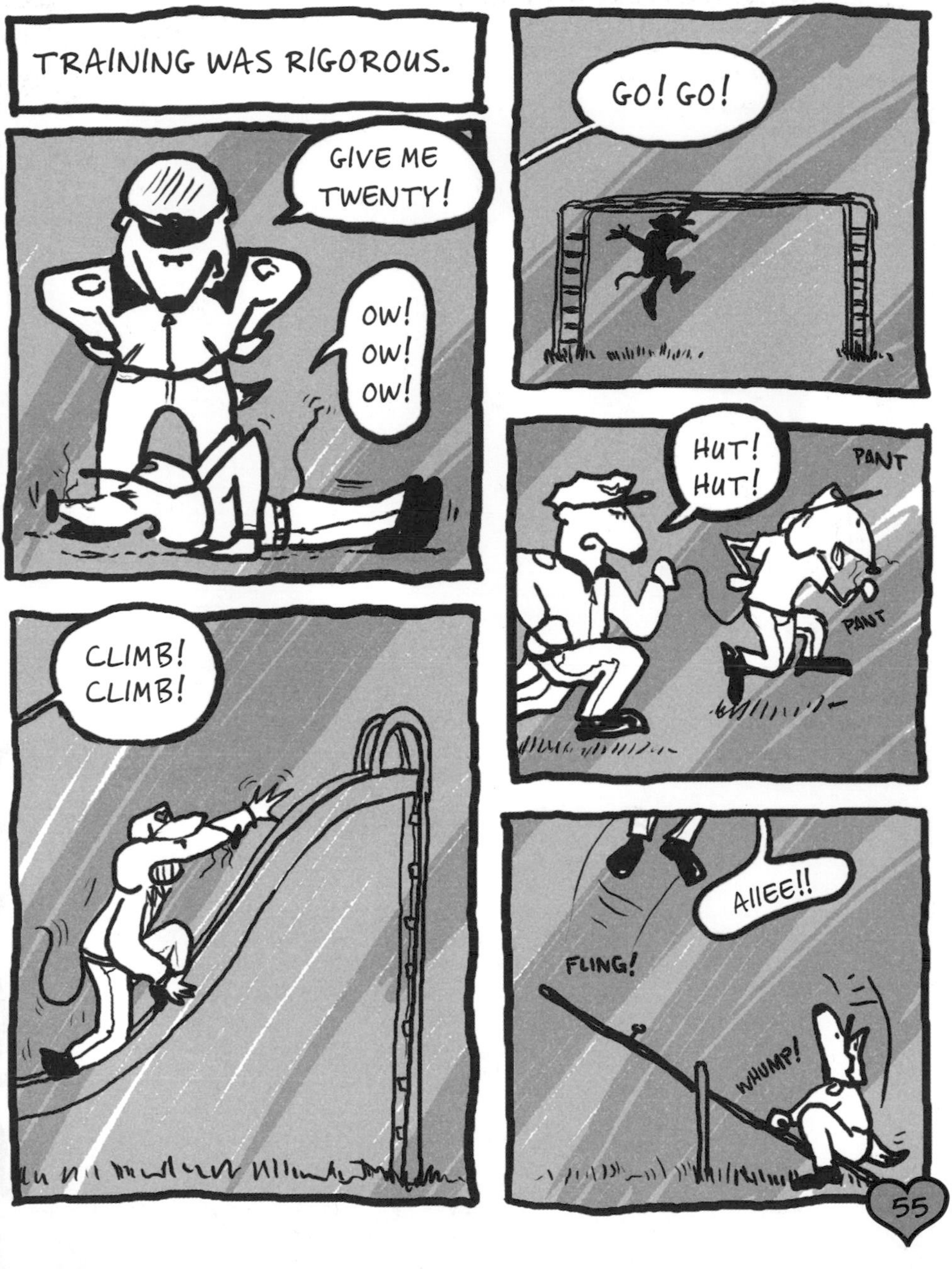
TRAINING WAS RIGOROUS.
GIVE ME TWENTY!
OW! OW! OW!
GO! GO!
HUT! HUT!
PANT
PANT
CLIMB! CLIMB!
AIIEE!!
FLING!
WHUMP!

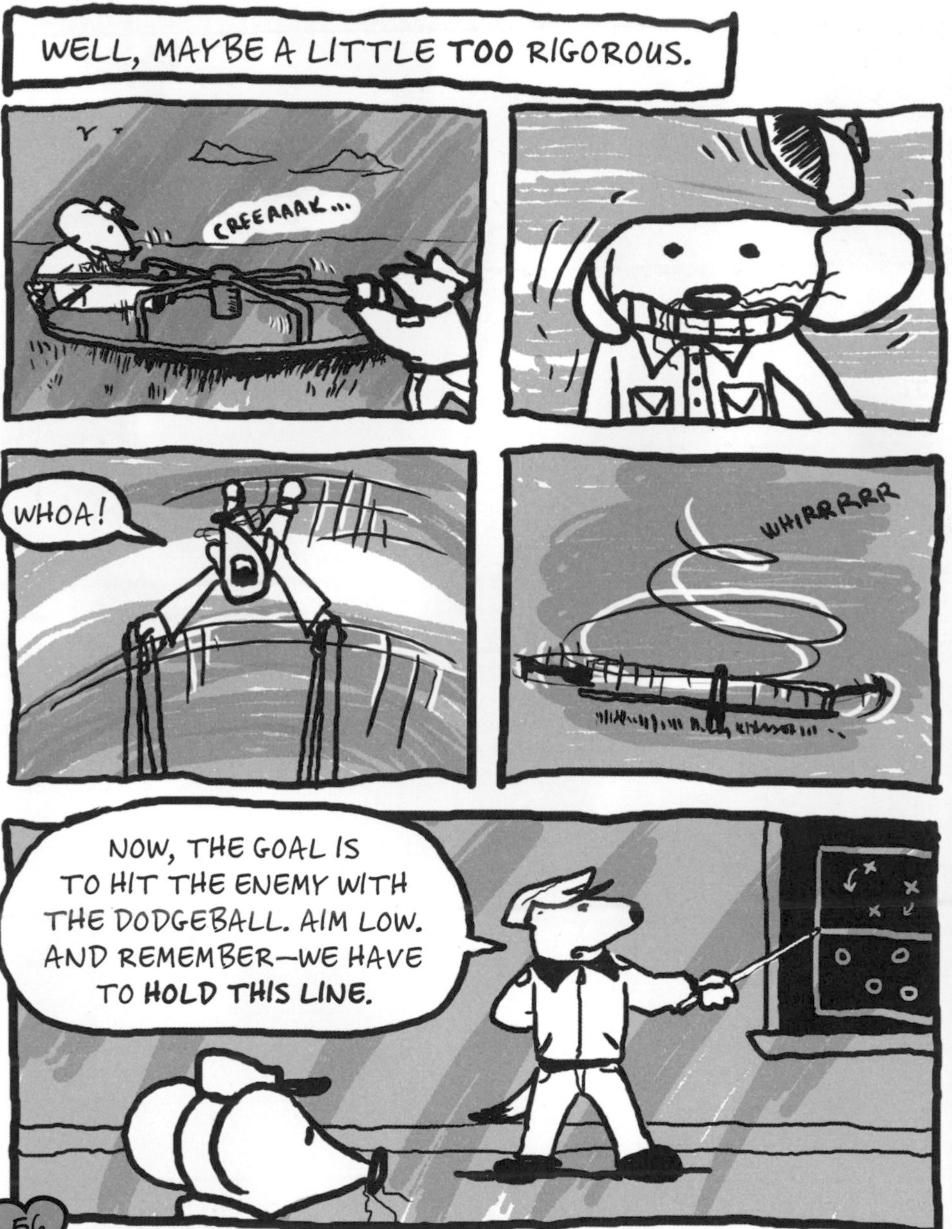
WELL, MAYBE A LITTLE TOO RIGOROUS.
CREEAAAK...
WHOA!
WHIRRRRR
NOW, THE GOAL IS TO HIT THE ENEMY WITH THE DODGEBALL. AIM LOW. AND REMEMBER—WE HAVE TO HOLD THIS LINE.

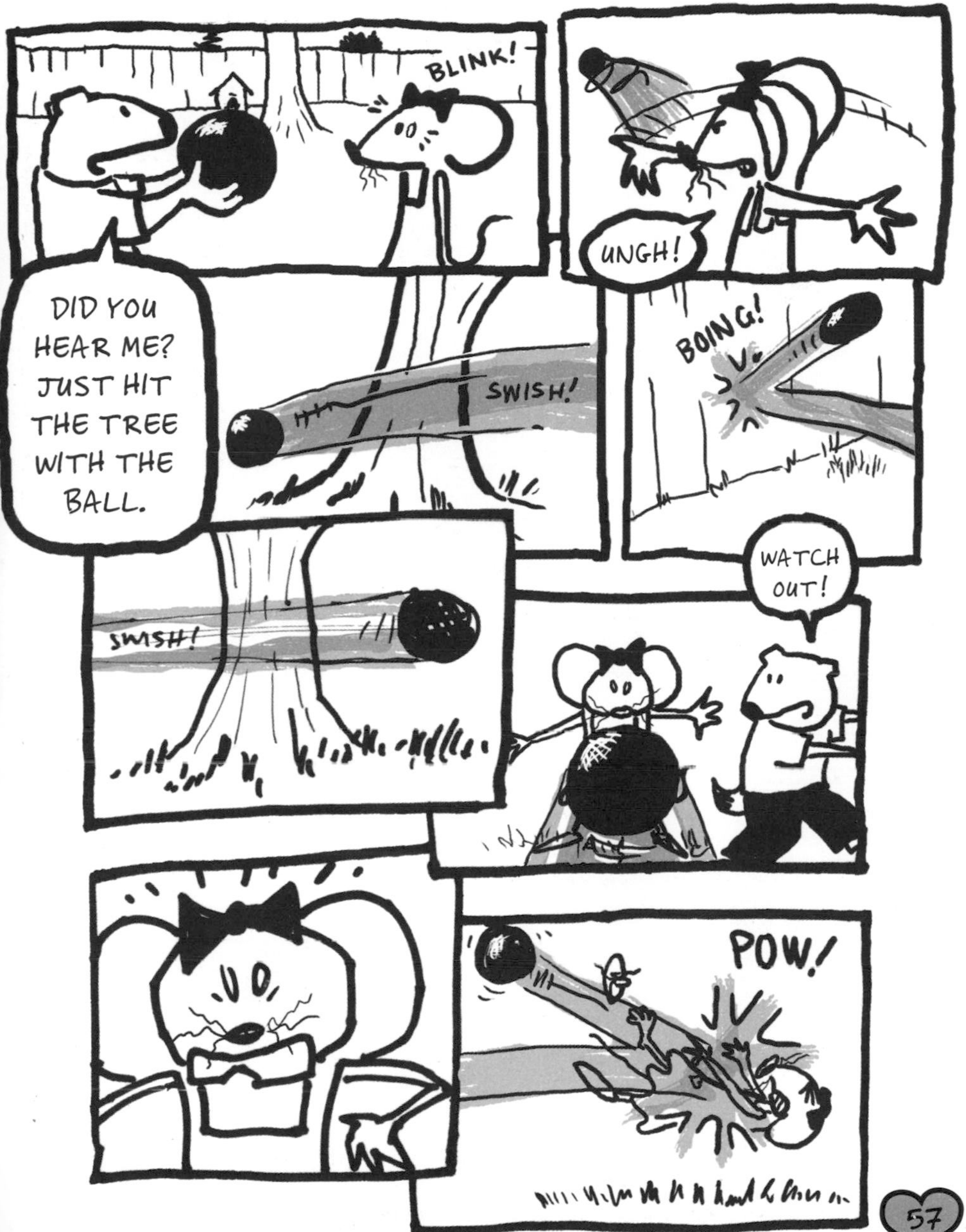
BLINK!
DID YOU HEAR ME? JUST HIT THE TREE WITH THE BALL.
UNGH!
SWISH!
BOING!
SWISH!
WATCH OUT!
POW!

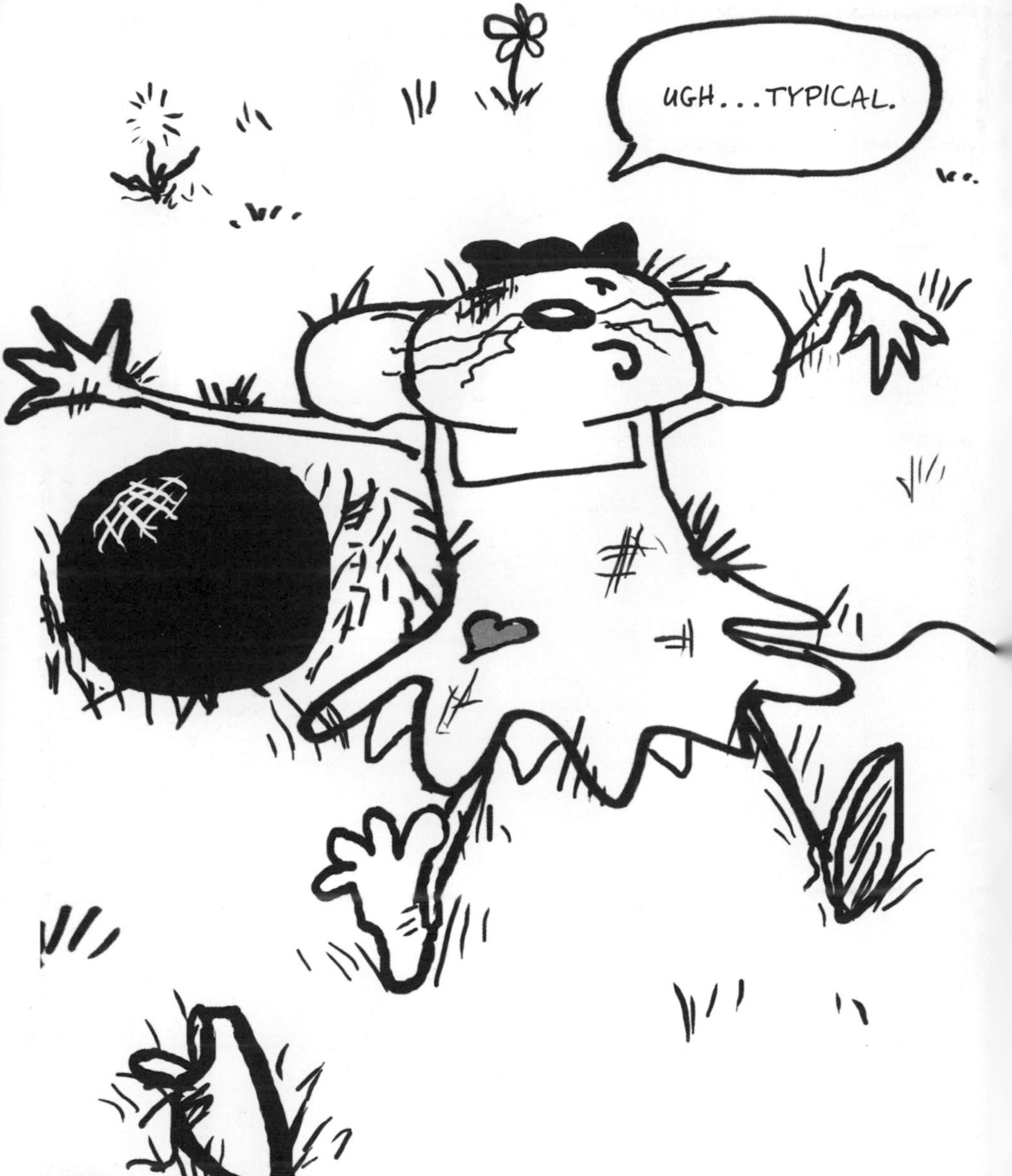
UGH...TYPICAL.

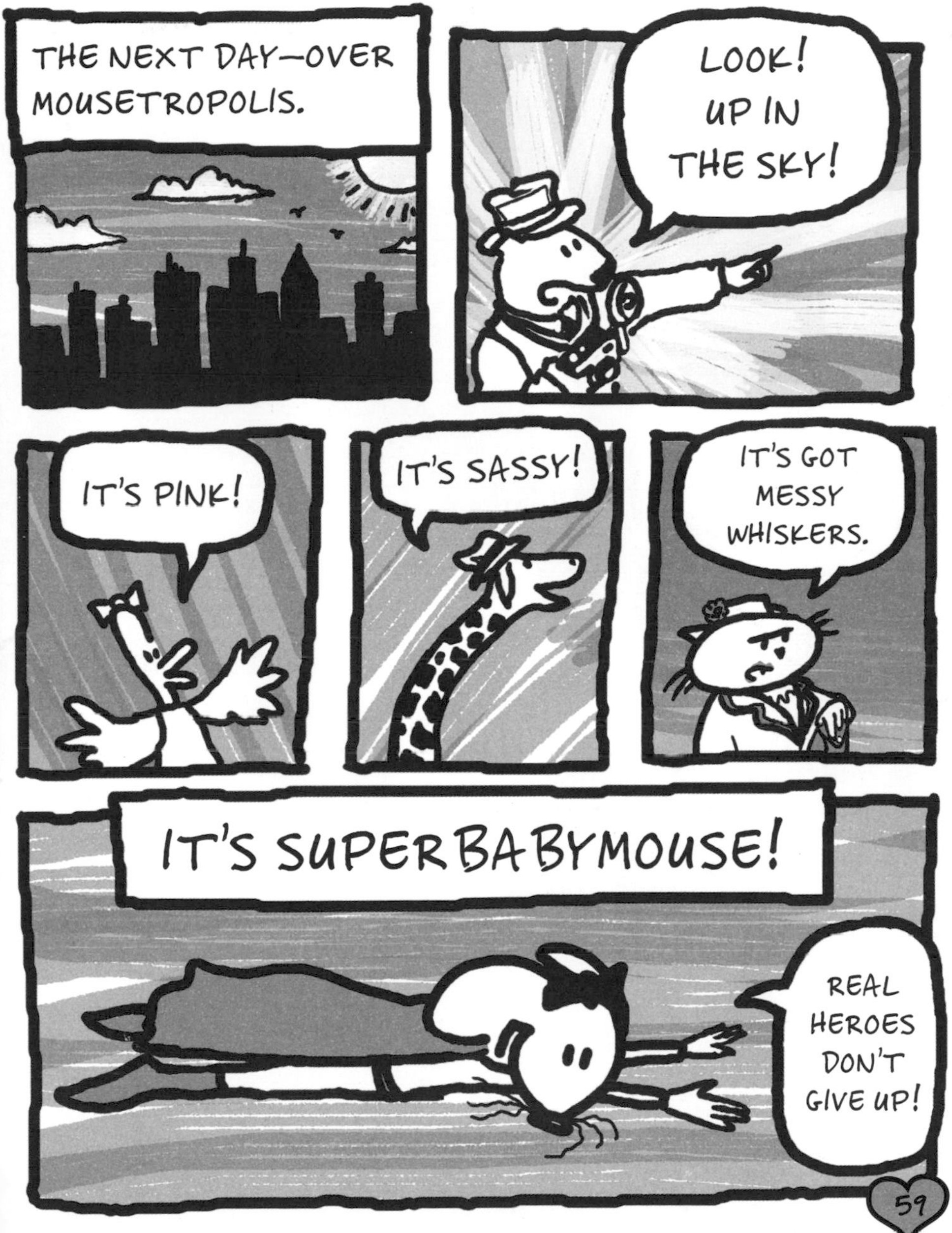
THE NEXT DAY—OVER MOUSETROPOLIS.
LOOK! UP IN THE SKY!
IT'S PINK!
IT'S SASSY!
IT'S GOT MESSY WHISKERS.
IT'S SUPERBABYMOUSE!
REAL HEROES DON'T GIVE UP!

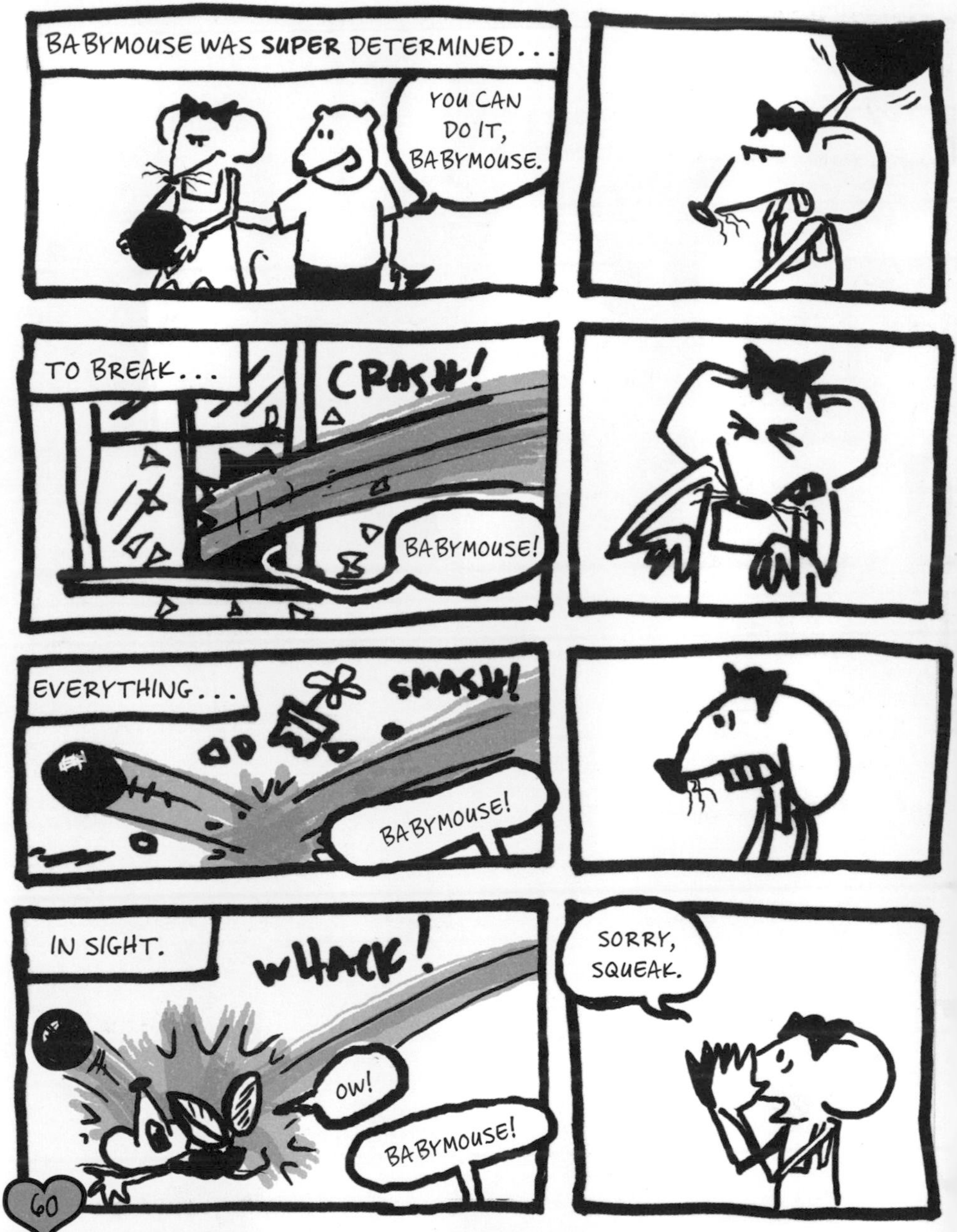

BABYMOUSE WAS SUPER DETERMINED...
YOU CAN DO IT, BABYMOUSE.
TO BREAK...
CRASH!
BABYMOUSE!
EVERYTHING...
SMASH!
BABYMOUSE!
IN SIGHT.
WHACK!
OW!
BABYMOUSE!
SORRY, SQUEAK.

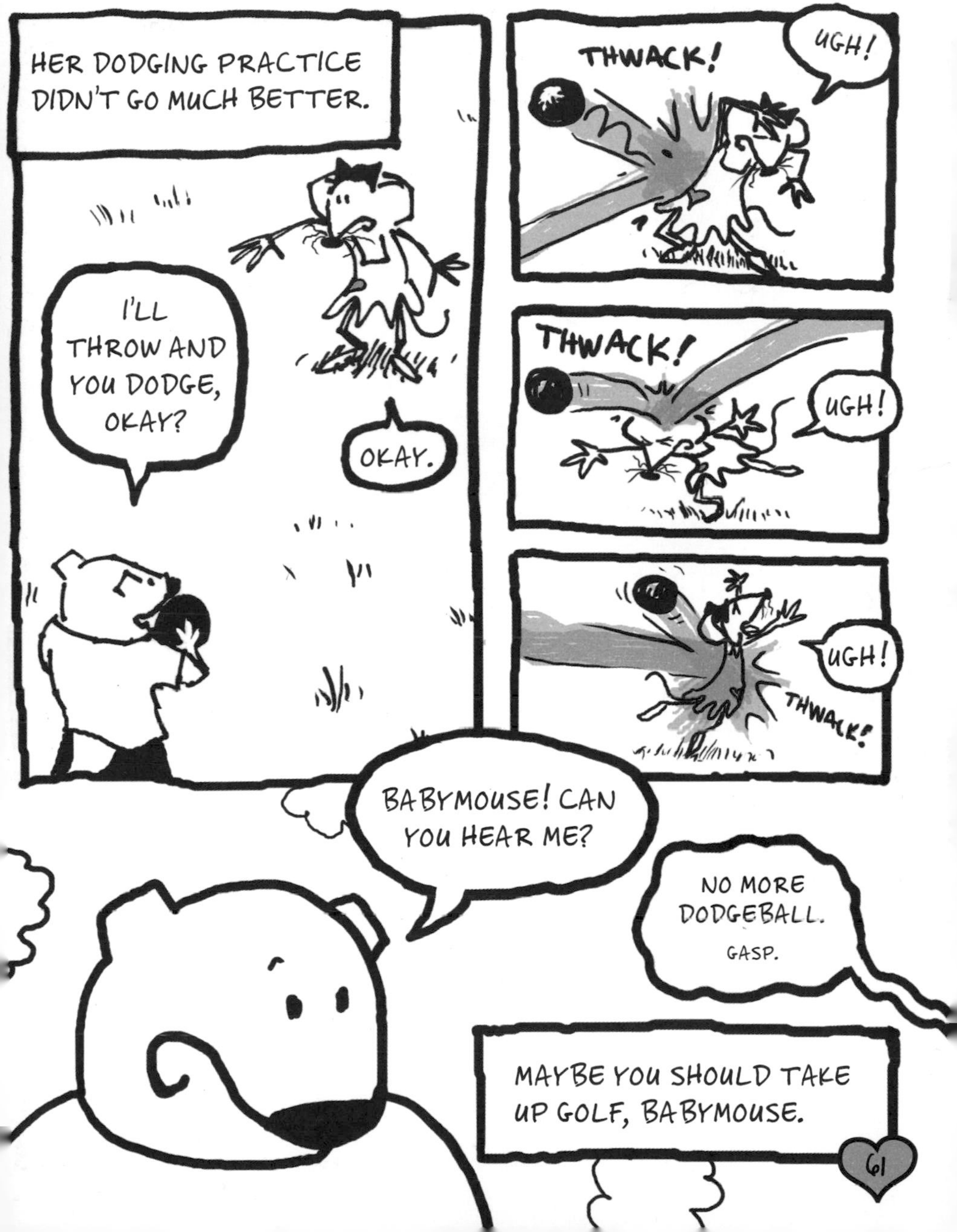
HER DODGING PRACTICE DIDN'T GO MUCH BETTER.
I'LL THROW AND YOU DODGE, OKAY?
OKAY.
THWACK!
UGH!
THWACK!
UGH!
UGH!
THWACK!
BABYMOUSE! CAN YOU HEAR ME?
NO MORE DODGEBALL.
GASP.
MAYBE YOU SHOULD TAKE UP GOLF, BABYMOUSE.

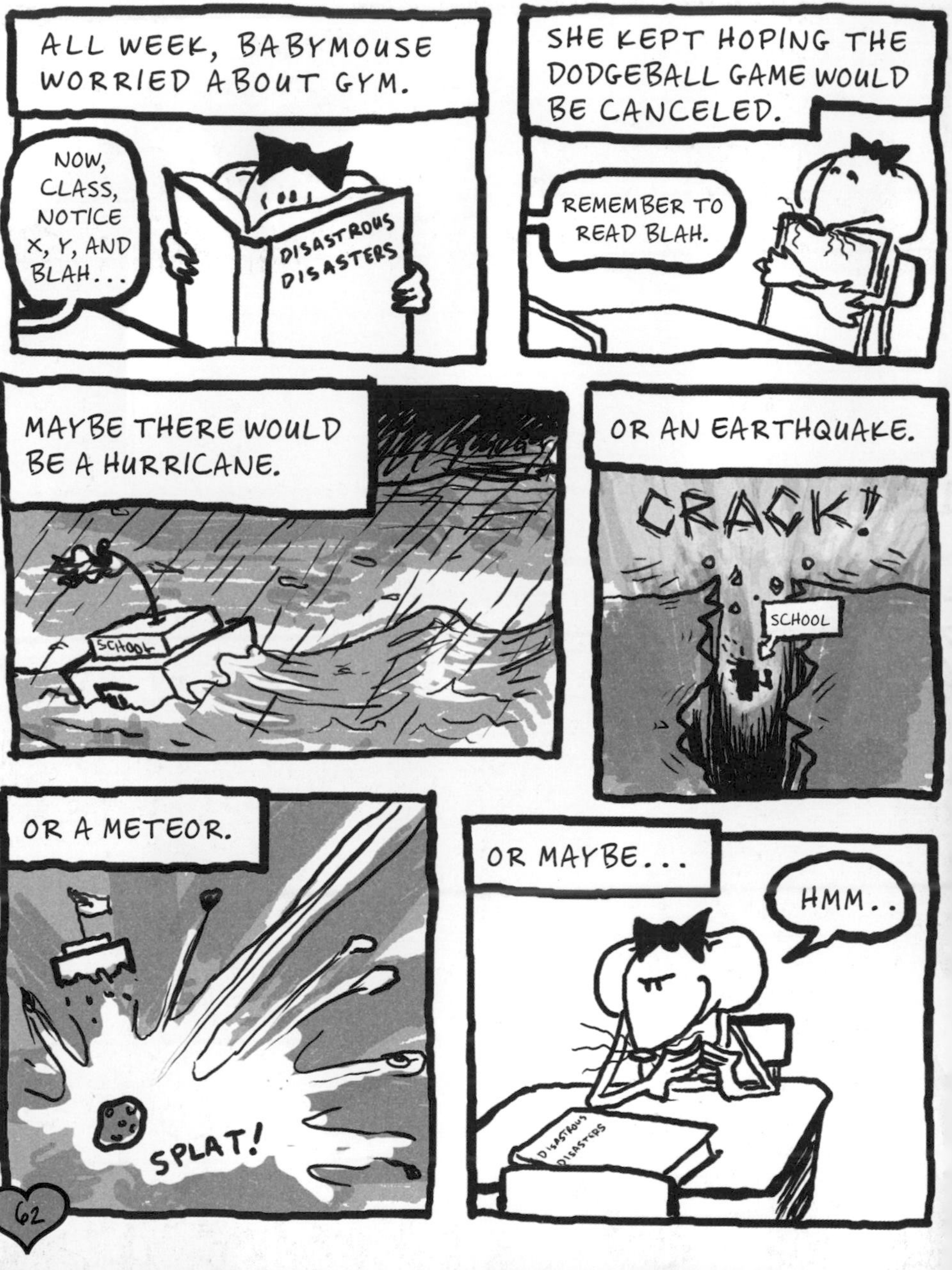
ALL WEEK, BABYMOUSE WORRIED ABOUT GYM.
NOW, CLASS, NOTICE X, Y, AND BLAH...
DISASTROUS DISASTERS
SHE KEPT HOPING THE DODGEBALL GAME WOULD BE CANCELED.
REMEMBER TO READ BLAH.
MAYBE THERE WOULD BE A HURRICANE.
SCHOOL
OR AN EARTHQUAKE.
CRACK!
SCHOOL
OR A METEOR.
SPLAT!
OR MAYBE...
HMM..
DISASTROUS DISASTERS

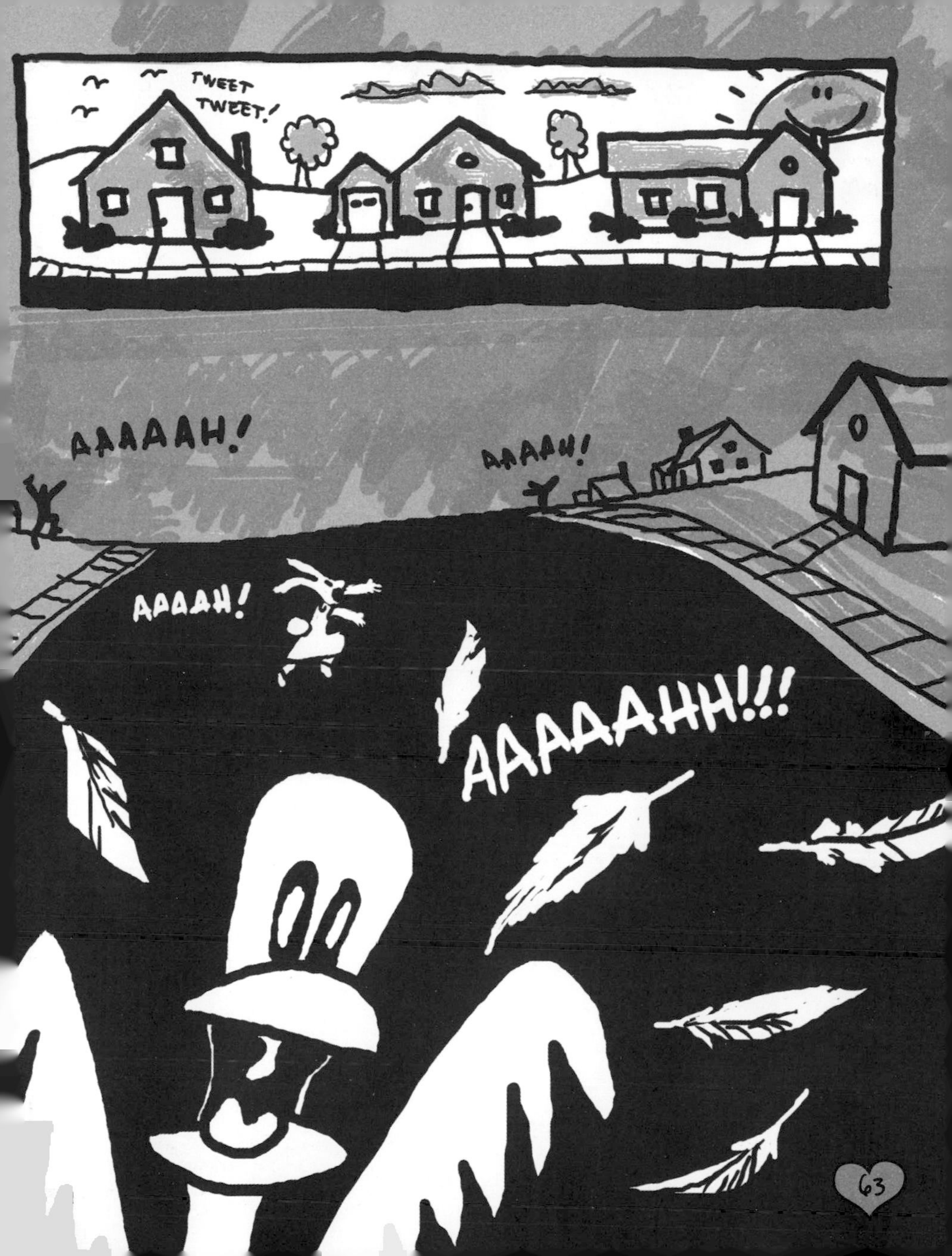
TWEET TWEET!
AAAAAH!
AAAAH!
AAAAH!
AAAAAHH!!!

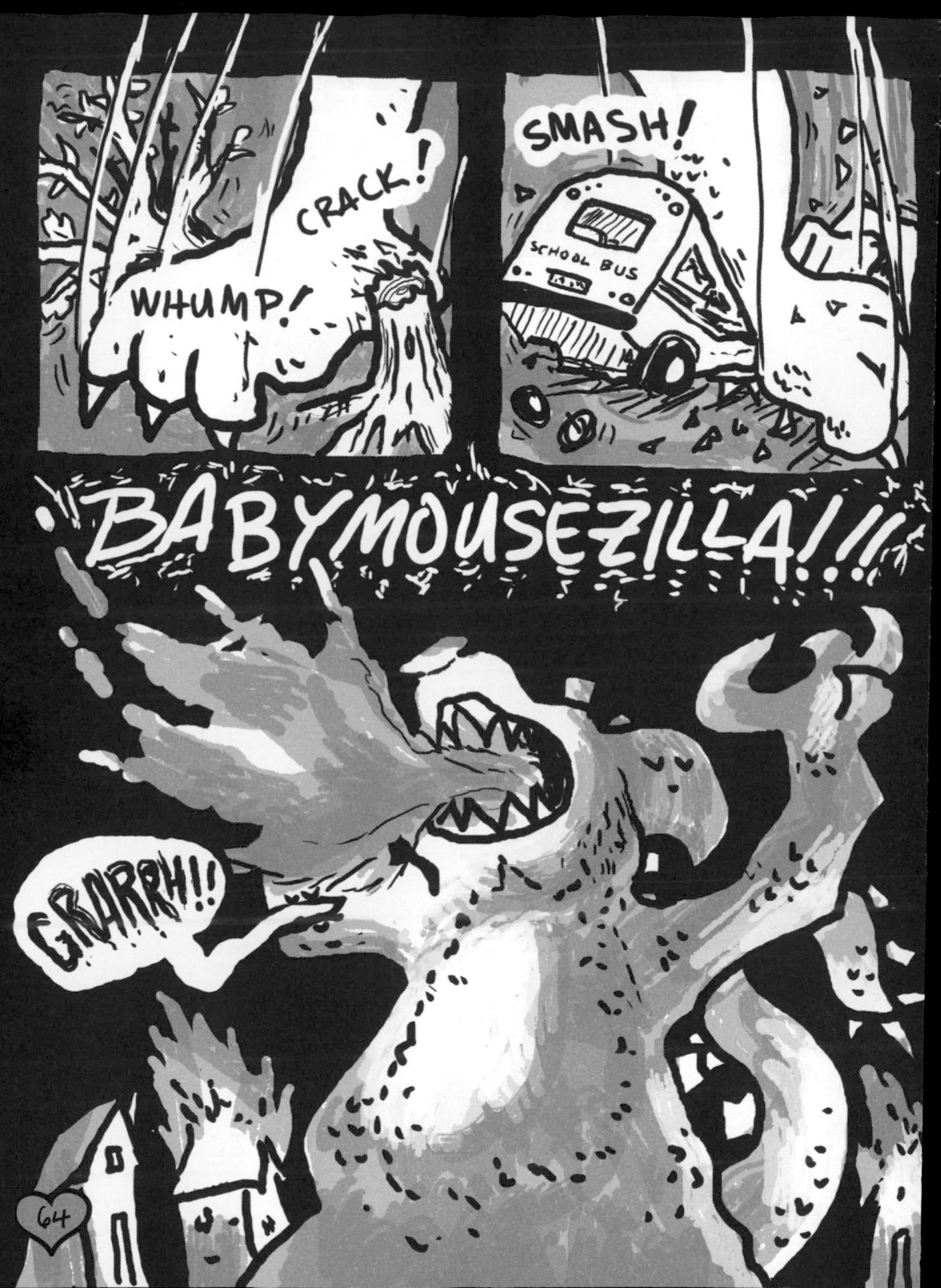

CRACK!
WHUMP!
SMASH!
SCHOOL BUS
BABYMOUSEZILLA!!!
GRARRH!!

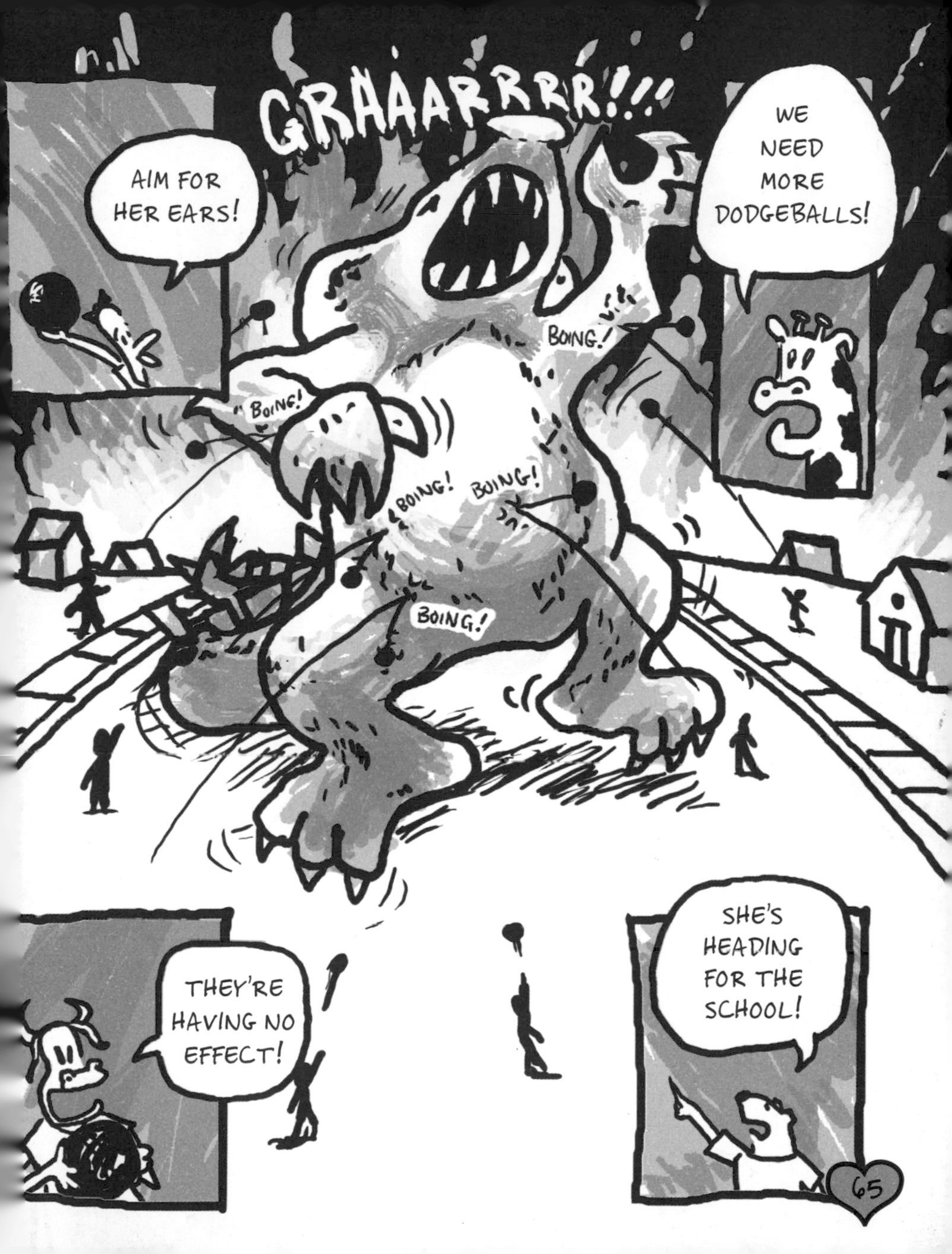
GRAAARRRR!!!
AIM FOR HER EARS!
WE NEED MORE DODGEBALLS!
BOING!
BOING!
BOING!
BOING!
BOING!
THEY'RE HAVING NO EFFECT!
SHE'S HEADING FOR THE SCHOOL!

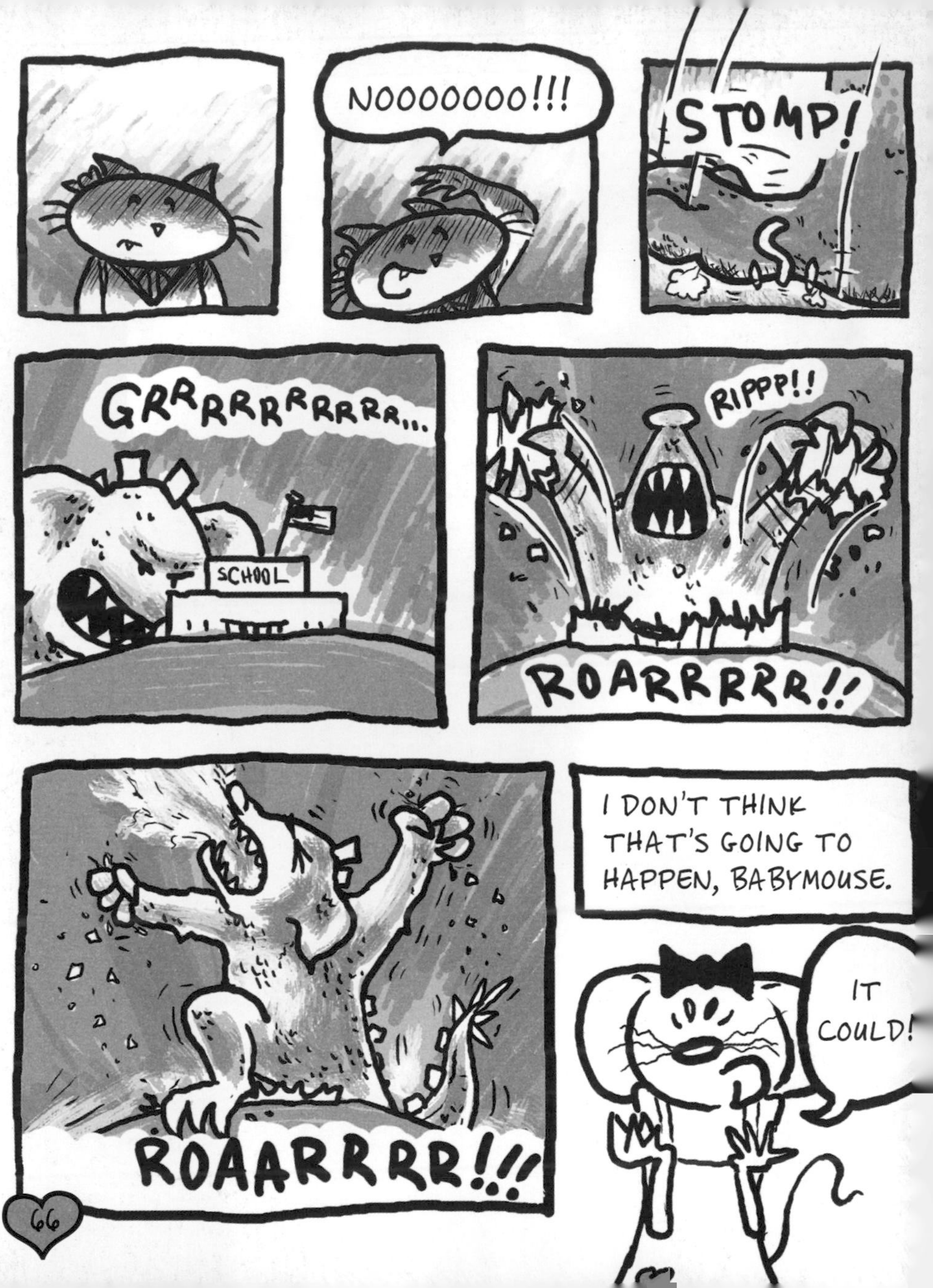
NOOOOOOO!!!
STOMP!
GRRRRRRRRRR...
SCHOOL
RIPPP!!
ROARRRRR!!
ROAARRRRR!!!
I DON'T THINK THAT'S GOING TO HAPPEN, BABYMOUSE.
IT COULD!

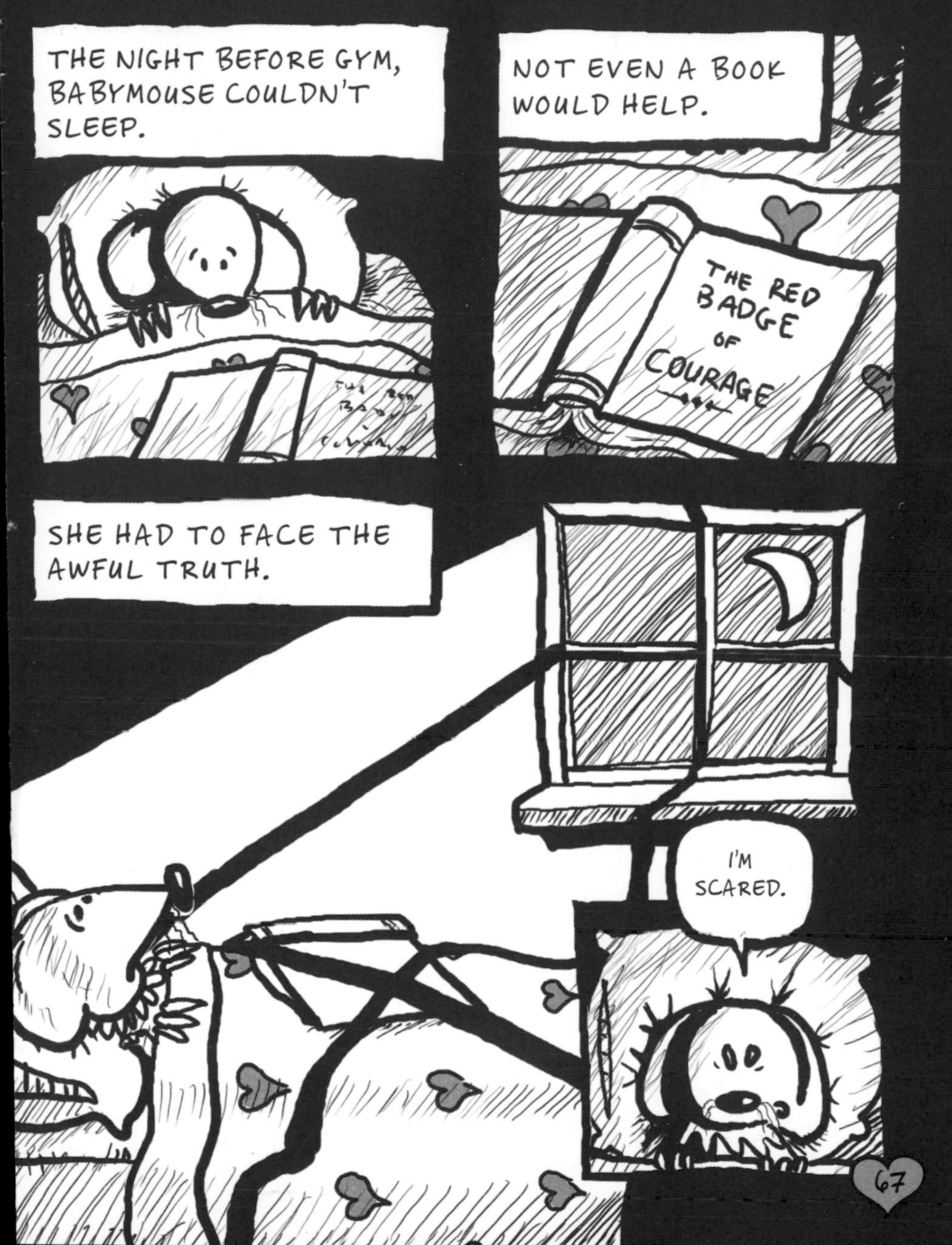
THE NIGHT BEFORE GYM, BABYMOUSE COULDN'T SLEEP.
NOT EVEN A BOOK WOULD HELP.
THE RED BADGE OF COURAGE
SHE HAD TO FACE THE AWFUL TRUTH.
I'M SCARED.

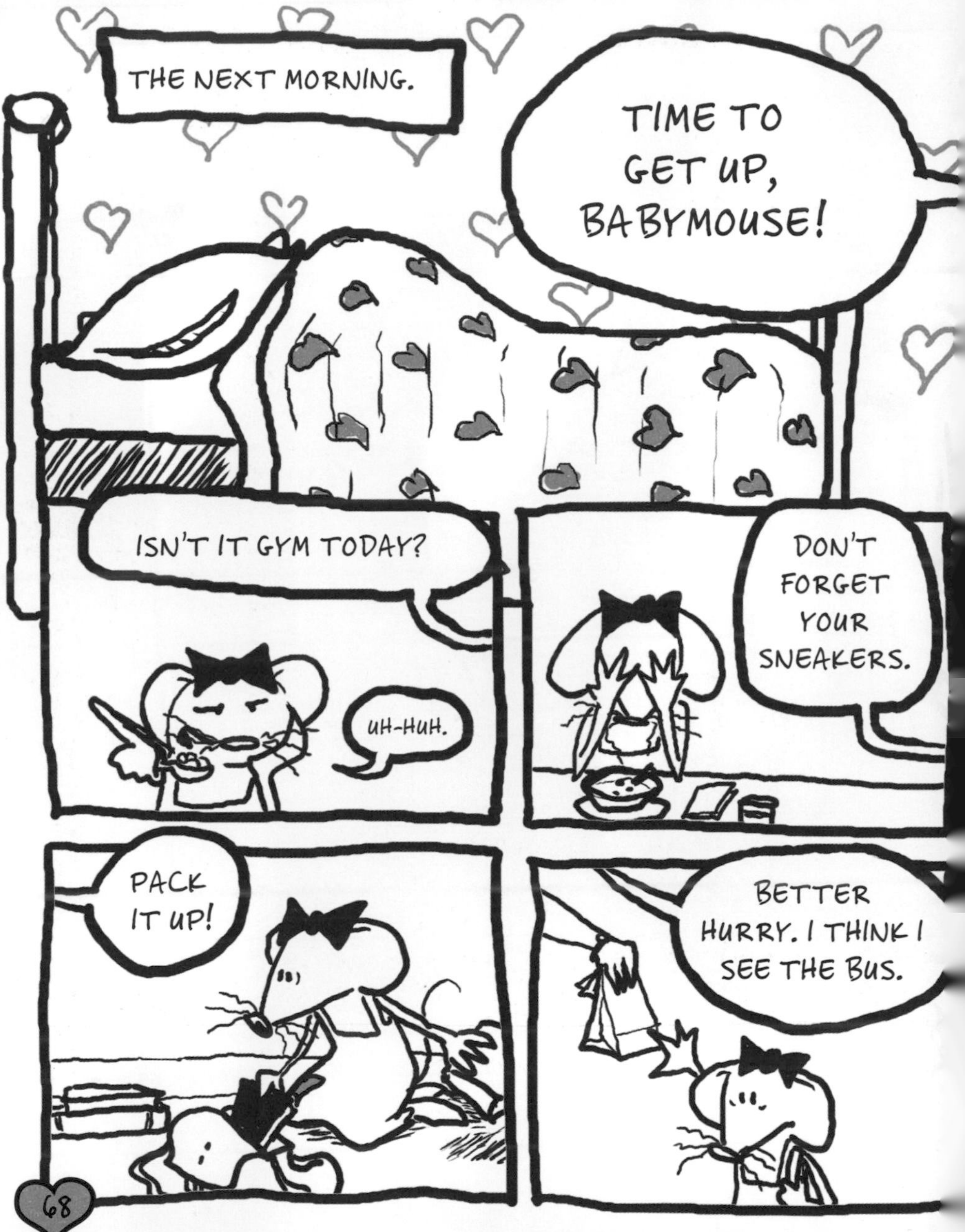
THE NEXT MORNING.
TIME TO GET UP, BABYMOUSE!
ISN'T IT GYM TODAY?
UH-HUH.
DON'T FORGET YOUR SNEAKERS.
PACK IT UP!
BETTER HURRY. I THINK I SEE THE BUS.

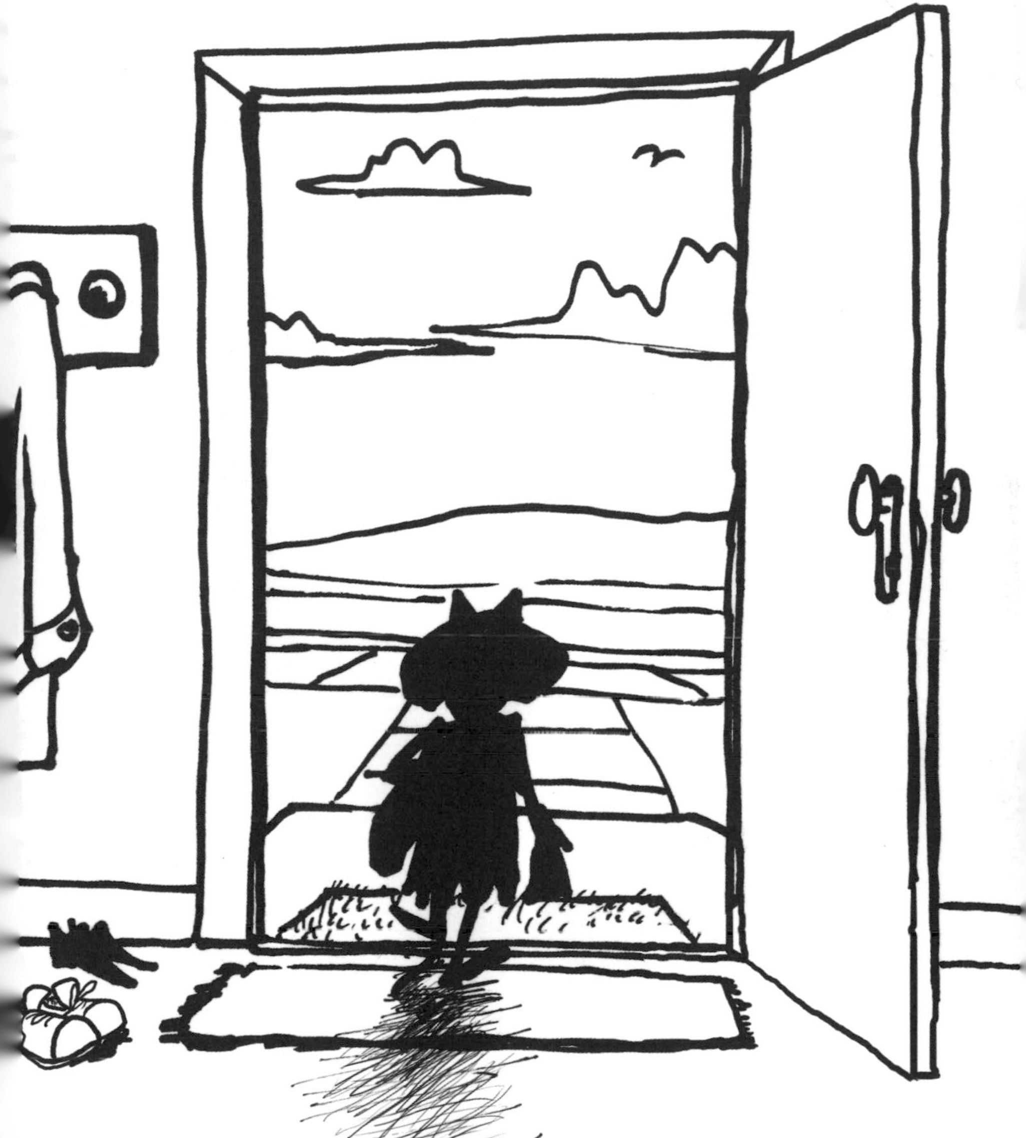

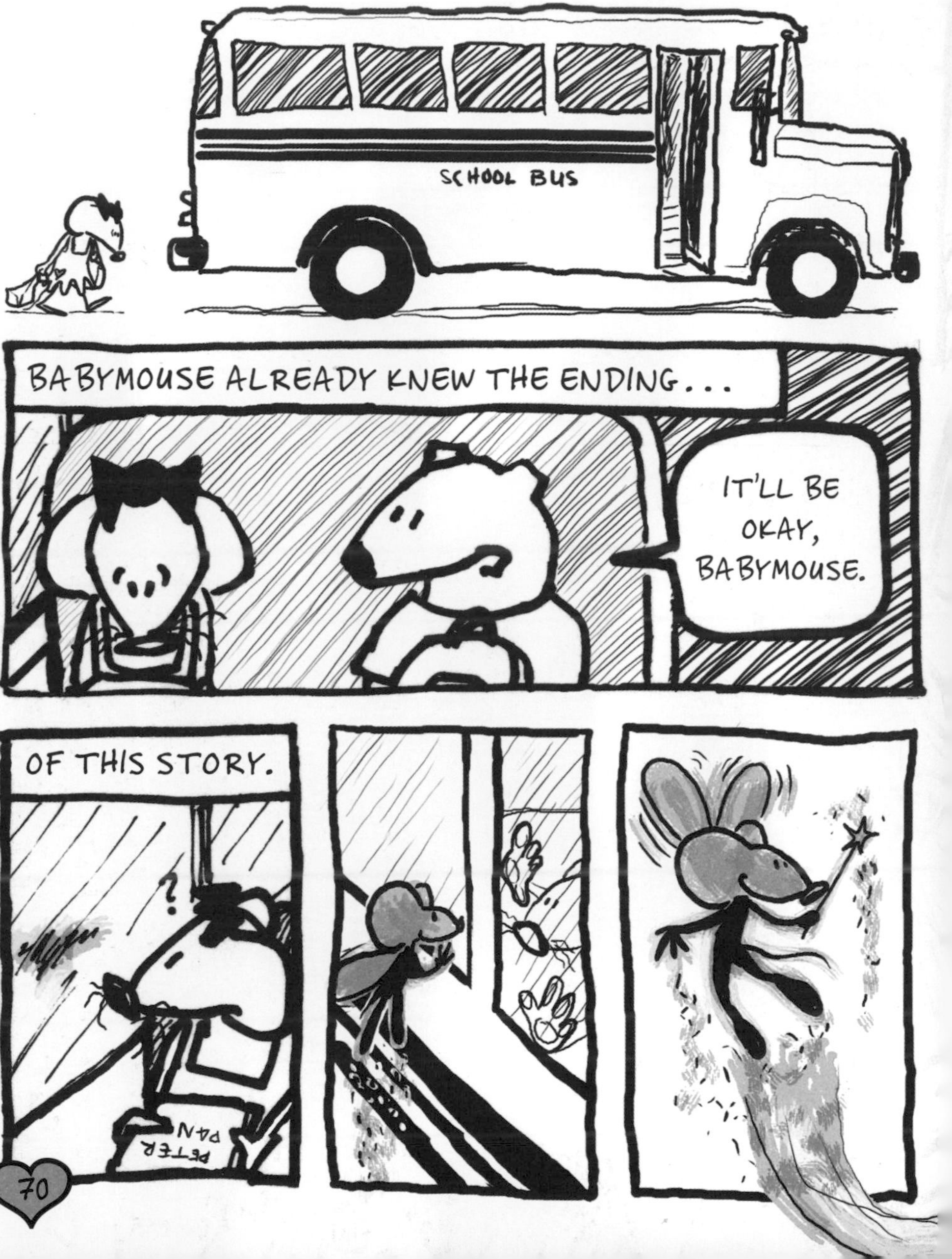
SCHOOL BUS
BABYMOUSE ALREADY KNEW THE ENDING...
IT'LL BE OKAY, BABYMOUSE.
OF THIS STORY.
?
PETER PAN

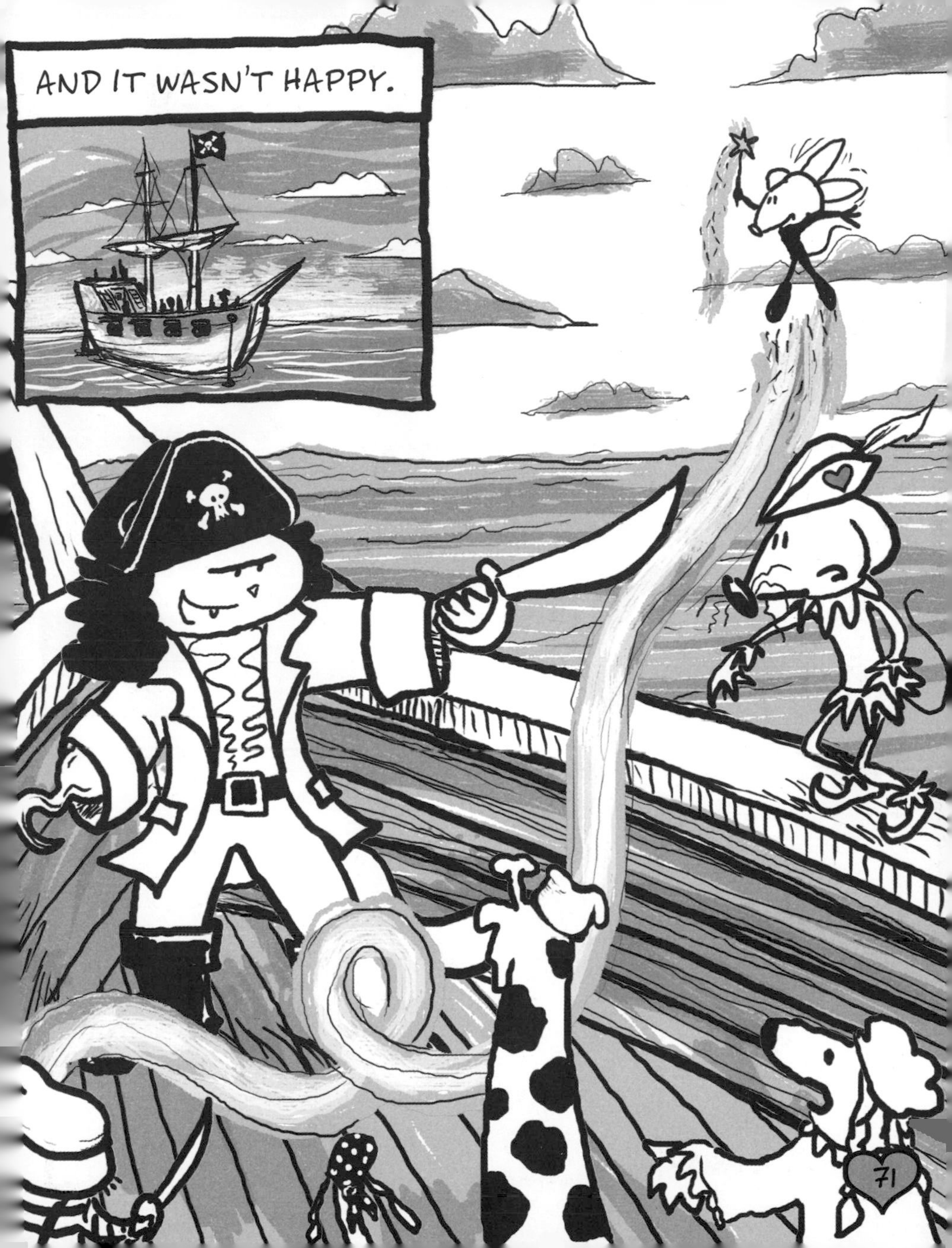
AND IT WASN'T HAPPY.

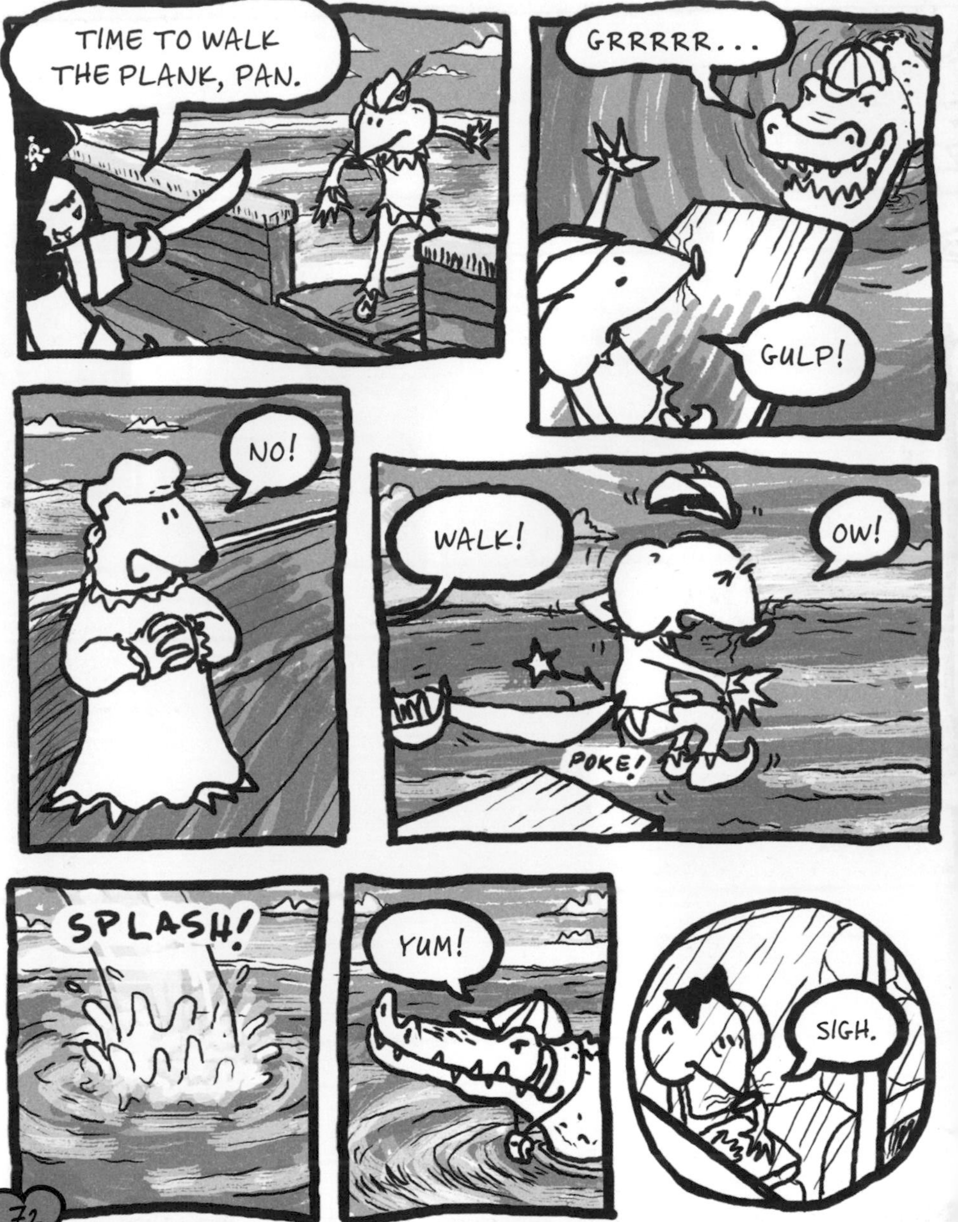
TIME TO WALK THE PLANK, PAN.
GRRRRR...
GULP!
NO!
WALK!
OW!
POKE!
SPLASH!
YUM!
SIGH.

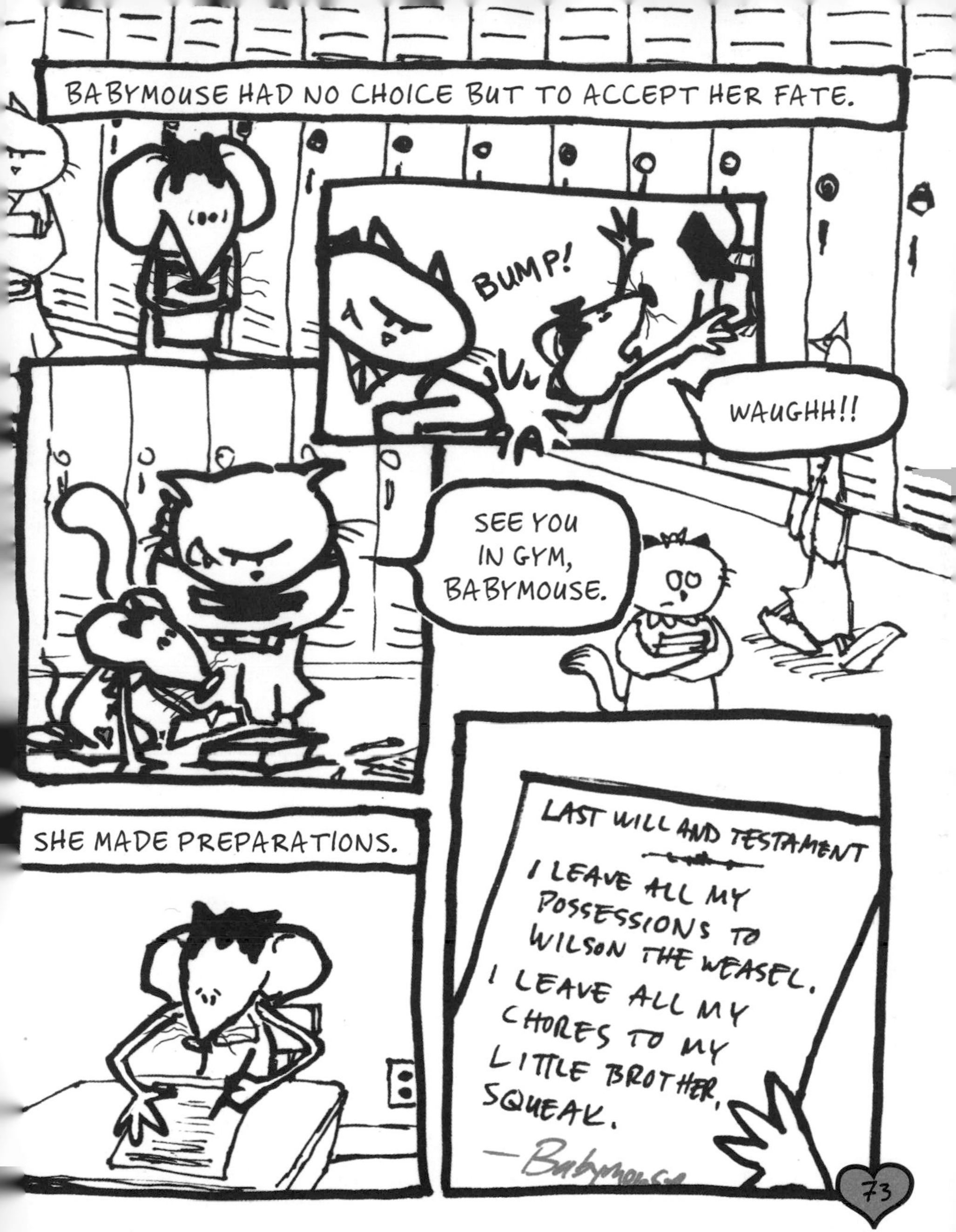
BABYMOUSE HAD NO CHOICE BUT TO ACCEPT HER FATE.
BUMP!
WAUGHH!!
SEE YOU IN GYM, BABYMOUSE.
SHE MADE PREPARATIONS.
LAST WILL AND TESTAMENT
I LEAVE ALL MY POSSESSIONS TO WILSON THE WEASEL.
I LEAVE ALL MY CHORES TO MY LITTLE BROTHER, SQUEAK.
—Babymouse

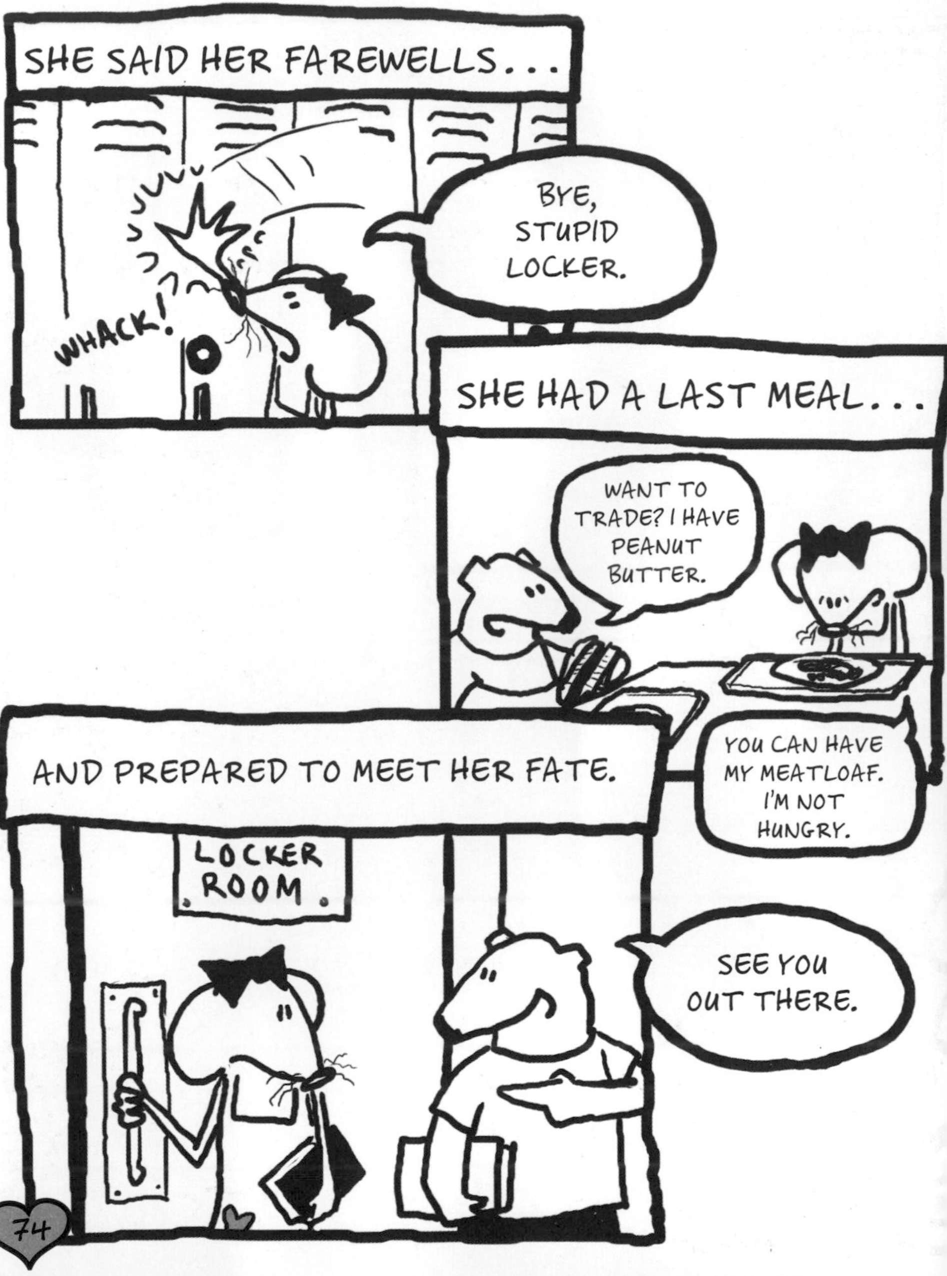
SHE SAID HER FAREWELLS...
WHACK!
BYE, STUPID LOCKER.
SHE HAD A LAST MEAL...
WANT TO TRADE? I HAVE PEANUT BUTTER.
YOU CAN HAVE MY MEATLOAF. I'M NOT HUNGRY.
AND PREPARED TO MEET HER FATE.
LOCKER ROOM
SEE YOU OUT THERE.

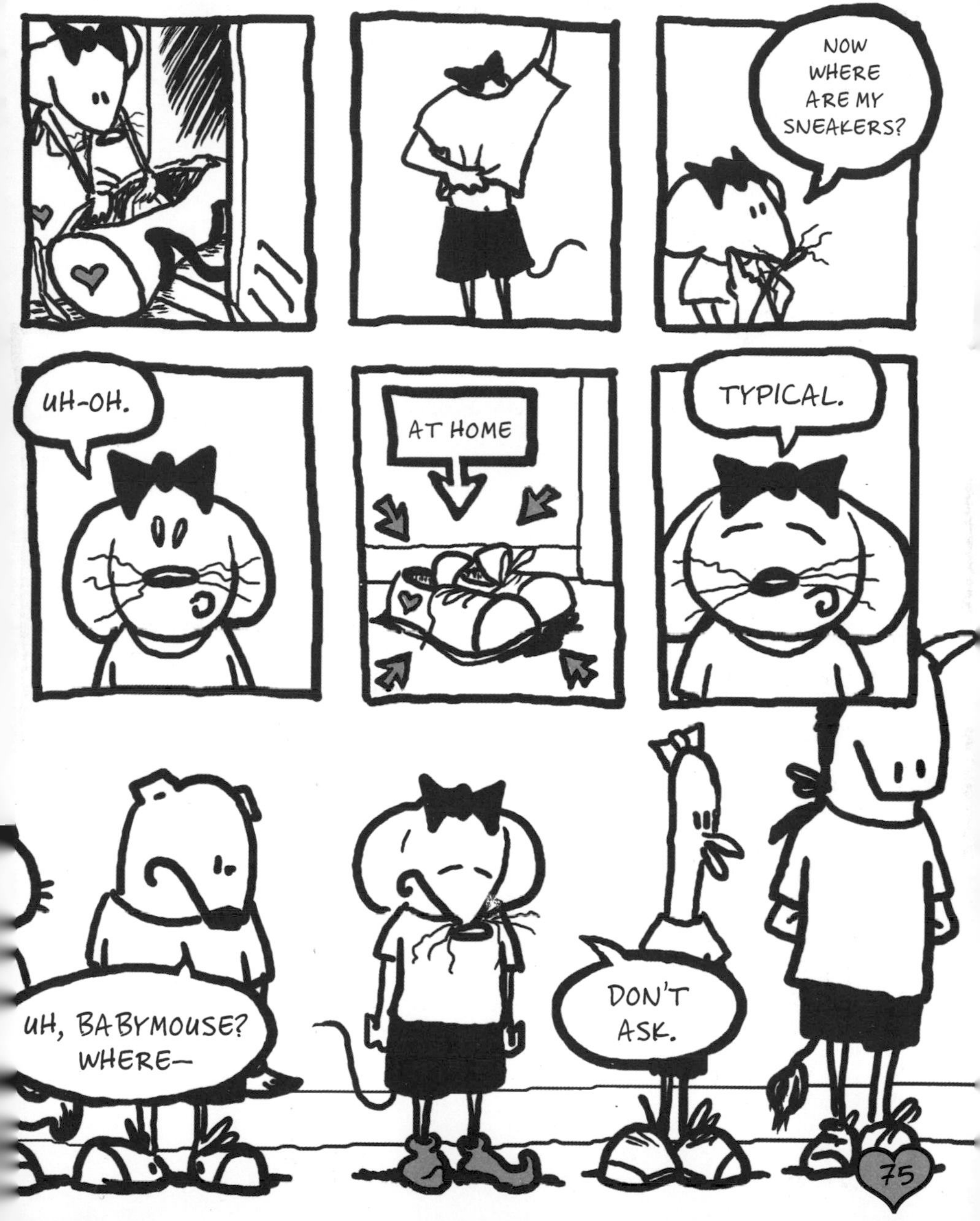
NOW WHERE ARE MY SNEAKERS?
UH-OH.
AT HOME
TYPICAL.
UH, BABYMOUSE? WHERE—
DON'T ASK.

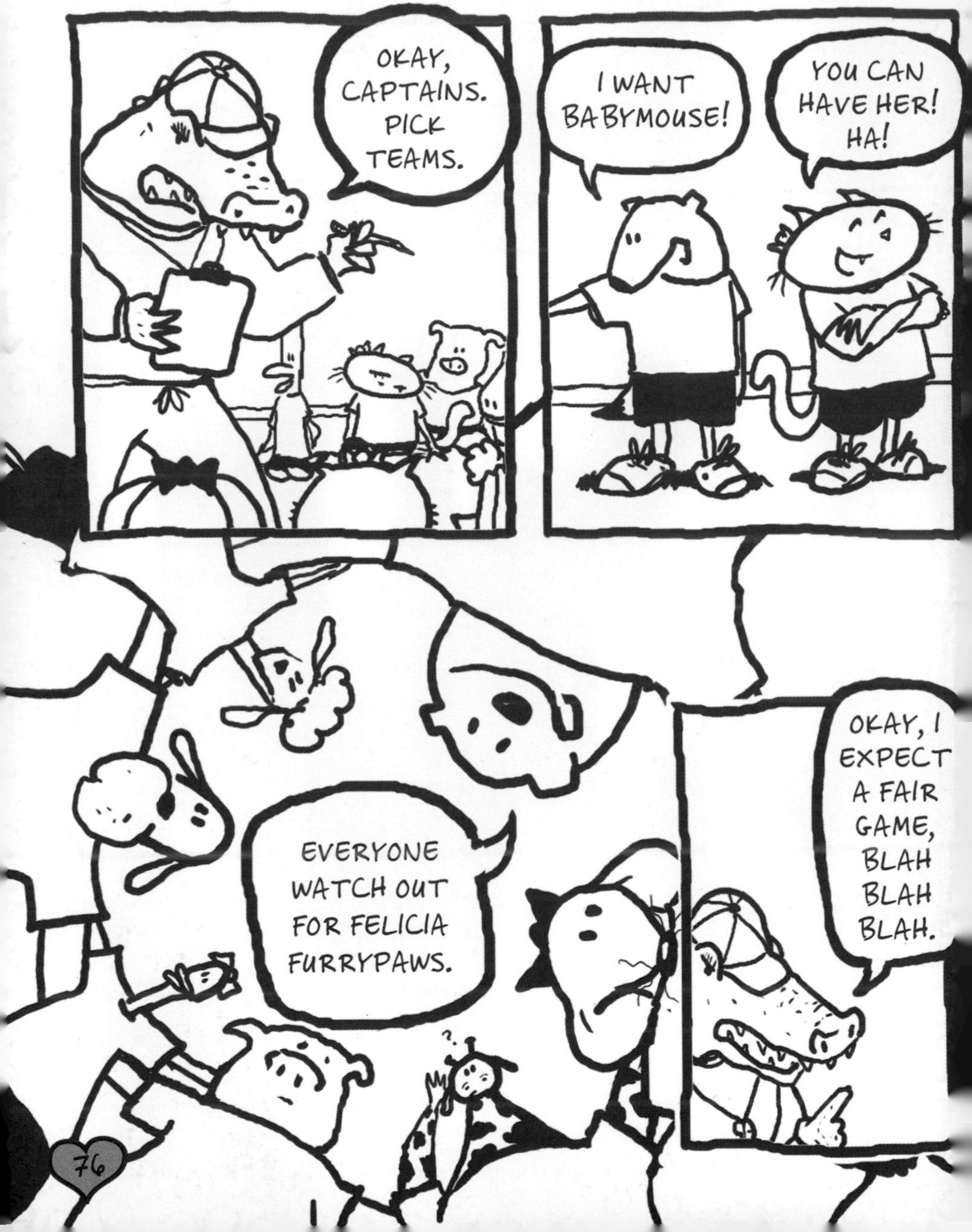
OKAY, CAPTAINS. PICK TEAMS.
I WANT BABYMOUSE!
YOU CAN HAVE HER! HA!
EVERYONE WATCH OUT FOR FELICIA FURRYPAWS.
OKAY, I EXPECT A FAIR GAME, BLAH BLAH BLAH.
?

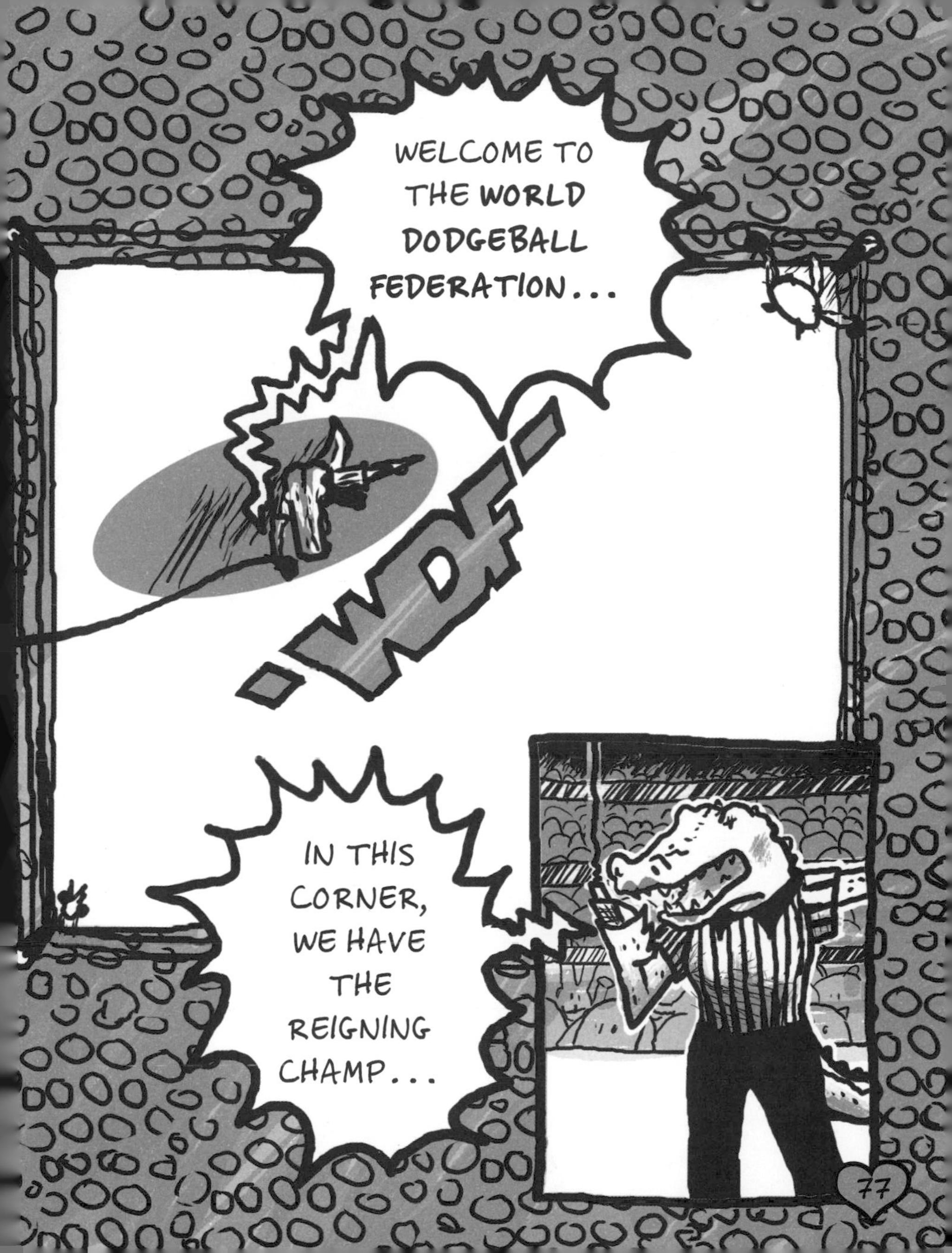
WELCOME TO THE WORLD DODGEBALL FEDERATION...
WDF
IN THIS CORNER, WE HAVE THE REIGNING CHAMP...

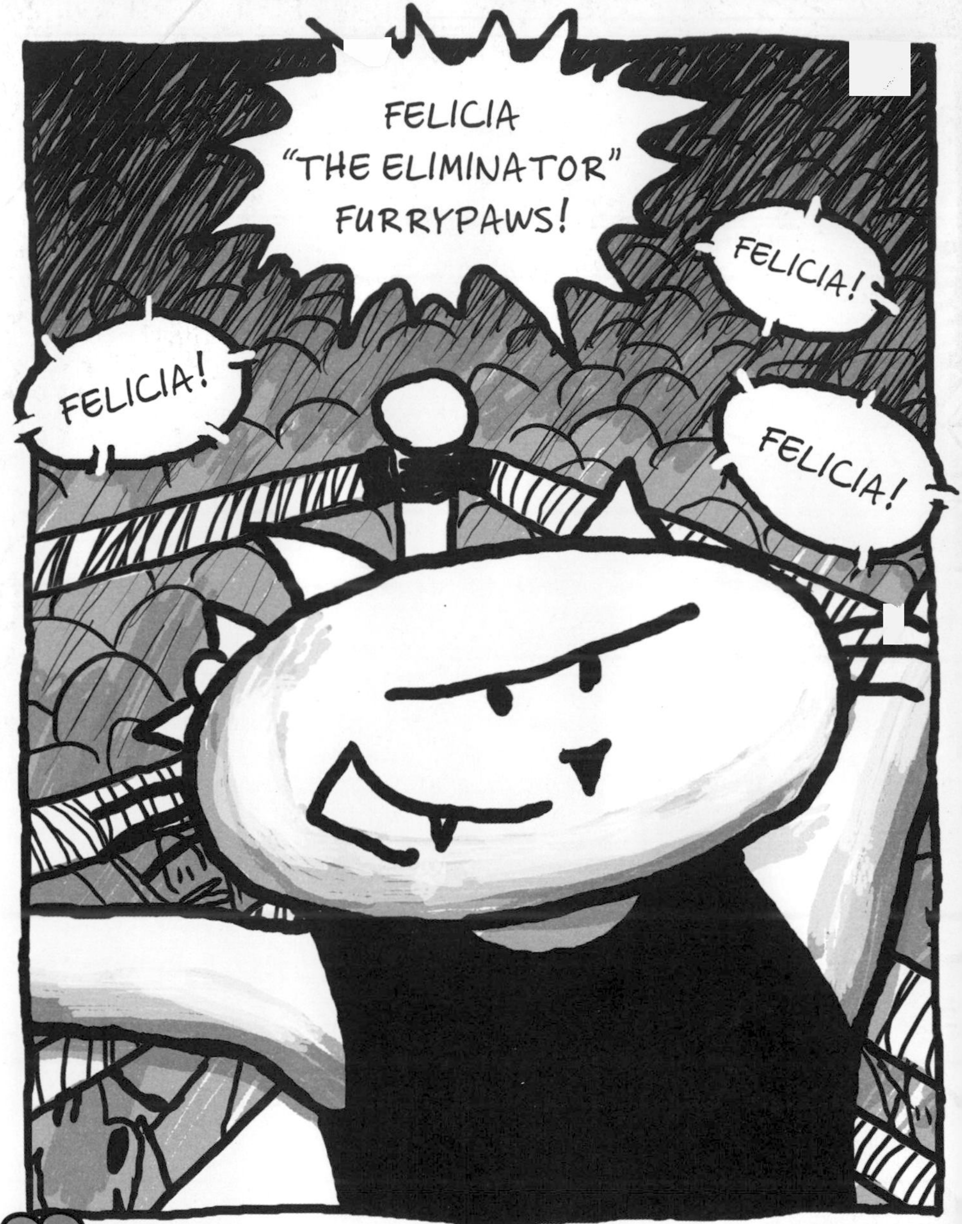
FELICIA
"THE ELIMINATOR"
FURRYPAWS!
FELICIA!
FELICIA!
FELICIA!

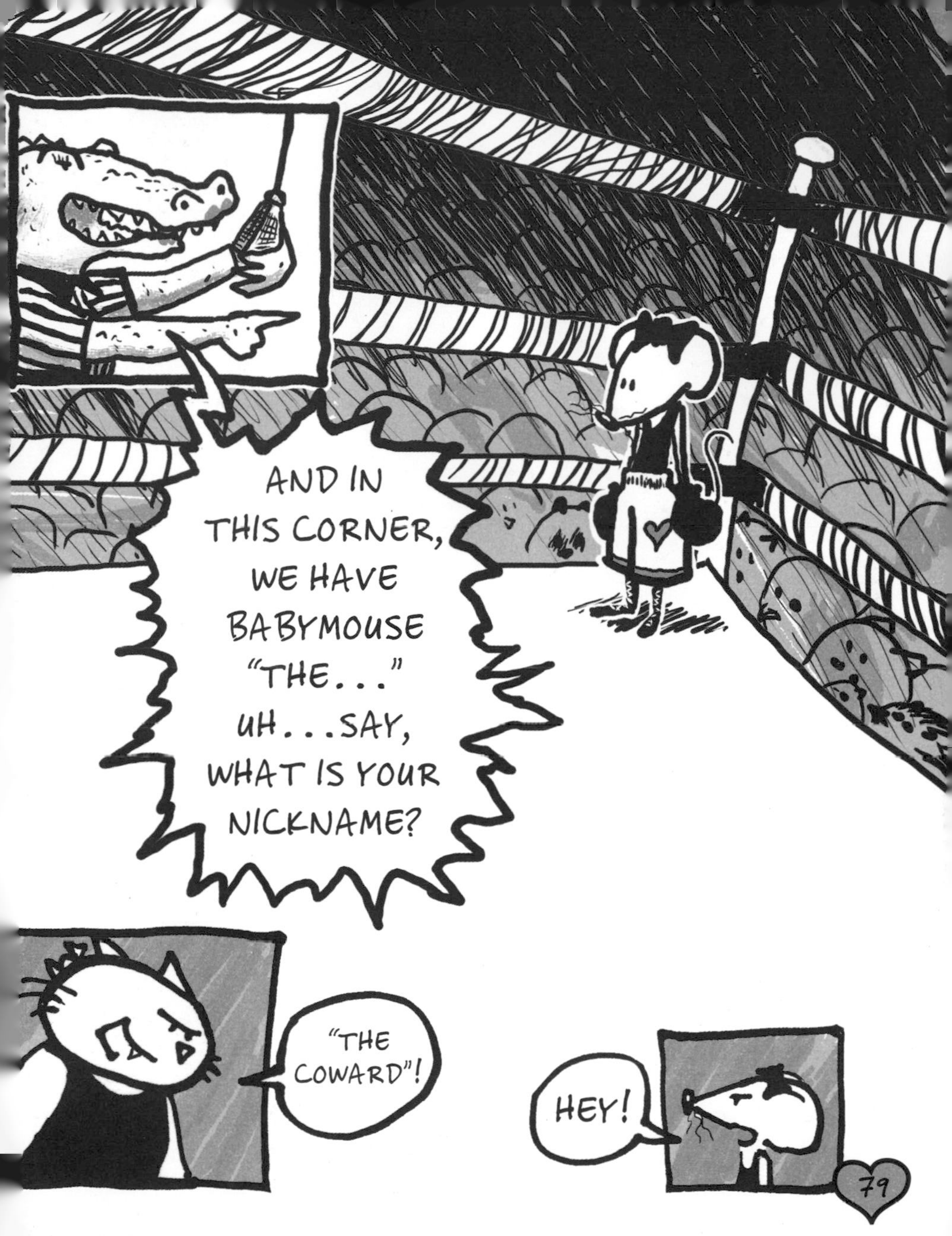
AND IN THIS CORNER, WE HAVE BABYMOUSE "THE..." UH...SAY, WHAT IS YOUR NICKNAME?
"THE COWARD"!
HEY!

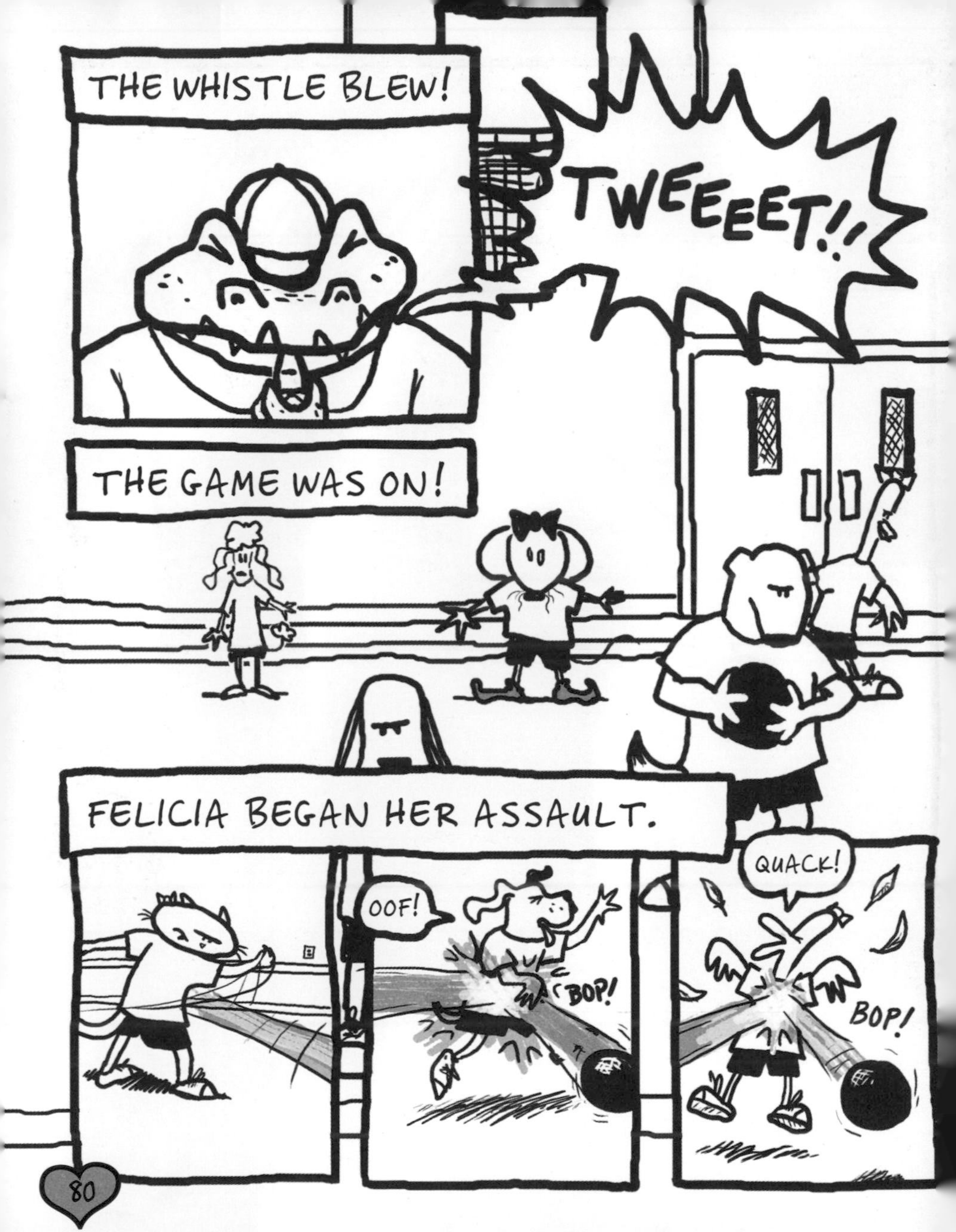
THE WHISTLE BLEW!
TWEEEEET!!
THE GAME WAS ON!
FELICIA BEGAN HER ASSAULT.
OOF!
BOP!
QUACK!
BOP!

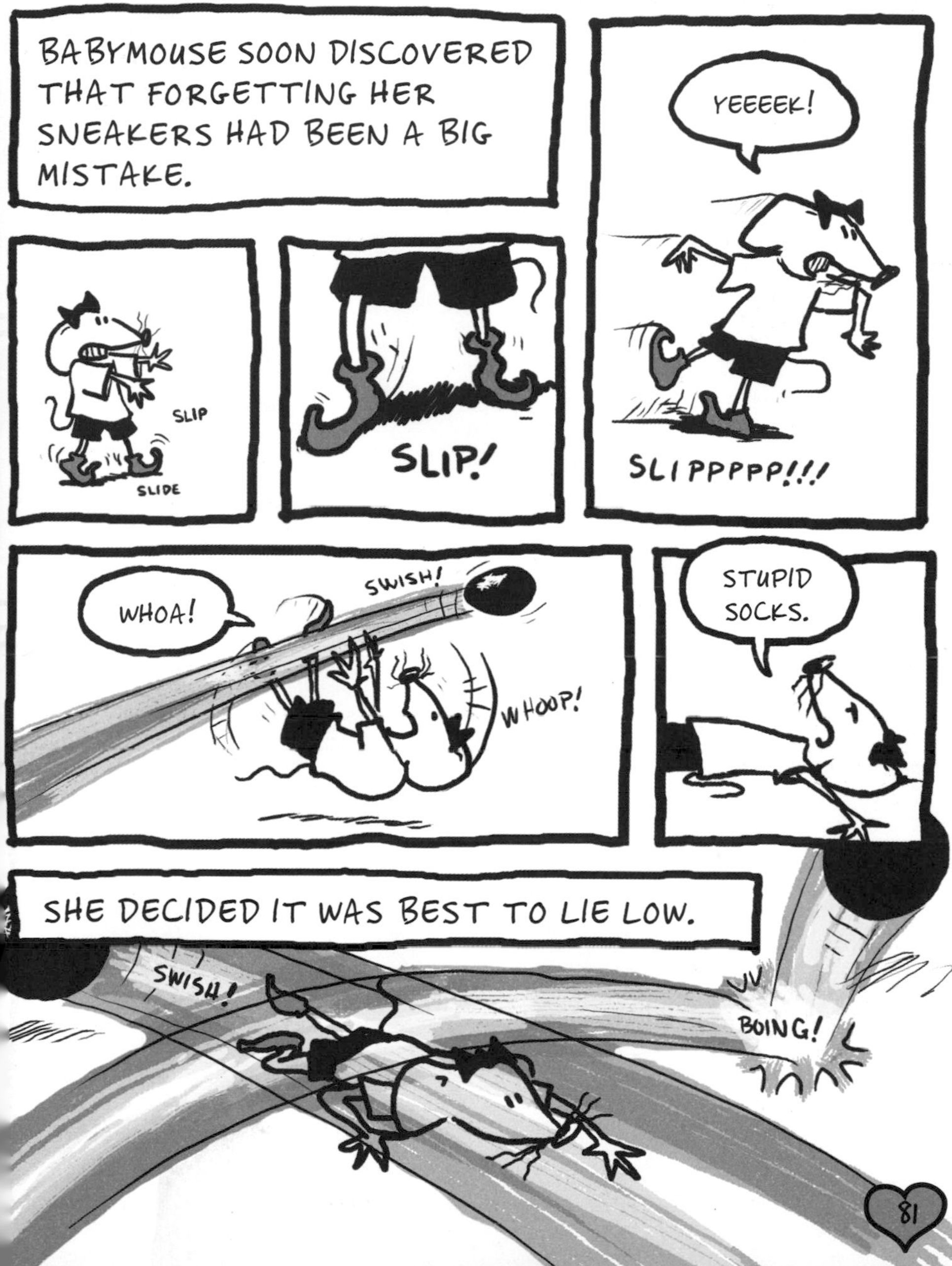

BABYMOUSE SOON DISCOVERED THAT FORGETTING HER SNEAKERS HAD BEEN A BIG MISTAKE.
SLIP
SLIDE
SLIP!
YEEEEK!
SLIPPPPPP!!!
WHOA!
SWISH!
WHOOP!
STUPID SOCKS.
SHE DECIDED IT WAS BEST TO LIE LOW.
SWISH!
BOING!

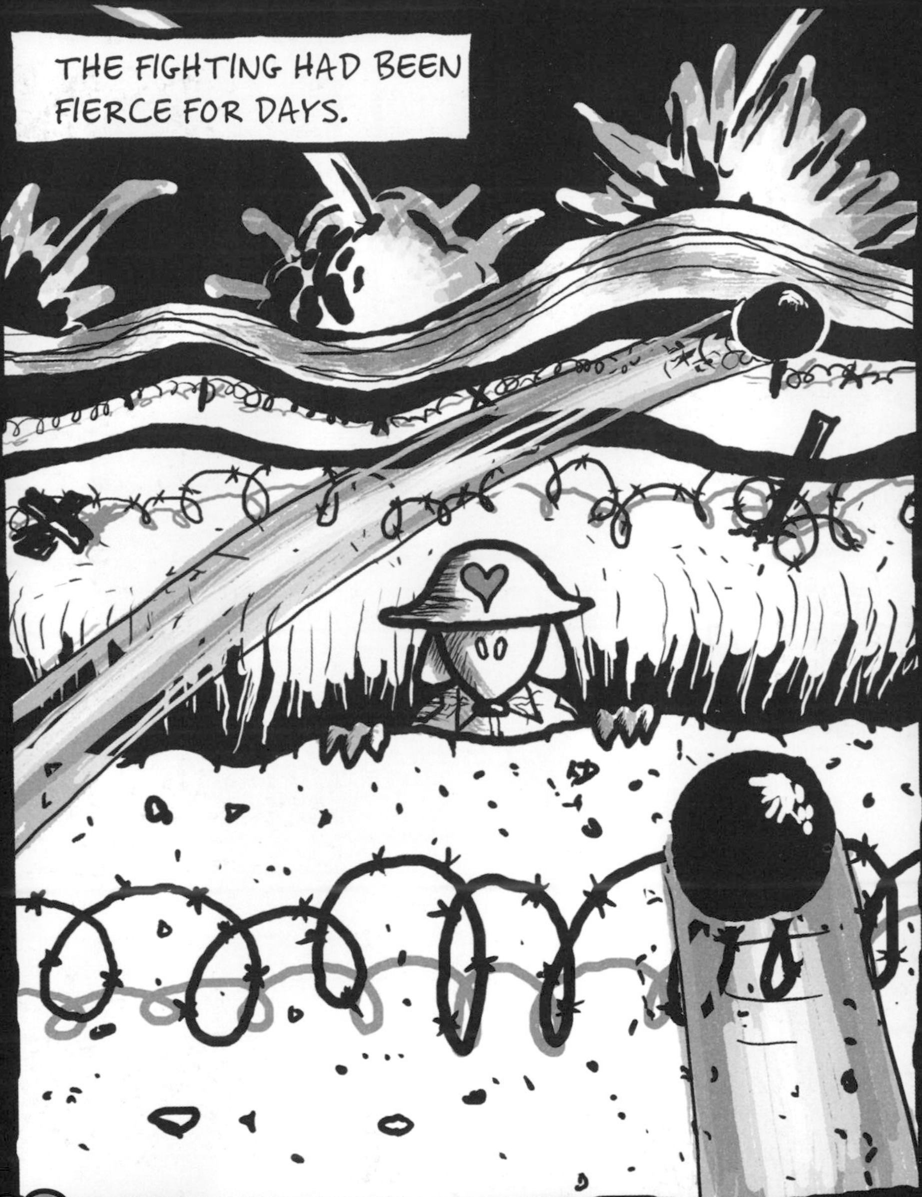
THE FIGHTING HAD BEEN FIERCE FOR DAYS.

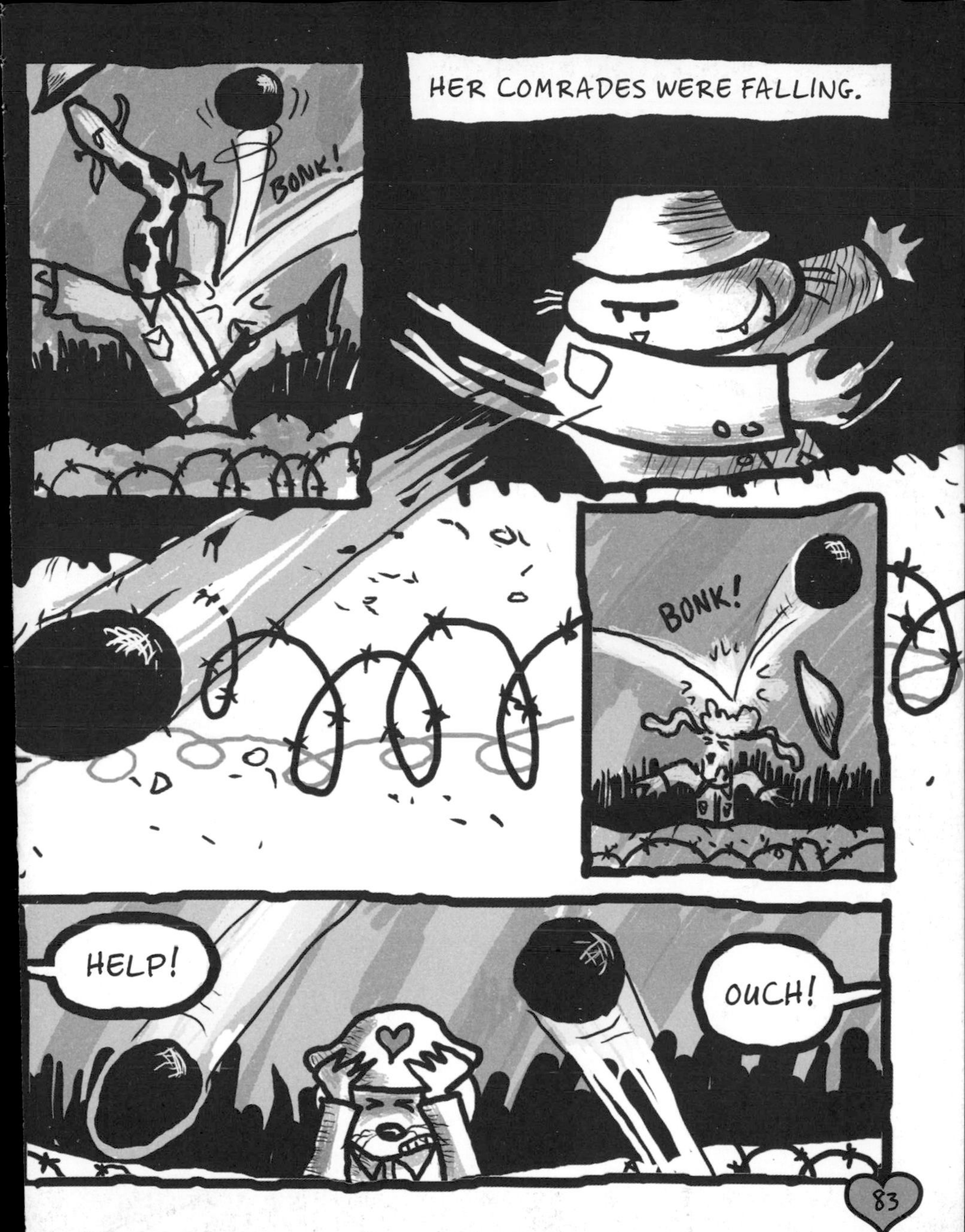

HER COMRADES WERE FALLING.
BONK!
BONK!
HELP!
OUCH!

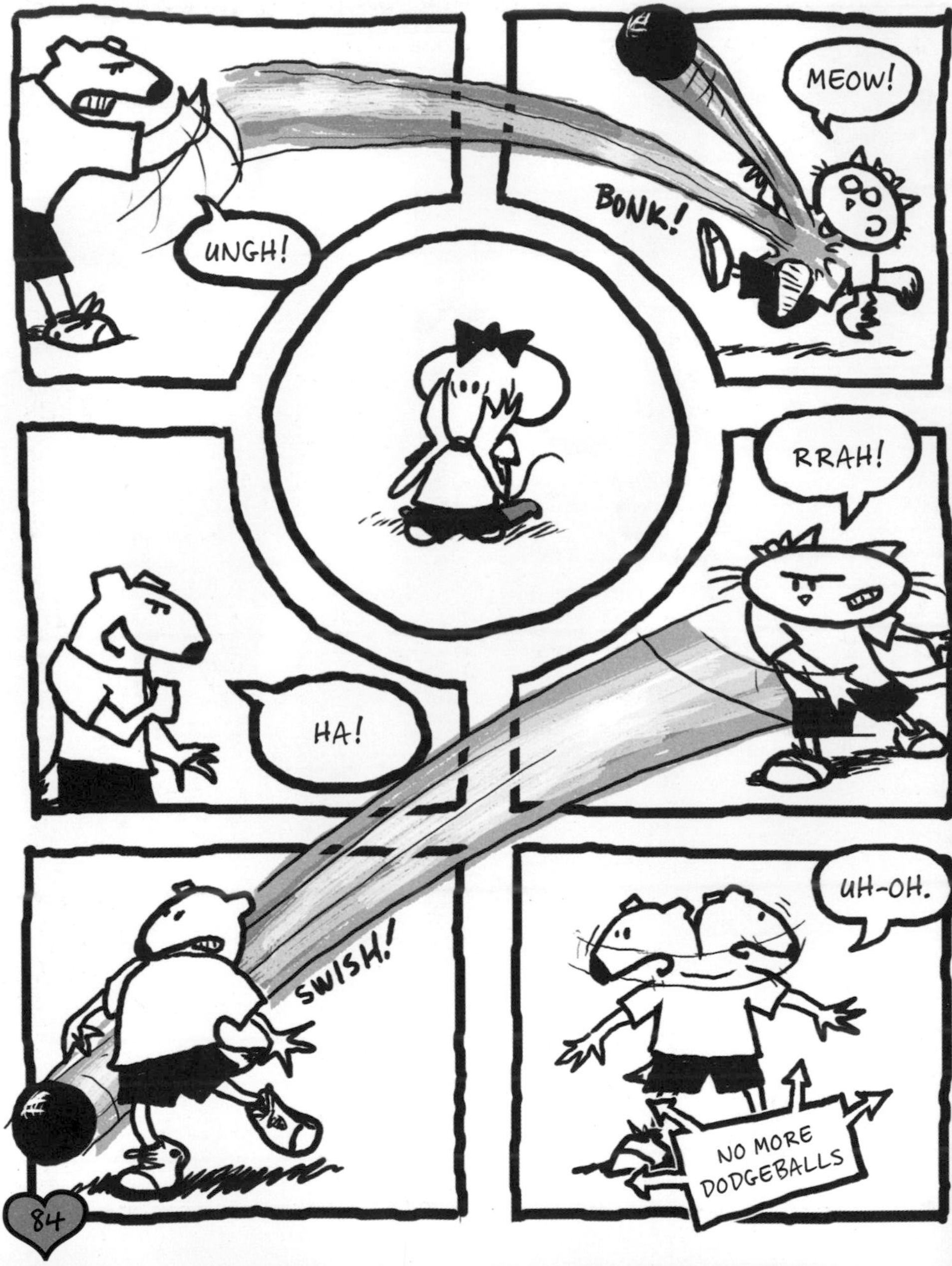
UNGH!
MEOW!
BONK!
RRAH!
HA!
SWISH!
UH-OH.
NO MORE DODGEBALLS

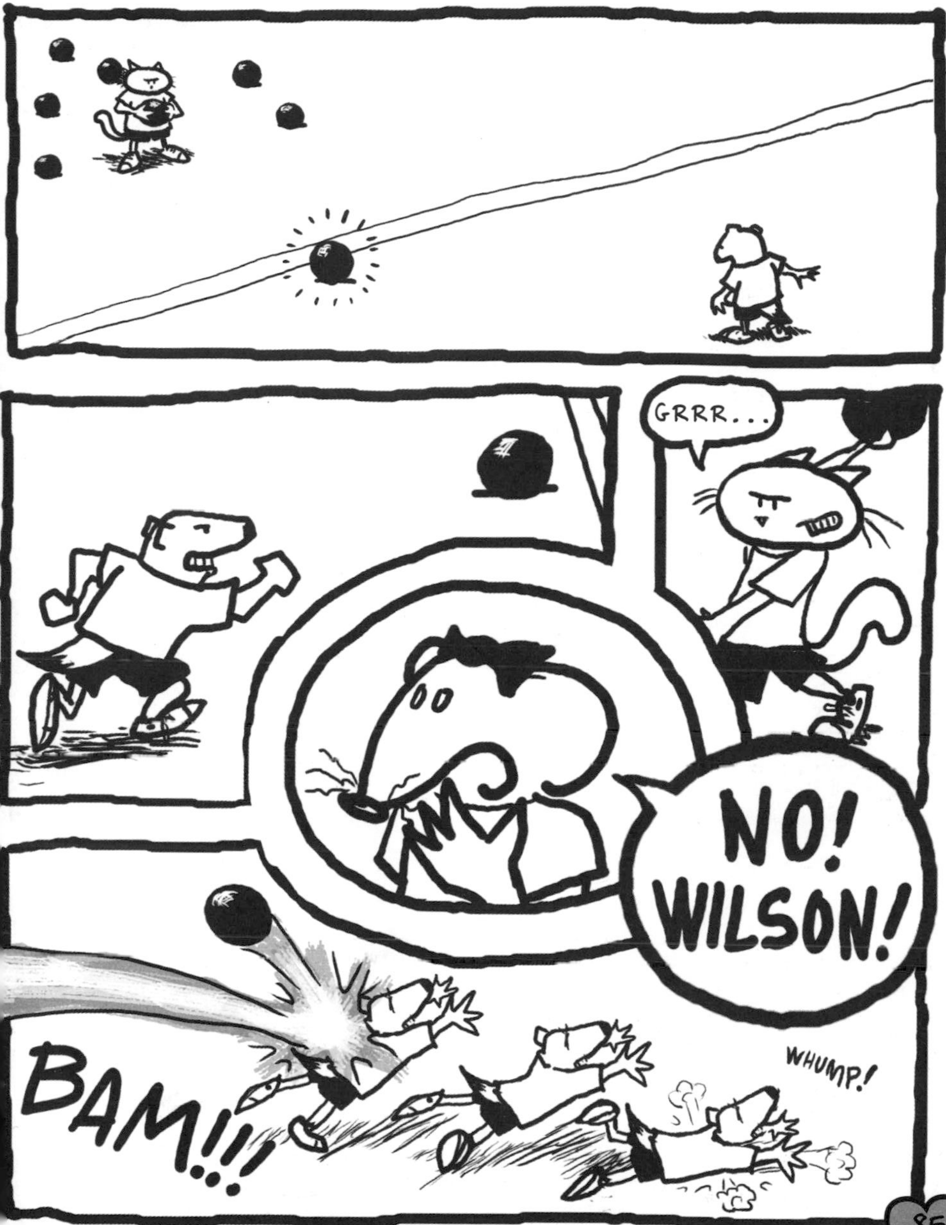
GRRR...
NO! WILSON!
BAM!!!
WHUMP!

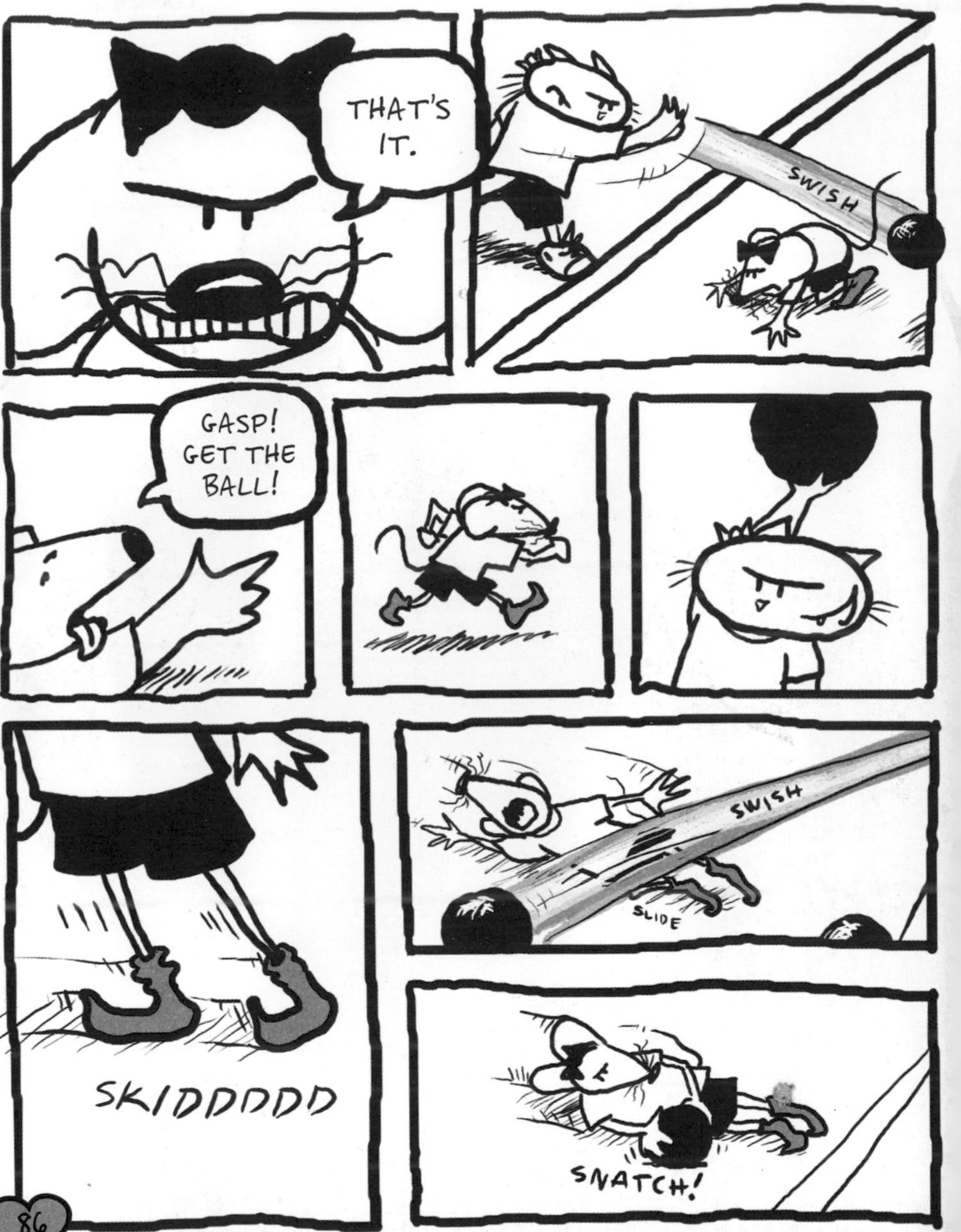

THAT'S IT.
SWISH
GASP! GET THE BALL!
SKIDDDDD
SWISH
SLIDE
SNATCH!

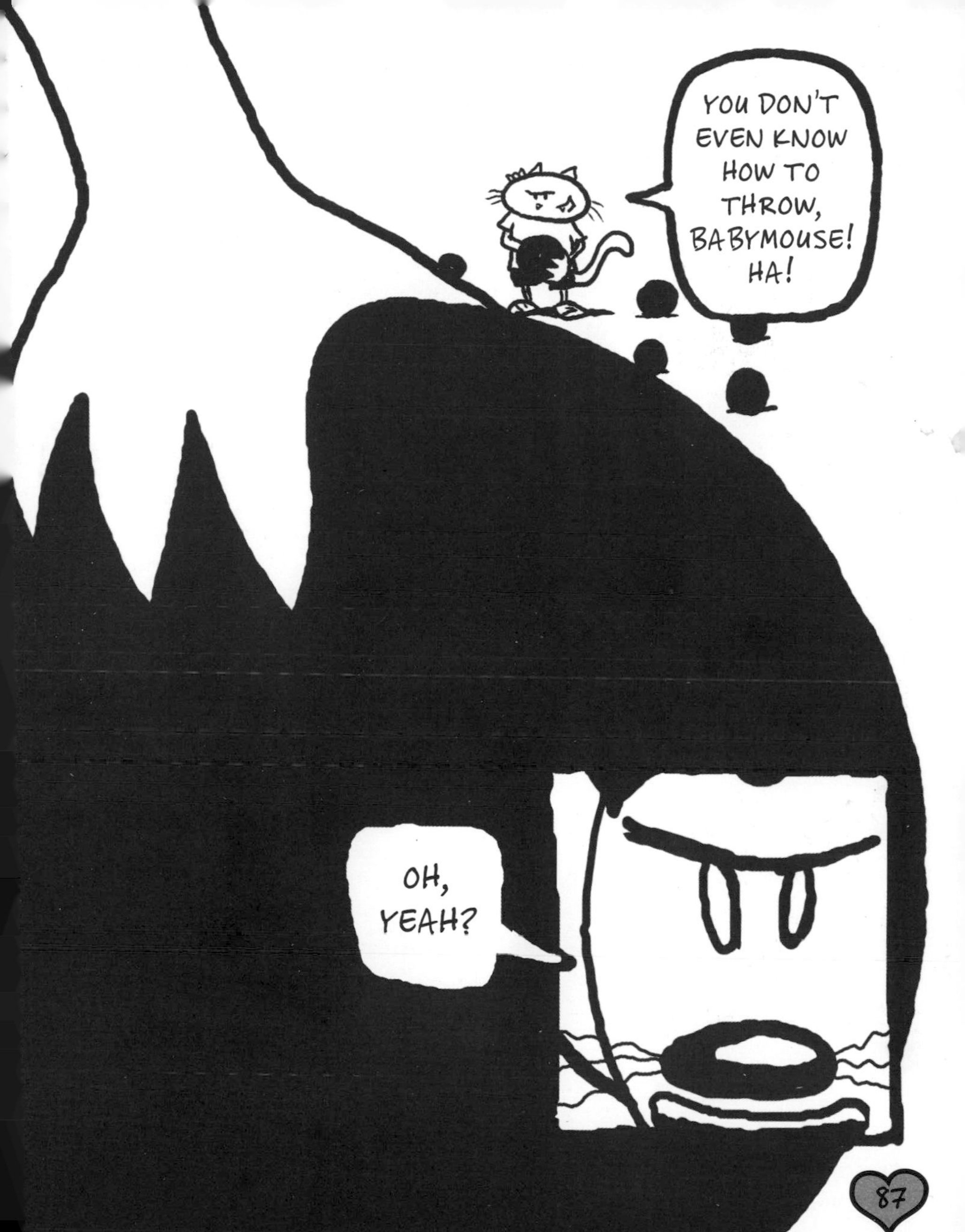

YOU DON'T EVEN KNOW HOW TO THROW, BABYMOUSE! HA!
OH, YEAH?

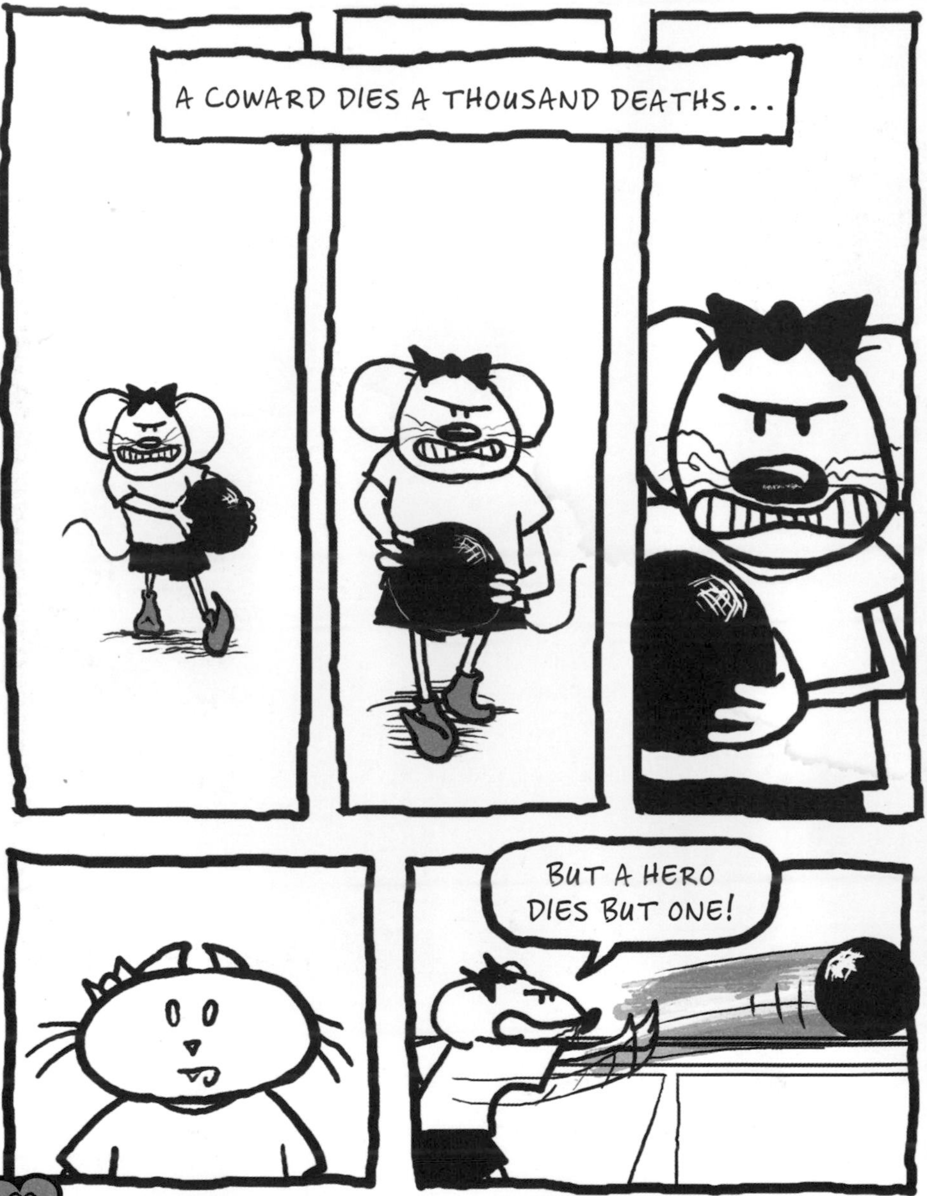
A COWARD DIES A THOUSAND DEATHS...
BUT A HERO DIES BUT ONE!

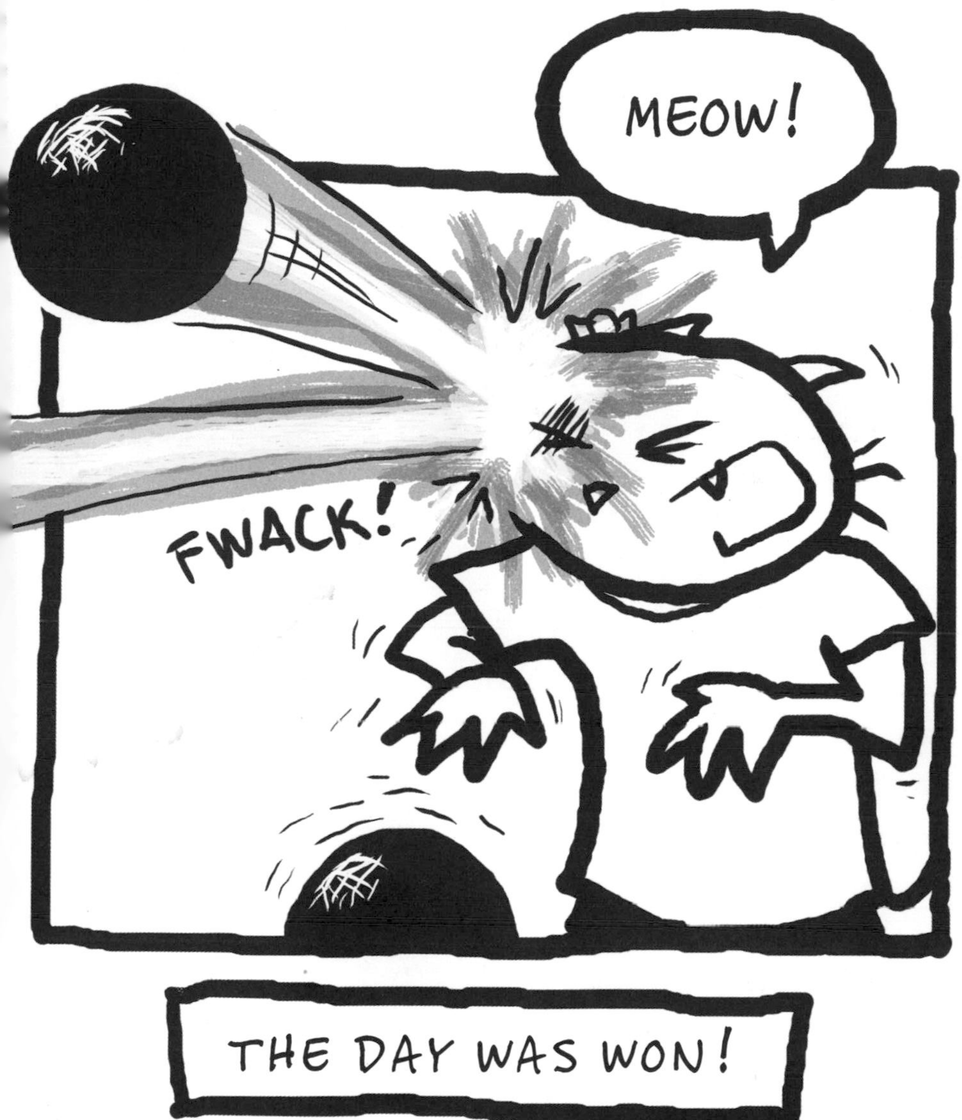
MEOW!
FWACK!
THE DAY WAS WON!

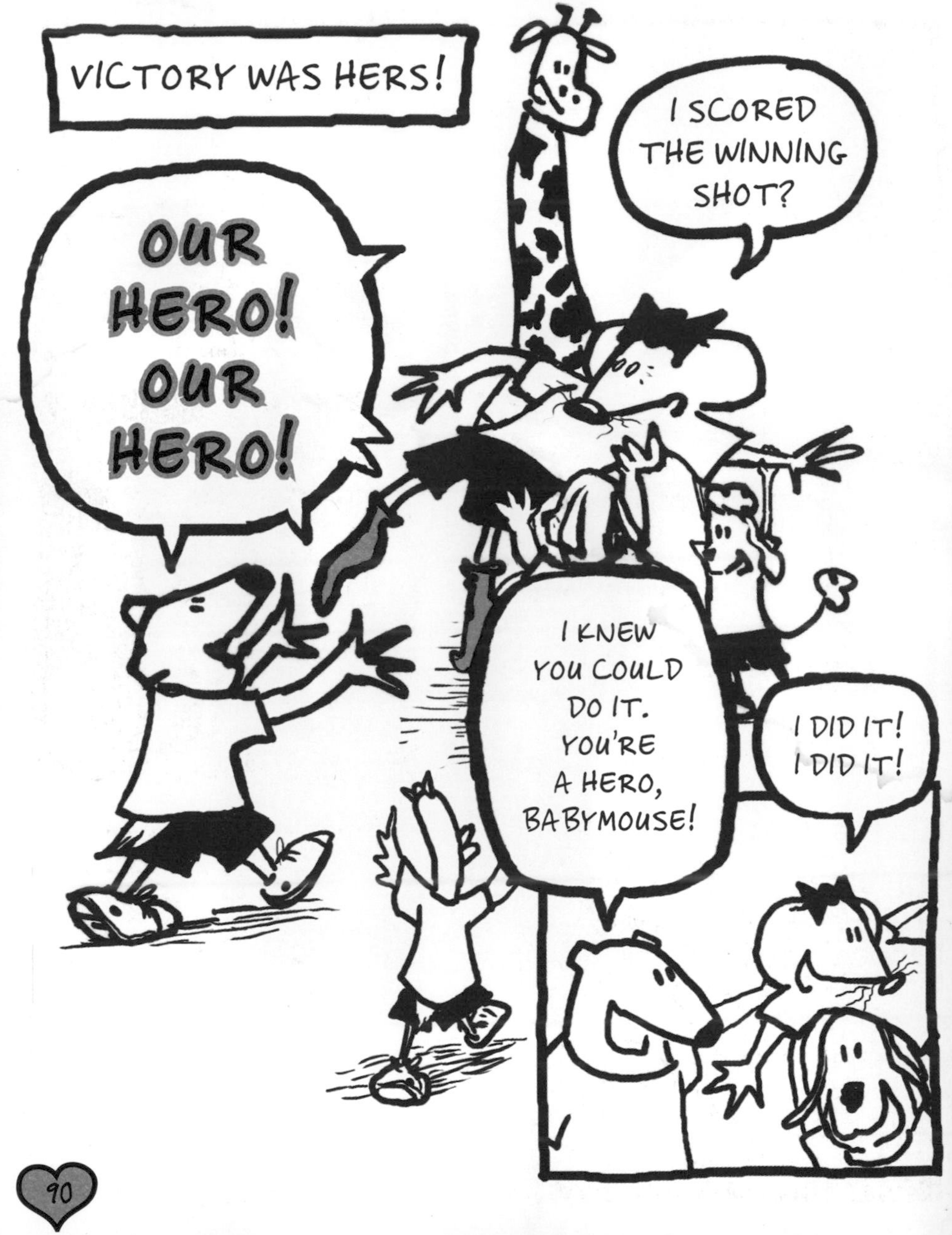
VICTORY WAS HERS!
OUR HERO! OUR HERO!
I SCORED THE WINNING SHOT?
I KNEW YOU COULD DO IT. YOU'RE A HERO, BABYMOUSE!
I DID IT! I DID IT!

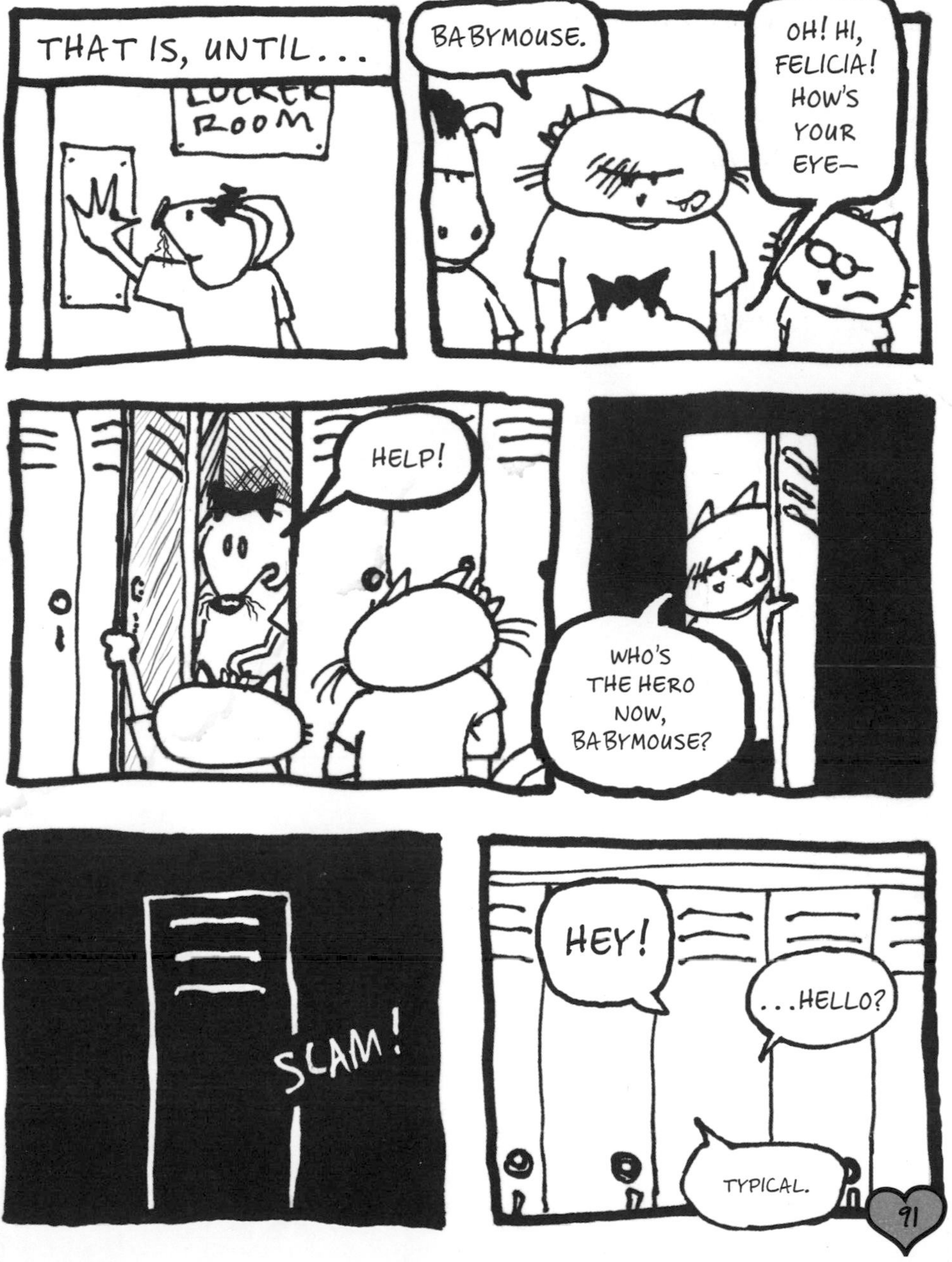
THAT IS, UNTIL...
LOCKER ROOM
BABYMOUSE.
OH! HI, FELICIA! HOW'S YOUR EYE—
HELP!
WHO'S THE HERO NOW, BABYMOUSE?
SLAM!
HEY!
...HELLO?
TYPICAL.

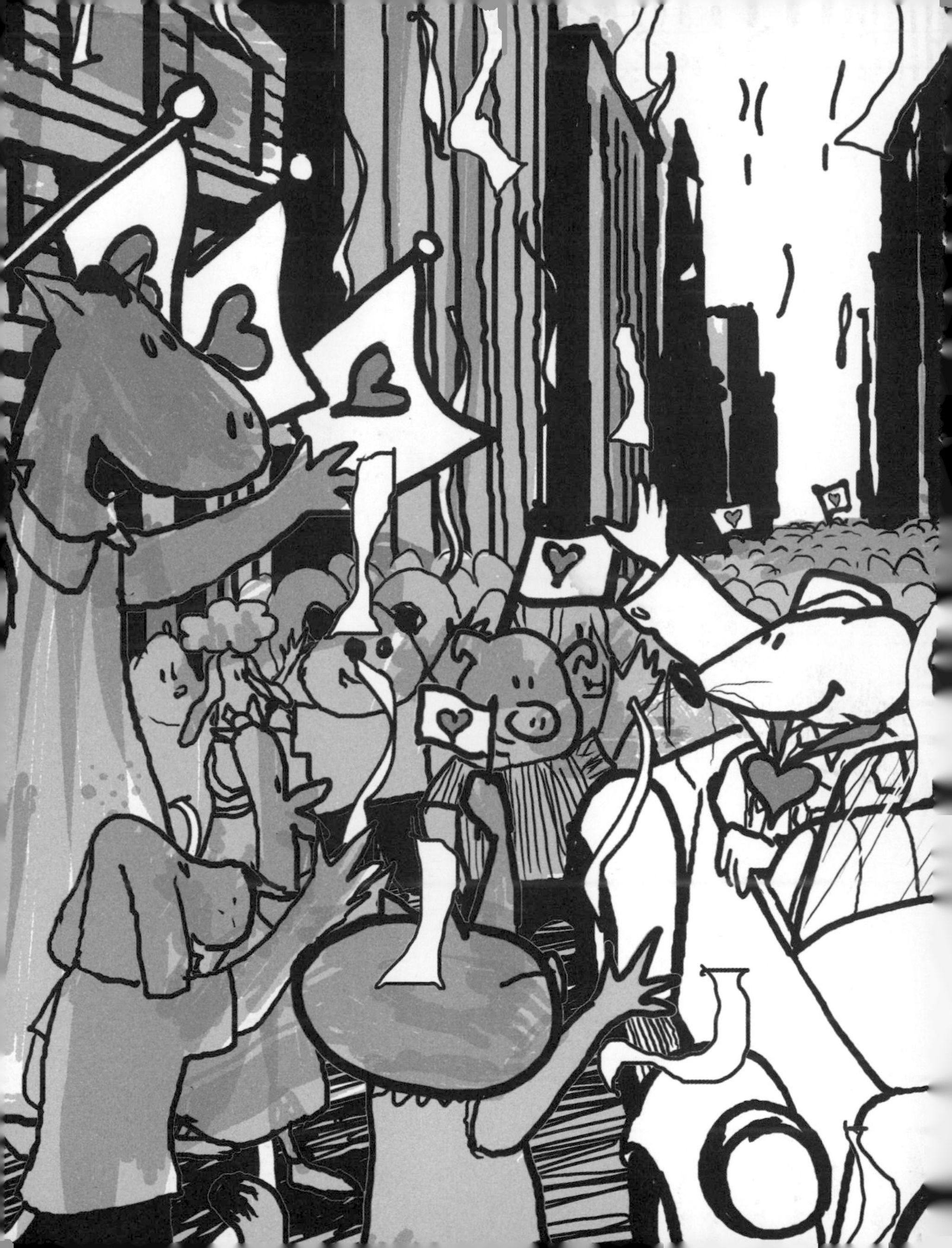

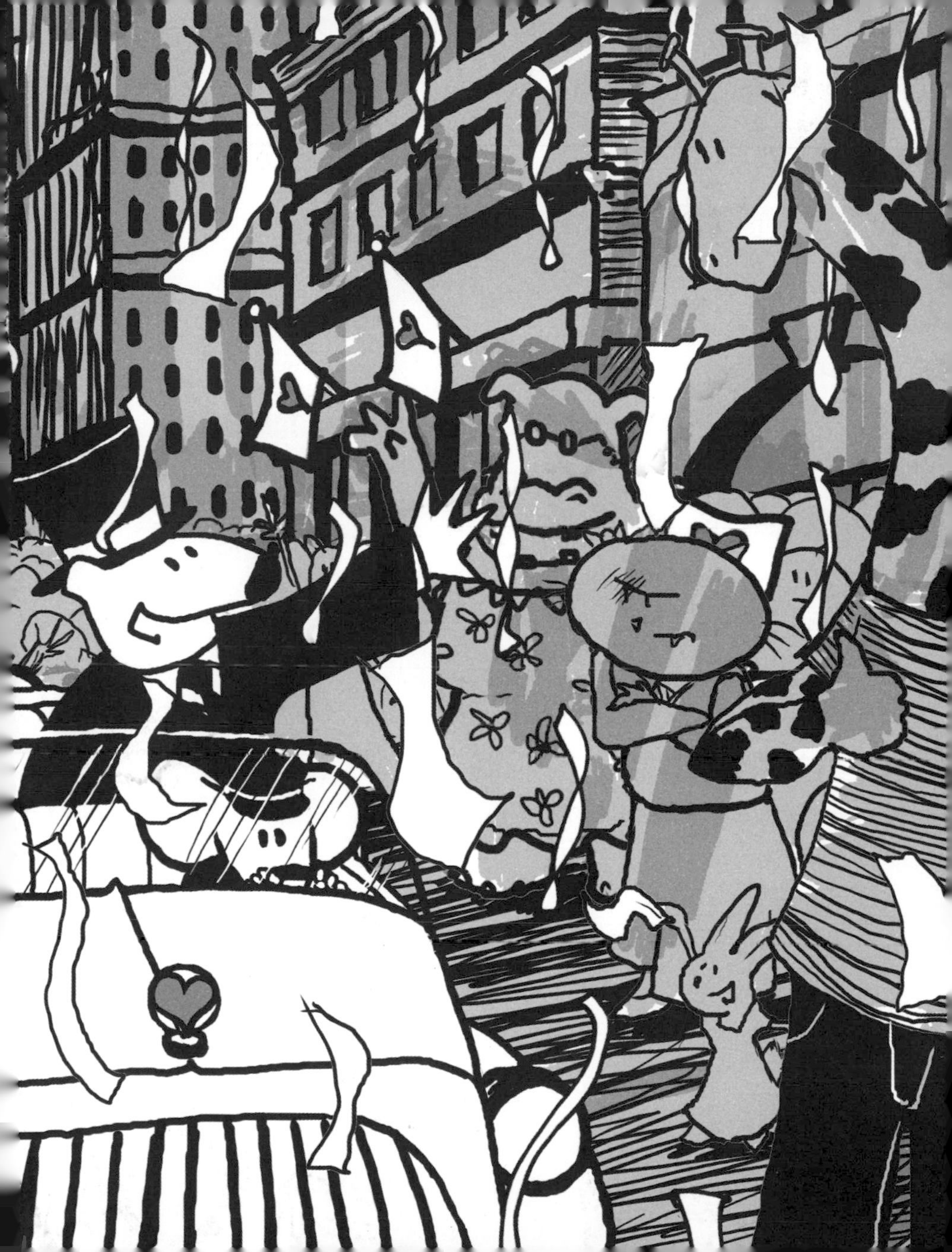

GET READY FOR THE SUN-SATIONAL NEW BABYMOUSE!

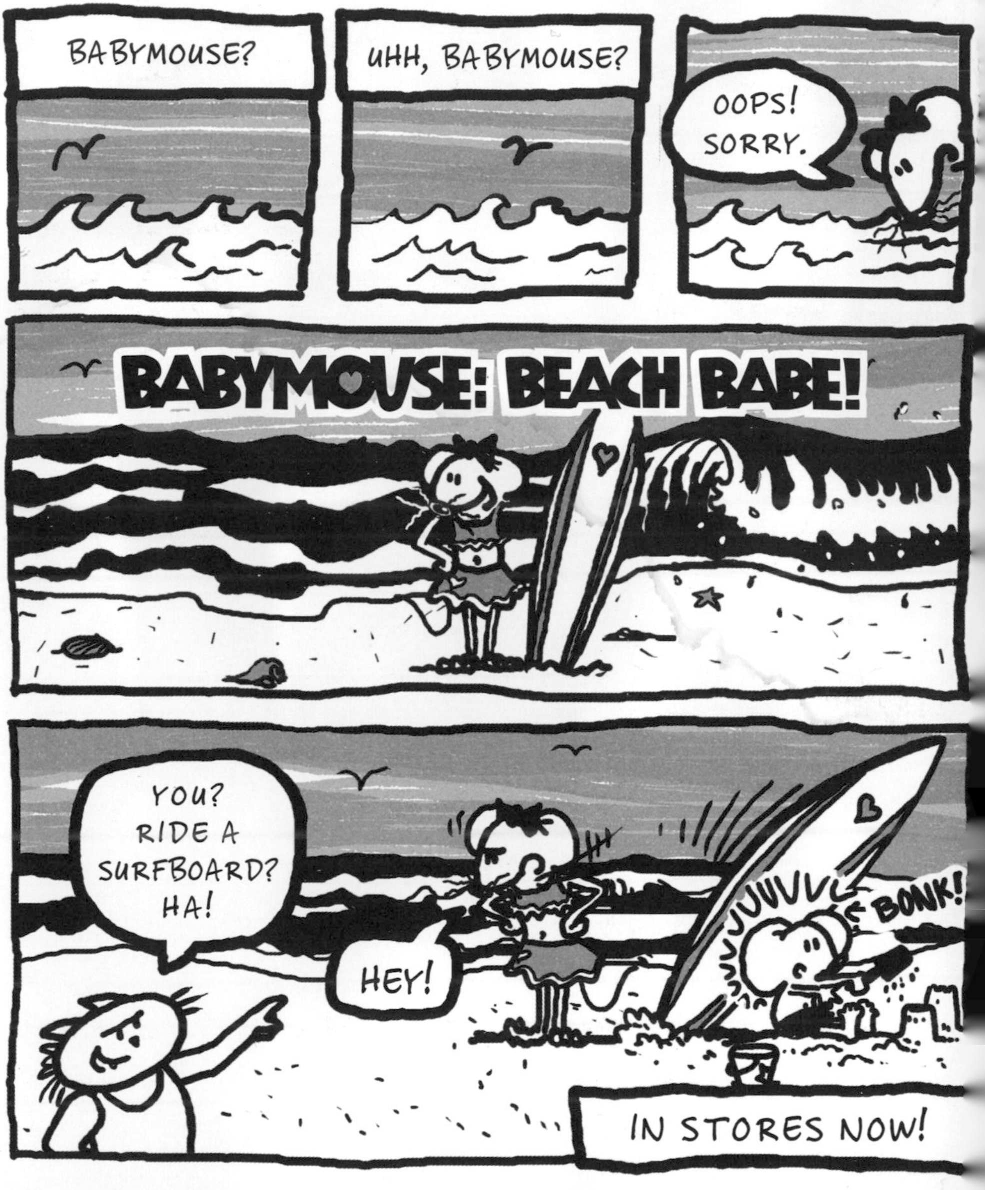
BABYMOUSE?
UHH, BABYMOUSE?
OOPS! SORRY.
BABYMOUSE: BEACH BABE!
YOU? RIDE A SURFBOARD? HA!
HEY!
VVVVVVVV
BONK!
IN STORES NOW!

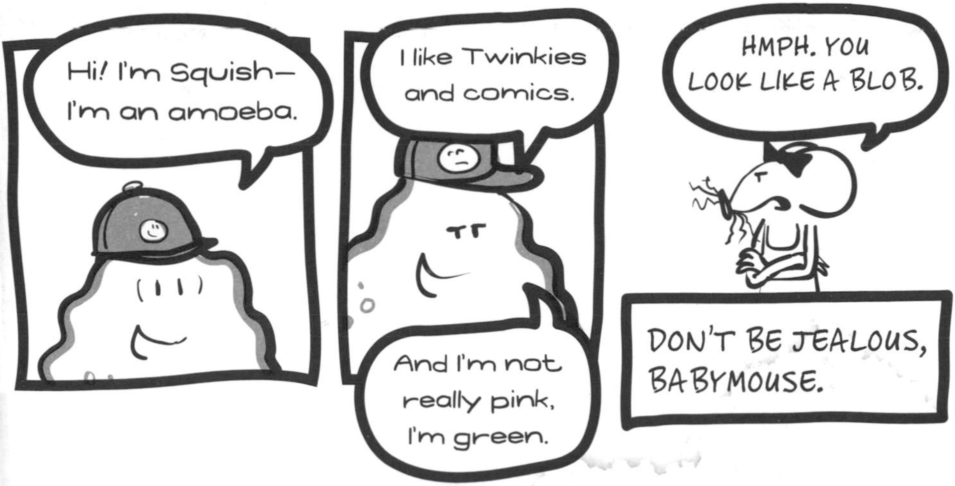
Hi! I'm Squish—
I'm an amoeba.
I like Twinkies
and comics.
And I'm not
really pink,
I'm green.
HMPH. YOU
LOOK LIKE A BLOB.
DON'T BE JEALOUS,
BABYMOUSE.

READ ABOUT SQUISH'S AMAZING ADVENTURES IN:

#1 SQUISH: Super Amoeba

#2 SQUISH: Brave New Pond

#3 SQUISH: The Power of the Parasite

#4 SQUISH: Captain Disaster

#5 SQUISH: Game On!

AND COMING SOON:

#6 SQUISH: Fear the Amoeba

★ "IF EVER A NEW SERIES DESERVED TO GO VIRAL, THIS ONE DOES."
—*KIRKUS REVIEWS*, STARRED

If you like Babymouse,
you'll love these other great books
by Jennifer L. Holm!

THE BOSTON JANE TRILOGY
EIGHTH GRADE IS MAKING ME SICK
MIDDLE SCHOOL IS WORSE THAN MEATLOAF
OUR ONLY MAY AMELIA
PENNY FROM HEAVEN
TURTLE IN PARADISE

THEY'RE REALLY GOOD! TRUST ME!